Praise for *Rise and Shine*

You just *thought* you knew Sleeping Beauty! **Sandra D. Bricker has done it again by bringing a story to life that we loved as little girls and made it for the big girl who lives inside us all.** What a great bed-time story!

EVA MARIE EVERSON, award-winning author,
The Road to Testament

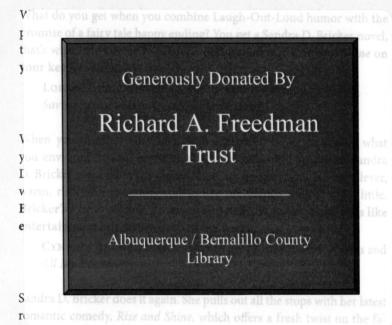

miliar. With an abundance of references to fairy tales, vintage sitcoms, and fun films, **be prepared to giggle at the most unexpected times.**

DEBBY MAYNE, author of the C⸱ Reunion series and *Dixie Belle*

Sandra D. Bricker is one of the few   use a light hand to address a hard subject,   I was hooked right from the begin   d unique lilt to Bricker's writing vo   ard that Happily Ever After for which she's k   end **this fun and heartwarming novel.**

JANICE HANNA THOMPSON, author of the Weddings by Bella series

Rise and Shine

Sandra D. Bricker

MOODY PUBLISHERS

CHICAGO

This is a work of fiction. Names, characters, places, and incidents either are the product of the author's imagination or are used fictitiously, and any resemblance to actual persons, living or dead, businesses, companies, events, or locales is entirely coincidental.

Published in association with the literary agency of WordServe Literary Group.

Edited by Cara Peterson
Interior design: Ragont Design
Cover Design: DogEared Design, LLC
Cover images: iStockphoto / #21653965 / #19965140 / #29826458

Library of Congress Cataloging-in-Publication Data

Bricker, Sandra D.
Rise and shine / Sandra D. Bricker.
  pages cm
  Summary: "Shannon Malone thought she'd found her happy ending when she married Edmund Ridgeway, but a diving accident on their honeymoon left her in a coma. Waking up to the news that she's thirty years old would have been daunting enough, but she also learns that Edmund has lost his interim battle with cancer and the world has marched on without her. Her gorgeous doctor, Daniel Petros, seems to know everything about her and becomes Shannon's tour guide into a whole new world of madness where reality television has taken over the planet and everyone's life appears to revolve around a tiny screen on their cell phones! As Shannon struggles to navigate through the changes—both in the world and in her—she also must discern real memories from imagined ones. Did she really ever wear capris pants and entertain in her living room, or was that Laura Petrie from her favorite classic TV show? And where is her beloved dog, Freeway? Oh, wait! That was Jonathan and Jennifer Hart's dog, not hers. Shannon's three elderly aunts flit through her life in true Sleeping Beauty style with her well-being always a priority. And Edmund's sister Millicent descends like the Evil Queen she is, trying to extract Shannon from any claim on the Ridgeway family fortune. When a tornado moves through town and Shannon is knocked unconscious, will Daniel's kiss awaken her once and for all?"—Provided by publisher.
  ISBN 978-0-8024-0630-9 (pbk.)
  1. Widows--Fiction. I. Title.
  PS3602.R53R57 2014
  813'.6--dc23
                                      2013050248

We hope you enjoy this book from River North Fiction by Moody Publishers. Our goal is to provide high-quality, thought provoking books and products that connect truth to your real needs and challenges. For more information on other books and products written and produced from a biblical perspective, go to www.moodypublishers.com or write to:

River North Fiction
Imprint of Moody Publishers
820 N. LaSalle Boulevard
Chicago, IL 60610

1 3 5 7 9 10 8 6 4 2

Printed in the United States of America

Prologue

Beqa Lagoon, Fiji
August 2005

"**I picked up** the workbook for class before we left Austin. Let's work on filling out the first exercise over breakfast, okay?"

"Shannon, may I remind you that we're on our honeymoon?"

Shannon looked up from the marriage class workbook she'd picked up before she and her husband of three days had left Austin.

"Babe, we can totally smoke the rest of the class by showing up prepared on the first night," came the reply. "They'll never expect us to have the first questionnaire filled out the day after we get back! Are we in this to show them who's boss, or what?"

Edmund chuckled and shook his head at his bride, hunched over the first page of the workbook like an Olympic runner crouched at the starting block.

Shannon paused to twist her long copper waves into submission, twirling them around her fist and forcing them into a messy bun secured with a second pen that she produced from her handbag. Her greenish eyes glistened with golden flecks as she lifted her eyebrows in anticipation and stared at him.

"So?" she prodded. "Are we gonna do this thing, or what?"

"All right," he conceded. No use dousing the fire. "But the shuttle arrives to take us to the marina in an hour, so we eat while we do it."

"Deal," she said, and her perfect merlot lips curved into a victorious smile.

That smile got him every time.

"First question," she announced. "Name the famous couple that you and your mate are most like."

"Famous couple," Edmund repeated, shaking his head as he poured coffee into both of their cups. He returned the carafe to the room service cart bellied up to the side of their patio table and asked, "What, like Antony and Cleopatra?"

"We're nothing like them," she corrected, making a large X in the air between them with her pen. "They were completely dysfunctional. She's totally vain and histrionic, and he's a big cheater." Suddenly, she froze for a moment and lifted one high, arched eyebrow. "You're not trying to tell me something here, are you?"

Edmund laughed, leaping to change the course of the train before it derailed. "No, Shannon. I'm not. So who would you say then?"

"I was thinking we're more like Rob and Laura Petrie."

"From that old Dick Van Dyke show?" he mused. "Nah. Too cozy."

"Yeah," she agreed. "Ooh! Wait. How about Jonathan and Jennifer?"

"Who?"

"That's it. We're the Harts."

"Who are they?"

"You know, *Hart to Hart*. Glamorous jet-setter couple who solved crimes together. She was a gorgeous redhead, and he was handsome and debonair, and—"

"I can see the resemblance to us now," he said, grinning. "But don't you ever watch television from this century?"

"This from the man whose mind went directly to ancient Rome."

A laugh burst out of him. "Well, how about Ross and Rachel?"

Shannon's mouth turned impossibly downward in that pout that took over her entire face every time someone mentioned *Friends*. Edmund counted down the seconds until her typical response. It would start with a whine—

"Ohhhh."

And then—

"I can't believe there's no more *Friends*."

"Maybe they'll syndicate."

"Maybe." But her weepy expression said syndication would never be the same for a fan who had planned her Thursday nights (and Friday mornings) around a group of thirty-somethings and a coffee house every week for the last decade of her life. "Besides, Rachel's the one with the money. And Ross is the brainiac."

"Are you comparing yourself to Ross?" he asked, confused. "Or are you saying I'm not a brainiac just because my family has money?"

"We're just not Ross and Rachel, babe."

"Okay then. How about Meredith and McDreamy from that new hospital show we watched the other night? What's the name of that show? You liked them, didn't you?"

"Yeah, I think I might like *Grey's Anatomy*," she answered. "But they've only just started. It's too soon to tell. We don't really know what kind of couple they'll be, or if they ever really will be one. I mean, I'm not sure they'll make it as a real couple."

"You do know they're not real, right?"

She ignored him. "She's too dark, and he's a player. They don't have the right stuff to last forever, so they're nothing like us. We're the Harts, okay?"

"Okay."

The hotel phone rang as she wrote down their answer, and Edmund went inside to pick it up. "What's the next question?" he called over his shoulder.

"Oh, this is an easy one," she returned. "Do the two of you have a song and, if so, what is it?"

Edmund grinned. He'd chosen to never reveal to Shannon that he'd seen *Titanic* with Sally Shafer, his first love, the girl he'd planned to marry; nor had he admitted that he didn't remember the tinny instrumental version of its theme song, which Shannon said had been playing in the elevator where they first met. If she wanted that to be their song, he felt no particular need to confess that it had ever had any other connotation for him.

She did look a little like Kate Winslet's Rose, come to think of it.

"Hello," he said as he pressed the receiver to his cheek and listened as the front desk clerk told him their shuttle had arrived ahead of schedule and could be asked to come back later.

"That won't be necessary. Send a cart and ask the shuttle driver to wait for us. We're just finishing up."

Edmund hung up the phone and crossed to the wide-open patio.

"They're early, right?" Shannon said with a sigh when she noticed him leaning on the chiffon-draped post. "Figures. Two hours late for our massage, and now an hour early for diving."

Her pen bounced across the tabletop when she tossed it, and she paused to stuff one last strawberry into her mouth before she bounded past him. She plucked the second pen from her hair and tossed it to him as buoyant red waves tumbled down her back.

"Just give me five minutes and I'm all yours until the end of time!"

Once upon a time, in a charming land
called Austin, an exquisite princess with fire-red hair
slipped into a deep sleep.
Her prince held vigil at her side,
hoping and praying that she would
one day open her beautiful emerald eyes again . . .

1

"I'm Dr. Petros. I'm just going to shine a light into your eyes for a closer look. Don't be alarmed, all right?"

The beam of light cut through her like a laser, and Shannon squirmed away from it.

"Can you speak? Do you know your name?"

She moaned, pulling away from the large hand holding the lid of her eye open. When she'd escaped it and the white shaft of light finally set her free, several solid black silhouettes moved in around her.

"Let's get an EKG, a chest X-ray, and some blood work right away," said the voice that had awoken her. Then, more softly, he asked, "Can you see me?"

She blinked several times before squinting to get a better look at the shadowy man standing over her. The darkness of him began to fade until a distorted—yet friendly—face emerged before her. She pressed her eyes shut and when she opened them again, kind, dark eyes seemed to smile at her.

Shaggy brown hair . . . a shadow of stubble across a dimpled, suntanned face . . .

"Welcome back," he said with what seemed like strange enthusiasm. "I'm Dr. Petros. Do you know your name?"

She tried to speak, but she choked on the words, coughing and sputtering for breath.

"That's okay," the doctor reassured her. "Your throat's going to be a little tight and dry for a while. Let's get the patient some ice chips," he said over his shoulder.

11

The patient.

Shannon clenched her jaw at the words. She tried to ask, "Where am I?" through her teeth, but she couldn't manage it without descending into another coughing fit.

"Here. Let's try this first," he said, and he spooned few ice chips from a plastic cup and offered them to her. "Open."

She did as she was told, and then she flinched as the chips hit her tongue.

"Just suck on those for a few minutes," the nurse who had fetched them advised. "Don't chew. Let them melt."

Frigid liquid cooled her parched mouth. When she opened her eyes again, the doctor stood over her, muscular arms folded across his chest, a lopsided smile once again lighting up his face. Despite her confusion, Shannon eyed him curiously. A stethoscope dangled from the neck of his white trench coat, and he wore several thin bracelets made of brown suede cord and small wooden beads where other men donned watches.

She pushed the last of the ice chips to the side of her mouth and tried to speak over them in the rasp that used to be her voice. "What kind of doctor are you?"

"I'm a neurologist."

Neuro. Nerves. Nervous system.

"Have I gone mad?"

The doctor huffed out a chuckle and shook his head. "No, you're not 'mad.'"

A sudden jolt of fear knocked the wind out of her and she gasped. "Am I paralyzed?"

Shannon kicked her feet beneath the scratchy white sheet and sighed in relief when they moved—though they did feel as if they weighed a few hundred pounds.

"Not paralyzed, either."

"Then why do I need a neurologist? What am I doing here?"

"You were in an accident," he replied.

"An accident? What happened?" A sudden flash of memory

made her gasp. "Edmund. Is Edmund all right? Was he hurt?"

"No, he wasn't hurt in the accident," he said, slipping the shiny stethoscope from around his neck. "You've been unconscious for quite a while. How about you let me check you out before you start asking your questions? I'm just going to listen to your breathing. Can you lean forward?"

Shannon's entire body felt weighted down, but she pushed against it. She jumped when the cold metal of his scope touched her back and she realized she wore one of those hospital gowns with the large, unfortunate opening in the back.

"Take deep breaths," he told her, but her lungs felt constricted when she tried. "Good. Just a few more."

When he finished, he guided her toward the softness of the pillow propped behind her and took a step back.

"You mentioned Edmund—"

"Where *is he*?"

"—but do you know your own name?"

"Shannon," she blurted, frowning. "Where is Edmund?"

"He's not in the hospital right now."

"What hospital is this?"

"Draper Long-Term Care Facility."

Long-term care.

"How long have I been here?"

"You've been here ever since your accident," he answered. "Do you remember your accident, Shannon?"

She shook her head. "Was it some sort of car accident? A head-on collision or something?"

"No, not a car." She thought he might have sighed as he looked at his shoes and shifted from one foot to the other. "Think back," he said once his dark brown eyes met hers again. "What's the last thing you remember?"

"I—I don't really . . ."

A distant beat intensified until she could hardly hear anything over it. Several seconds thumped past before she recognized it as her own heartbeat drumming in her head.

"Do you know your address?" he asked, and Shannon grimaced, first at the doctor, and then at the plump, middle-aged nurse standing next to him looking so hopeful that she might remember basic personal information. Stranger still, Shannon realized she was having trouble doing it. "How about your phone number?"

The side of her head began to itch. Why couldn't she think of her own phone number? What was wrong with her?

"You said you're a neurologist," she said slowly. "My brain's messed up, isn't it?"

"It's just a little over-stimulated at the moment," he told her, and he touched her hand. "Let's try this, Shannon. What's the first number that comes into your mind?"

After just a fraction of a pause, she said with confidence: "78737. Is that my phone number?"

The nurse muttered something to the doctor, and he nodded.

"What? What is it?"

"Well, that's a ZIP code," he prompted, and understanding dawned inside her.

"Right!" she exclaimed. "Austin, Texas, 78737! It's our address."

The doctor smiled. "Good. Can you think of the rest of it?"

Shannon bit down on her tongue and held it there between her teeth as her brain itched and itched. She wanted to scratch it, she really did, but—nothing.

"What is wrong with my head?" She growled in frustration, smacking her hand against the bed railing. "And why are my arms strapped down?" she asked, noticing her arms for the first time and looking up with alarm. "What, am I a prisoner?"

"It's okay, Shannon," he said as he loosened the side straps and set her arms free. "That was for your own protection. When you woke up, you were flailing. What do you say you get some rest for now. This is your nurse, Angela. She's going to take some blood, and in a little while we'll get you a quick chest X-ray and an EKG.

Once I have a look at everything, I'll come back and check on you again, okay?"

"No, wait," she said, rubbing her sore and swollen forearm. "I have so many questions."

"And I'll answer every one of them when I come back, I promise."

"Are you going to call Edmund?"

"You just focus on getting some rest. I'll see you very soon." At the door, he smiled at her. "Welcome back, Shannon."

She watched his head disappear, long dark hair moving freely. That kind of man wasn't her type, really. Edmund had been fair all the way around—light skin, eyes, and hair. Still, she couldn't escape the thought as it came.

He's very attractive, a voice in her head seemed to whisper. Shannon gave it a violent shake, trying to replace the image of shaggy Dr. Petros with one of Edmund. But nothing came.

Why can't I remember?

"Do you know my husband?" she asked Angela as she lifted Shannon's hand and squeezed her index finger.

Angela shook her head and shushed her. "This is just a quick stick," she said, but the warning came as no real notification at all. Before Shannon could process the words, a small cylinder pressed against the tip of her finger inflicted an instant sting.

"Youch!" she howled. The nurse squeezed it until a drop of blood flowed out, which she transferred to the end of a small blue strip protruding from some sort of meter. "What is that?"

"Just monitoring your glucose," the nurse said reassuringly.

"My glucose. Why?"

"Standard procedure for patients waking up from a coma."

"A coma." Shannon narrowed her eyes and focused on the nurse's apple-cheeked face. "I was in a coma?"

"Indeed you were. Now you have some ice chips in the cup, and I want you to suck on them for a while. The doctor has ordered some initial tests, and they should be here in just a little bit." She placed a wired remote into Shannon's hand. "If you need anything, you just push this button, okay? I'm at the other end of it. Do you want your shows on?"

"My—my shows?"

Angela nodded toward a metal rack angled into the corner of the room. A black box sat on the top shelf, wired to the television hanging above it. The three shelves below it held DVD cases.

"All your favorites are there. Would you like to watch something?"

All my favorites. How would you know my favorites? she wondered.

"The complete *Dick Van Dyke Show*," she said as she approached the rack, angling her head to read the labeled cases. "Let's see, there's some *I Love Lucy*, some *Hart to Hart*, the complete collection of *Friends*."

Friends.

The corners of her mouth turned downward, but she wasn't quite sure why.

Looking back at her, the nurse asked, "Any of that sound appealing?"

Shannon shrugged. Suddenly, a thought occurred.

"Wait—*every* episode of *Friends*?"

"Would you like me to put in season one?"

Questions bombarded her tired brain, and she shook her head and closed her eyes. "No," she finally replied. "I think I'll just . . ."

Dropping her head back to the pillow behind her, she let her words trail as a cloak of weariness pressed down on her.

"That's right," Angela said, and she moved to Shannon's bedside and stroked her hair. "You just take it easy for a little bit. You've had a big day."

She heard the soft thump of the nurse's rubber shoes as she padded out of the room. The next thing she knew, a lanky young man with a sing-song voice asked her to lean forward so he could place a plate behind her for the portable X-ray.

"Sorry we took so long," he said as he gingerly arranged the tubes that bridged the distance between her arm and the plastic bags of fluid hanging from the rolling stand next to the bed.

"Did you?" she commented. "I must have dozed off."

"Oh yeah, Dr. Petros ordered your tests three hours ago. But we've got a couple people out this week."

Three hours, she thought. It felt like moments ago when the doctor had left the room. The cute doctor with the wavy brown hair and expressive dark eyes . . . Shannon gave herself another mental shake.

"Petros," she said aloud. "Is that Greek?"

"Sure is. Dreamy, isn't he?" the male nurse said with a wide, toothy grin. "Dr. Daniel Petros. I wouldn't be surprised if some of the others here doodle his name like grade-school girls."

"Now when I tell you to, hold your breath so I can get a good picture, okay?"

"Okay."

"On three. One, two, three. Hold it."

● — ● — ●

The elderly woman on the other end of the line seemed to stop breathing. Daniel had heard that thundering silence more times than he could count; more times than he even liked to think about. He repeated his introduction.

"Hello? This is Dr. Petros at Draper Long-Term Care."

"Is it Shannie?" the woman asked with an emotional rasp that reminded him very much of her niece's throaty voice when she had asked, "Where am I?" In all those years that he'd been caring for Shannon Ridgeway, he'd never imagined her voice as a husky one. He wondered what a little more time getting reacquainted with speech would do to it.

"Yes, ma'am. I'm calling with some fairly spectacular news."

The woman sputtered, but her questions didn't quite find her voice.

"Shannon is awake, Mrs. Winters."

Daniel waited. Five seconds went by, then ten.

"Did you hear me, ma'am? Shannon is awake."

"I'll be right there."

And with a slam, the call disconnected, leaving Daniel with a soft hum in his ear. He laughed out loud as he hung up the phone and leaned back. His desk chair creaked as he did, and he shook his head and raked both of his hands through his hair. He so seldom had the opportunity to deliver truly happy news. Phone calls to the families of his Draper patients typically began with, "I'm so sorry to have to tell you . . ."

He looked up to find Angela Westborne leaning on the doorjamb, watching him with a smile.

"What is it?"

"The EKG was just taken."

"Good grief, it's about time."

"I called down to light a fire underneath them. You'll have all the results within thirty minutes."

"The X-ray, too?"

"And the blood work."

"Very good, Angela. Thank you very much." When she continued to hover in the doorway, Daniel raised his eyebrows and asked, "Something else?"

"Pretty unusual, isn't it?"

"What's that?"

"Waking up after almost ten years the way she did."

"Oh," he said, barking out a laugh. "Unusual. Yes. It's unusual."

"Not like most of our patients."

"No, she's not. And to tell you the truth, Angela, I'm relieved to finally get to make a call like that to the family."

"You called them then," she said thoughtfully. "I'm sure they were thrilled."

He chuckled again. "She just said she'd be right here and hung up on me."

The two of them shared a laugh over it, and Angela's entire demeanor softened as she tilted her head slightly and looked at him.

"Shannon Ridgeway has become very special to all of us here, hasn't she, Doctor?"

"Well, it's been nearly ten years," he pointed out. "In my case, I've been her doctor every day since she was first admitted six months after her accident."

The look on Angela's expressive face spoke volumes. Daniel recalled that she'd discovered him having lunch in Shannon's room more than once, even found him asleep in the recliner next to her bed one night when he'd avoided heading home and decided to watch an episode or two of those old classic TV shows Edmund had asked him to play for her from time to time.

"I'm just happy she's the patient who woke up for you."

"Not for me," he corrected. "For herself."

"When will you tell her about Mr. Ridgeway?"

"Once her aunt arrives. I think it will be easier news to hear with family in the room to comfort her instead of a bunch of strangers."

Angela tapped the doorjamb several times and smiled. "I'll bring you the results once they're in my hands."

"Thank you."

Easier news to hear.

The news of what had happened to Edmund would not be easy under any circumstances. Mere tolerability seemed like the best he could hope for, and Daniel bowed his head and prayed for just that.

Prepare the ground, Lord. Please. Help her cope with what's to come.

● — ● — ●

"Could you ask my doctor to come back, please? He was here quite a while ago and said he'd return in an hour, but I haven't seen hide nor hair of him."

The male voice on the other end of the speaker replied, "Sure thing." Shannon waited, but he had nothing more to say, so she dropped the call button and let it sag over the side of the bedrail.

She tossed her head back into the stack of pillows the X-ray technician had fluffed and placed behind her, and she released a growl of frustration. The buttery walls of her hospital room slowly crawled in a kaleidoscope pattern, and Shannon clamped her eyes shut in an effort to stop the movement.

"You said she was awake?"

Shannon's eyes launched open and her head popped up, sending the room into another spin. "Ohh," she moaned, and she dropped her head again and closed her eyes.

"Shannie?"

She eased her eyes open slowly and squinted at the elderly woman hovering over her bedside. Tears glazed the woman's steel-gray eyes as she covered her mouth with the sausage-like fingers of her very round hand. Silver hair, pulled into a neat little circle at the top of her head, looked as if it had been combed upward over a pillow of air. Something about that funny bun reminded her of something, but what?

"Oh, Shannie, you just don't know how long we've prayed for this!"

The woman's voice sat very high at the back of her throat, breaking with emotion as she spoke.

I know that voice.

"Can you speak, dearie?"

She hadn't meant to gape at the woman, but Shannon could see that her astonished expression had wounded her.

"You said she was talking to you?" the woman asked the tall Greek doctor with the shaggy dark hair.

"Yes. She's able to speak," he confirmed. "I think she's just feeling a little overwhelmed at the moment." He moved toward her and took Shannon's hand. "Shannon, do you remember me? I'm Dr. Petros. We met a little while ago."

She managed a nod, but she couldn't take her eyes off the woman who had begun to weep softly.

"Are you feeling all right?" the doctor asked.

"Y—you never came back," she muttered. "You said you were coming back to answer my questions."

"I know," he replied, his attention diverted to the screen on the monitor behind her bed. "I wanted to get your test results."

"And did you?"

"I did. Shannon, do you recognize your aunt?"

My aunt.

She narrowed her eyes and regarded the woman with caution. "You're . . . my aunt?"

Nodding hopefully, she dried her tears. "Yes. I'm your—"

"Aunt Mary?" she blurted, and an unexpected wave of relief washed over her. She remembered this woman. Pushing herself upright, she took a closer look. "Aunt Mary, you look terrible! Are you sick?"

Mary chuckled and touched her turkey neck. "No, dearie. I'm not sick. I've just aged since the last time you saw me."

The doctor touched Mary's arm and they exchanged a strange look between them. He scraped a chair toward the side of the bed and nodded at Mary. "Why don't you sit down so we can all talk for a while."

"It's so good to see your pretty eyes again," Mary told her, smiling. "I've missed those eyes! The last time I saw them, you were looking at me over the top of your wedding cake as you cut into it. Do you remember that, Shannie?"

A rushing wind moved through her ears, and a bright flash of the elaborate strawberry-filled chocolate cake with scrolled fondant imprinted on the back side of her eyes. Her hands flew instinctively to her temples as she exclaimed, "What is *wrong* with me?"

The time for an explanation had come. She had so many questions, and she wanted answers.

"You were in an accident," the doctor told her, using a tone of voice people tended to think of as calming. It was not having that effect on Shannon.

"What kind of accident?"

"Do you remember going diving? On Fiji?"

Shannon frowned, remembering only fragments.

"You were diving, and the tank had a malfunction. By the time they got you to the surface, you were already unconscious. In fact, you were several minutes without oxygen . . ."

His words trailed off into a tunnel, and Shannon struggled to follow them. She saw his lips moving, and the echo of his voice took on a metallic quality as it clanked at her. He continued to speak as he leaned over her and replaced the oxygen tube she'd removed before they arrived.

"Deep breaths," he instructed as he came back into focus. "Slow and deep."

Shannon clamped the tube to her nose and closed her eyes as she inhaled. When she opened them again, her aunt glared at the doctor as he inspected the monitor behind her again.

"So that's why I'm here," she surmised. "Because of the diving accident."

"Yes," he said. Stepping back, he folded his arms across his chest the way he had when she'd first met him, and he smiled in the same way too, that deep dimple at the center of his chin flashing at her. "You've been in a coma ever since that time. You spent several months at Austin-Bryant Regional Hospital—"

"Months!"

"—and you were transferred here to Draper Long-Term Care that Christmas."

"Christmas," she repeated, and her eyes darted to her aunt. "What about Edmund? Where is he?"

And with that, Mary descended into tears, burying her face in her hands.

"Aunt Mary? Where is he?"

"Let's approach this a little more slowly, Shannon," the doctor suggested.

She scowled at him. "What's your name again?"

"Dr. Petros."

"Dr. Petros," she repeated. "Where is Edmund?"

"We'll discuss your husband in just a moment, Shannon. I just want to make sure you're clear on what led up to this day. Is that okay with you?"

She gulped around the dry spot at the back of her throat and sighed. "So I was in a coma through Christmas. How long ago was that?"

Dr. Petros reached over and set his hand to rest overtop hers. "Almost ten years."

2

The room began to gyrate, and Shannon pushed the oxygen nozzle deeper into her nose as she inhaled several times.

"Could you repeat that?" she finally asked. "I thought you said—"

"Almost ten years," the doctor answered softly.

Shannon's eyes had widened to the point that they ached and burned, and the inner corner of her left one twitched sporadically. She met her aunt's gaze, and she cocked her head slightly. "Aunt Mary?"

"I'm afraid he's right, Shannie."

"I've been—*what?*—sleeping all this time?"

"We started to notice some increased brain activity about a month ago," Dr. Petros informed her, and she felt as if she were an outside observer. She could hardly grasp the fact that it was *her* brain activity they were discussing.

"But it didn't last long," he continued. "Then a couple of days ago, it started up again and you eventually opened your eyes."

Shaking her head, Shannon held up her hand to stop him from speaking. After he'd been silent for a few seconds—or it could have been minutes for all she could trust of her sense of time now!—she grunted in protest. "You said *ten years?*"

"Yes."

"So . . . what year is it?"

"Twenty fourteen," Mary piped up.

"Two thousand fourteen," she said in shock. As a new realization suddenly struck, Shannon whimpered. "Poor Edmund! I've been in a coma since we got married?"

"Oh, dearie, that boy was—" Mary faltered, starting to cry. "He—he was a *saint*! He hardly left your side. He slept right there in that chair," she said, pointing out a leather recliner in the corner of the room as she wiped her eyes. "The nurses finally started bringing him meals because he just refused to leave you."

A smile twitched at one corner of Shannon's mouth. "Where is he?" she asked, realizing again how anxious she was to see him. "Will you call him? Does he know I'm awake?"

Mary bit her lip, crying harder, and Dr. Petros placed a soothing hand on her shoulder.

"What is it?" Shannon asked him. "Where is Edmund?"

His expression frightened her, and her heart began to pound, harder and faster, harder and faster.

"He got tired of waiting and he finally gave up and—and left me?"

"No!" Mary shouted. "He would never! That boy loved you so much! But he—he—"

Her aunt's eyes darted to the doctor's pleadingly as she struggled for words. The doctor took up the explanation.

"Edmund fell ill three years ago."

"He-he's—*sick*? What's wrong with him?" she jabbered. "Is he here at this hospital?"

"No," he replied gently. "Shannon, you've had more than your share of shocking news for one day, but the truth is, Edmund was diagnosed with a very aggressive form of malignant brain cancer several years ago."

"No!" she gasped.

"It's called gliobastoma, or GBM," he continued, "and it presents with nausea and headaches at first. Later, there are seizures and neurological deficit to the temporal and frontal lobes—"

"Stop!" she shouted, holding up both hands. "Stop talking!"

"I know it's overwhelming, Shannon, but we're here to help you—"

"Please! Would you please just stop talking for a minute?"

She tried to lift her knees, but her heavy legs wouldn't budge, so she simply leaned forward as far as she could manage and began to rock from front to back as tears streamed down her face. She didn't know how much time passed while they sat silently with her. When she finally pulled herself together, she felt ready for more details.

"Is he at Bryant?" she asked, wiping the tears away. "I want to see him."

"No, he's not at Bryant," Dr. Petros said.

"Well, where is he?"

When her aunt started whimpering again, Shannon felt something heavy finally settle on the center of her chest and she couldn't breathe. Suddenly, she began to hear again all the past tense descriptions they'd used, thudding like a bass drum in her memory.

". . . that boy was a saint . . ."

". . . He slept right there in that chair . . ."

". . . he loved you so much . . ."

". . . Edmund fell ill three years ago . . ."

"No," she began. "Wait . . ."

"Oh, Shannie. Oh, honey. I'm so sorry."

She stared at them in bewilderment, the pounding of her heart thudding in her ears.

"I'm sorry," Dr. Petros said.

The silence that followed felt hollow and awkward. When he crouched near her side, she shrank back on the bed, as if distancing herself from whatever awful thing he had to say.

"You're sorry? What do you mean? Why are you sorry?"

A biting frost of cold perspiration created a film over her upper lip and across the back of her neck. Her eyes stung, and she realized she'd forgotten how to blink.

"You don't mean—what do you mean? Just tell me where Edmund is!"

"Shannon," the doctor began gently, "Edmund died two years ago."

She shook her head in quick denial. "No." A roller coaster of emotion ticked slowly up its track as Shannon weighed the words. How was that even possible? Edmund couldn't be—

The coaster peaked, and her breath caught somewhere in her throat as her insides plummeted. She looked to her aunt to deny the doctor's horrible declaration, but what she saw in Mary's face brought no comfort.

"I'm so sorry, dearie."

"No," Shannon managed. "Aunt Mary, no! Edmund?"

Her aunt nodded sorrowfully. The doctor's eyes darted toward the floor.

"He's . . . *gone*?"

The flames of grief in Mary's eyes set Shannon's heart ablaze.

Yes. She finally understood. She'd come back after such a long time, greeted by this unimaginable, cruel truth. Edmund was gone.

3

Shannon crumpled, her confusion giving way to sudden, violent grief. For a long time she lay there, gasping and sobbing. Finally, Dr. Petros removed the oxygen tube from her nose when she hiccupped. She thought she heard him leave the room, but he returned with a box of tissues and handed them to her.

"He—he died—" she broke off. "I wasn't there! He was alone!"

"No, no, child," Mary said. Her aunt rushed toward her, and the bed bumped when she sat down on it and wrapped her chubby arms around Shannon, tugging her into an embrace. "My sisters and I were with him until the very last moment. And he had that awful sister of his. No, Edmund was never alone."

The faces of her other two aunts skittered across her mind, but their names stayed hidden in the murky shadows hovering like a dense fog.

"Thank you," she muttered. She couldn't have handled hearing that he had been alone when he died.

Died! How could it be?

"He was always family," Mary reassured her. "Our family. I wouldn't have left him."

It was small consolation when she should have been there herself, for all of it. Realizing she didn't even know how much she had missed, she blew her nose and it honked like a trumpet into the wad of tissue.

"Were you his doctor?" she asked Dr. Petros.

"Only at first. My colleague, Dr. Roose, performed the first surgery, but I was the one to tell him about the cancer."

Aunt Mary drew a shaky breath and added, "Edmund and Dr. Petros became very good friends, Shannie."

She looked up at him with wide, watery eyes. "You did?"

"I got to know him fairly well," he acknowledged. "He was a remarkable man."

Shannon gulped back a new wave of emotion. How could this stranger be talking about her Edmund as if he knew him?

"What . . . will I ever do without him, Aunt Mary?"

"We'll figure that out together. The good Lord has brought you back to us, and that's good enough for today. We'll manage the rest of it tomorrow."

But what use is waking up after ten years if I have to wake up to a world without Edmund?

She wondered, too, what that world could possibly hold for her. It was all so unfathomable.

A distant melody played somewhere within her, and a moment later she recognized the urge to pray. There had been a time—she was almost sure of it—when prayer was the first and last inclination for her. Good times, bad times, everything in between. It seemed like there had always been prayer.

But prayer to a God who had stood idly by and allowed this to happen? Or worse—had caused it? Why would He do this to her? Why would He wipe out ten years of her life? Take her from Edmund just as they'd found each other? And take him away before she could come back to him? Shannon couldn't wrap her mind around it all.

She closed her eyes tightly and shook her head, bitter resolve closing in on her heart with vice grip pressure. There would be no prayer today; no communing with a God who had stolen her husband away before they'd even started the life they'd planned, the same God who had snatched her parents, leaving her with nothing but a saintly old aunt who took her in out of duty.

She opened her eyes, and it took several blinks to bring Aunt

Mary into focus again. She knew she was being unfair. Aunt Mary had loved her and given her a happy home. But she couldn't be both father and mother to a child. Shannon swallowed the emotion creeping up the back of her throat, casting down with it the inclination to thank *Him* for such an aunt.

No, there would be no praying to that God today. Or maybe any other day either. Shannon didn't know if she'd ever want to speak to Him again, in fact.

●　—　●　—　●

"Dr. Petros, you asked me to let you know when Shannon Ridgeway completed her first physical therapy session."

Daniel glanced up from the laptop screen and removed his wire-rimmed reading glasses. "How did it go?" he asked Angela.

"Carrie says she did remarkably well for a woman who hasn't left her bed since 2005."

"Thank you, Angela. Make sure she copies me on her notes sooner rather than later."

Daniel's chair groaned as he leaned back into it. Against all odds, Shannon had been awake for two weeks, and yet there had been no inclination to celebrate the miraculous event. The ten years that had stretched between her honeymoon and her awakening had been nothing more than the blink of an eye for her, and her heart had crumbled into pieces at the news about Edmund's death.

The storm of agony raging in her green eyes at the news had tormented him after work that night, and many nights since. Never before had one of his patients awakened so dramatically and faced such emotional odds. His first call had been to Josiah Rush, his colleague at Austin-Bryant, asking him to cover his patient rounds there for the day so that he could stick close to Draper and keep an eye on Shannon.

"So now she's your only patient," Josiah had stated dryly.

Daniel hadn't wanted to admit it, but he couldn't really deny it either: he was making Shannon Ridgeway top priority. He sighed. "Just for the next day or so."

"Fair enough. Whatever you need."

That was the nature of his kinship with Josiah; unflinching honesty and unquestioning loyalty. That kind of friendship didn't always bloom within the medical community. Josiah, an African American, told him that he'd just felt sorry for Daniel, the only Caucasian in the mix of incoming doctors, but the truth was the two of them had been fast friends since the day they had met.

Daniel rubbed his stubbled cheek briskly and wished he'd thought twice about shaving that morning. After detouring to the private head—the bathroom attached to his office—just long enough to take care of the thick shadow darkening his face, he stopped at the floor desk to look through a couple of charts and made his way to the end of the main hall. He stood outside the door and prepared himself for another look into those sad green eyes. With a bracing inhale, he pushed the door open and walked in.

To Daniel's complete surprise, the corners of Shannon's mouth tilted upward slightly. It appeared somewhat pained, but her eyes almost sparkled when she saw him, and he appreciated the effort to greet him.

"How do you feel after your PT session this morning?" he asked her, scraping a chair toward the side of her bed and sitting down.

"Honestly?"

"Of course."

"Exhausted."

Daniel chuckled. "I'll bet."

"Carrie says you want us to work together every day, but I was kind of hoping you'd let me go home." She hesitated and shook her head. "Wherever that is."

"You have a home, I assure you," he told her. "It's one of the reasons I wanted to have a chat with you this morning. Do you remember the house you and Edmund purchased? The one you

32

were going to move into when you returned from Fiji?"

Her face seemed to go rigid, shadowed with consternation as she considered his question. "Kind of," she replied slowly. Brightening, she asked, "So I have a place to go?"

"You would have had somewhere to go anyway, Shannon. Your aunt has been actively involved in your care all these years. But yes, you have a home of your own that's waiting for you. It's been furnished and prepared for your return."

"How?" she asked. "I mean . . . *How?*"

"Edmund held on to the belief that you would come out of the coma," he explained. "He could never bring himself to move in without you, but he prepared the place for the two of you in the event that you rallied."

"Rallied," she repeated with a snicker. "I'll bet the place is cob webs and dust bunnies by now."

"No, there's been a semi-annual cleaning service. And I'll call them and schedule a deep clean as soon as we see how you progress."

"You know the number of the cleaning service?"

He'd hoped full disclosure could wait a day or two. "I've been keeping up with it."

"You?"

Daniel sighed and shifted. "By the time Edmund got sick, he and I had become pretty good friends. We played golf together every now and then, attended the same men's group at church—"

"Wait. Edmund *went to church*? I had to drag him—" She fell silent and her eyes grew instantly stormy and distant. When she finally spoke again, her voice turned gravelly and low.

"Well, it's nice to know he went on his own without me having to shove him through the doors."

"Yeah, he went to United Point of Grace for two years before he passed away."

She tucked her hair behind her ear and stared out the window for a long moment before she turned back and smiled at him. "I don't really remember if he ever . . . I mean, I didn't even know—

well—" She started over. "So he roped you into custodial duties, huh?"

"I was happy to do it." Daniel's throat felt dry. "He wanted to make sure you had everything you'd need if you—"

"Lived?" She raised her reddish eyebrow into a perfect arch, and one corner of her lips twitched slightly.

"Well, yeah."

The casual laugh they shared eased the tension.

"Okay, so I still have a house and some furniture. Good to know."

He smiled at her. "Anyway, we can go over all the details when you're stronger. Right now, I'd like to talk about your care if you're up to it."

She relaxed into the pillows behind her. "Go for it."

"Are your memories coming back yet? Or do you still feel a little cloudy?"

"More than a little cloudy."

"I'd like to schedule some sessions for you with a therapist."

"Carrie. Right."

"No, another kind of therapist."

"Oh." She seemed to grasp his meaning. "You think I need to have my head examined. Like by a psychologist."

"Or a psychiatrist, yes. You've been through some pretty severe trauma, Shannon. It might help you develop some coping skills."

He half expected an argument. In fact, in the light of learning what to expect from this patient now that she'd awoken, he gently braced himself for one. Instead, however, she nodded slowly. "I guess that's a good idea."

"Good."

"Maybe he can help me swim to the surface," she said hopefully. "I feel like I'm always reaching for something I can't quite grasp."

"Like what?"

"Well . . ." She scratched the side of her head and groaned. "Like my aunts. I can see them in my head, but I can't think of their names. And it's driving me batty."

"Would you like a little help?"

"Yes!" she exclaimed, sitting up straight. "Do you know them?"

"Well, you remembered Mary."

"Yes." She leaned forward and lowered her voice to a near-whisper. "But she's always been my favorite. Don't tell them though."

"I promise." Daniel smiled and released a sigh.

"The one is tiny and round with jet-black hair," she recalled. Squeezing her face with both hands, she added, "And her face looks like she's been sucking on something really sour."

He chuckled. A pretty accurate description. "That's Lora."

"Aunt Lora." She seemed to try the name on like a new hat, stepping back from the mirror to decide whether it fit. "Lora."

"And Mary's other sister—"

"She looks more like Aunt Mary, only tiny and round like Lora. When she smiles, her eyes disappear into straight slits across her face."

He nodded. "That's Lonna."

"Lora and Lonna?" she asked, and her small nose crinkled. "Where did a name like Mary come into it?"

"Lora and Lonna are fraternal twins, I think."

"Oh, well that makes sense. I guess."

Her eyes glazed as she processed the information, and Daniel watched her closely. "Any solid memories coming back to you?"

"Here and there," she said. "Flashes, you know?"

"Like what?"

"It's silly really. But I think I remember dancing."

"Dancing."

"Yeah, in a living room somewhere. A bunch of people were watching, and I was doing this dance number for them."

Edmund hadn't ever mentioned Shannon having a penchant for dance. Daniel scratched his jaw as she continued.

"It was a strange song, too. Some old Calypso number or something."

"Calypso!"

35

"I know, right?" she grimaced. "Probably a dream and not a memory?"

He chuckled. "I don't know."

"I don't know if I was singing or someone else was, but the lyrics were weird. Like . . ." She squinted as she tried to remember, and then she began to sing. *"True, mon, true. Dat is de actual fact. True, mon, true . . ."*

Daniel cackled and slapped his hand on the side of the bed.

"What?" she cried. "What's funny? Do you know that song?"

"That wasn't you." He snorted. "That was Laura Petrie."

"Who?"

"Did you notice the DVDs in the corner?" he asked, pointing out the metal rack standing next to the recliner. "Edmund dragged all of these classics in and he played them for you just about non-stop." He stood up and walked over to the shelf and began to read off some of the titles. *"Hart to Hart, The Andy Griffith Show, Breakfast at Tiffany's, My Fair Lady, Funny Girl—"*

"Barbra Streisand!" she bellowed, grinning victoriously.

"Nice," he congratulated her with a nod. "And apparently your favorite, *The Dick Van Dyke Show*. That's an oldie. Black-and-white."

"Rob and Laura Petrie," she said with a deep sigh. "I remember them."

"That song you remember? That was a dance number Laura Petrie did in the living room."

"How do you know? Do you watch those old shows?"

Daniel weighed his next words. "I've been known to watch them sometimes."

"I'm not sure . . ." As he watched her struggle with a memory, he thought she looked a little like a kid at the back of the class who couldn't quite make out the words on the chalkboard at the front. "But I think I remember . . ." She grunted in frustration. "Someone named Alan Brady?"

"Very good!" he exclaimed. "Rob Petrie was the head writer for a variety show—"

The two of them said it in unison: "The Alan Brady Show!"

"Right!" Shannon recalled. "Laura always wore those cute little capris pants. And those tight—" Breaking off, she scrunched up her face and dropped her head to peer down at her chest. Bunching up the loose-fitting gown in her fist, she pulled it away from her body and grinned. "Well. She had a little something to fill out those sweaters."

Daniel couldn't help but laugh as he replaced the DVD case in his hand and crossed the room to sit down in the chair beside her bed.

"Oh, and Rob was really uncoordinated, right?" she asked.

"Uncoordinated?"

"Yeah, he tripped over the ottoman all the time."

Daniel could almost hear the opening music of the show. "Every time."

"You'd think Laura would have just moved it, right? I mean, if he's going to stumble over it every time he comes in the door . . ."

"I guess you're right."

She seemed to drift away for a moment and, when she blinked back into the present, she asked, "Did they have a dog?"

"A dog? No. I don't think so."

After a moment: "Do I have a dog?"

He chuckled. "No. No dog."

"Hmm."

"Are you remembering a dog?"

"Yeah. A scruffy little thing," she told him. "Not much to look at, really. But I get the feeling that I really loved him."

"Maybe when you were growing up?"

"Maybe." After another moment, she tipped her head and muttered, "Freeway."

Daniel grinned. "Freeway?"

"Yes. His name was Freeway. Does that mean anything?"

"Freeway belonged to Jonathan and Jennifer Hart."

"Do I know them?"

"*Hart to Hart*. It's another old television show. From the '70s."

"*Ohhh. Riiight.*" She tilted her head again and asked, "Did I ever watch anything from this century?"

"Edmund used to say that all the time," he answered with a laugh.

"Did he?"

Daniel nodded and grinned. "He said except for *Friends*, in terms of television, you were a child of the sixties, born twenty years too late."

Born twenty years too late for her shows. Reborn ten years too late for her life with Edmund.

And there it was again: that stormy torment churning her emerald eyes into dark pools of pain.

4

"**Your other aunties** live in Phoenix now," Mary explained as she toddled about the bed tucking in the corners of Shannon's clean bed sheet. "They'll come as soon as they can and stay at my house for awhile."

"Lora and Lonna," she piped up triumphantly.

"Yes! They both squealed like children on Christmas morning when they heard the news. We're so happy to have you back with us, Shannie."

She wished she could say she felt the same, but she hadn't quite been able to work around to that yet. Instead, she pushed the corners of her mouth up into a smile and tried to ignite it with her eyes. Mary's expression told her she hadn't reached the end zone with the effort.

"I know," Mary said, and she took Shannon's hand between both of hers as she thumped down on the side of the bed. Patting it noisily, she continued. "You can't expect to be acclimated to all of this yet, dearie. You've had quite a shock."

Her aunt's sweetness propelled an emotional reaction, and tears crested in Shannon's eyes until she couldn't see much more than the blurred round shape of the woman sitting beside her.

"You go right ahead and cry. Don't you think twice about it either. Do you remember what Grandma Malone used to say about crying?" She didn't wait for Shannon's reply, but she had to admit she didn't remember her grandmother, much less her views on shedding a few tears. "She said crying is our way of letting out the steam before the whole cooker explodes and you have rice all over the ceiling."

Shannon snickered. And the more thought she gave to it, the funnier it seemed. Finally, she snorted and began to belly laugh.

Grabbing her stomach with both arms, Shannon groaned. "Oh! Why does that hurt? Why does laughing hurt?"

Mary looked at her with round, innocent eyes. "Maybe because you haven't done it in ten years. It's probably like that walk we took on Auntie Lonna's ranch. Do you remember?"

Shannon shook her head. "I wish I did."

"Lonna let the chickens get out, and you pitched in to help us round them up before her husband Cecil found out. You and I had to go clear across the pasture before we got that last one. I could hardly get out of bed the next morning. My rubber legs buckled right underneath me the minute my feet hit the floor and I tried to stand up. I hadn't had that much exercise in a month of Sundays." She squeezed Shannon's hand. "You don't remember that? We joked about it for years afterward. You called me Aunt Gumby."

"Sorry. I don't."

Mary patted her hand and gave her a loving smile. "No matter. It will all come back to you, just like you've come back to us, Shannie. You just let your brain wake up in its own time. Nobody ever has a rosy day when they've been roused from bed with a bucket of ice water. A nice banana bread baking in the oven, some tea steeping in the pot, a little warm walnut butter. That's how we'll greet your brain now. Slow and easy."

Shannon giggled. "You know what I do remember, Aunt Mary?"

"What's that, child?"

"I remember how much I love you."

Tears sprang to Mary's eyes. "That's a good start, dearie. That's a very good start."

● — ● — ●

Dr. Petros had arranged for one of the Austin-Bryant psychiatrists with whom the Draper staff collaborated to come and meet with Shannon in her hospital room. She'd gone into it carrying a backpack of very high hopes strapped to her back, but she felt like one good bump in the road might shake the bag free.

"That's it?" she asked Dr. Benedict when she ended the session with a placating smile.

"I think we've done very well for our first time."

"Are you serious?"

The doctor wore her brownish hair in a tight bun at the back of her head, and she brushed away a wisp that had escaped. With her hazel eyes fixed on Shannon through her black cat glasses, she added, "You need to have a little patience with yourself. You've been *Missing in Action* for a very long time. You'll catch up to yourself. Just give it some time."

"Dr. Benedict, time has already proven that it is not my friend. I can remember Edmund, but I can't remember his touch. I know I studied graphics, but I can't remember a single detail about it. How am I supposed to figure out the canvas of my life now when I can't bring along a single brush stroke of my life then?"

The doctor sighed. "You're just a little out of sync. But I'd say that's a small price to pay when you weigh it against the fact that you're alive. You've come back to life, Shannon. Against all the odds."

Back to life. The words taunted her. *Back to what life?*

"I'll see you again in a few days," Dr. Benedict said as she gathered her things. When she reached the doorway, she turned around and smiled. "This was a good beginning, Shannon. We'll get there."

She didn't have it in her to feign encouragement, so she simply nodded and willed the doctor to leave. Moments after she disappeared into the corridor, Shannon heard the exchange of whispers. She leaned forward in the hope of detecting the origin, and she jerked backward into a mock-casual lounging position as Dr. Petros turned the corner into her room.

"So how did it go with Dr. Benedict?" he asked her.

"Good beginning," she replied.

"Really?"

"That's the word on the street."

Daniel chuckled as he pulled a penlight out of the pocket of his white lab coat. "Look at the wall behind me," he instructed, shining the light at one eye and then the other. "Follow my finger." When he'd finished, he poked the penlight back into his pocket. "Any headaches, blurry vision, discomfort?"

"I'm a little blurry late in the day, but it's not too bad. Discomfort—well, that's another thing."

"Pain?"

"Extreme," she snapped.

"Can you describe it?"

"I think so. It's my brain. It throbs, all the time. This pounding kind of throb with an out-of-beat kind of rhythm."

"Your brain."

"Yes."

He crossed his arms across his chest and shifted his weight to one side. "Expound, please."

"Expound," she repeated bitterly. "Okay, Doc. How's this for expounding? I want to go home so much that it aches, and yet I can't remember the home I'll be going to. You and Dr. Benedict and Nurse Angela are all very nice, but you—" She had been about to tell him she didn't like him, but that wasn't exactly true.

"I don't want to depend on you. And I resent you because I know when I do leave this place, I'll remember everything about you. But my husband, my family, whatever friends I might have left? Not so much."

Daniel sighed. "I'm sorry, Shannon."

"Sorry enough to grant my parole?"

"No," he stated. "Not sorry enough to do that."

She turned away from him and sighed, but it manifested as more of a hiss.

"But what I can do is try to make us more palatable while you are here." He picked up a brown leather case from the chair by the door and opened it as he crossed back to her. "Your aunt said you asked her to bring you some books to read."

"Is that not allowed? I figured if I could have all those movies and—"

"No," he interrupted, "of course it's allowed. I want you to be comfortable while you're here. I just thought this might be easier than having your aunt toting books back and forth."

He handed her a small leather case, and Shannon opened it and stared down at the gray screen inside it.

"What is it?"

"It's a Kindle."

"What's a Kindle?"

He considered a moment, then pulled a chair next to the bed and sat down.

"There are several different types of electronic devices now that act like a book. A Kindle is one of them."

"Oh." She stared down at it without blinking. "What book is it?"

Was it her imagination, or did he just snicker?

"The Kindle acts like a sort of computer," he explained, and he reached through the bedrail and flicked the button at the bottom of the contraption. "It stores a lot of books. This is the one I used before I got my Android tablet—which is another type of computer —so it's got a couple hundred on it. But if you want some more up-to-date reading material, we can restock it for you."

Shannon was thinking fast. The idea of different types of computers rang a bell. The difference may have been important to her before—something to do with her work?

"There were really only two kinds of computers before—right? Are there more now?"

"Not exactly. There are still two major types, but there are more products now, and these e-readers—that's another name for the Kindle—are one example. Here. Take a look at this."

With a few strokes, he did some magic on the Kindle that brought a long list to the screen.

Hemingway, Fitzgerald, Koontz . . .

"All these books are in here?" she asked, lifting it and turning it over curiously.

"Yep."

Patterson, LaHaye, Peretti . . .

The next line stopped her in her tracks. "Ooh! Nicholas Sparks. I like him."

"Yeah, I think there's a couple of his on there."

"Wait. You read Nicholas Sparks?"

"I read everyone. I'm pretty voracious. For you, it's classic TV. For me, it's books."

"Well, you knew a thing or two about *The Dick Van Dyke Show*, as I recall."

His smile ignited sparks in his dark eyes as he looked at her. "I have you to blame for that," he said. "We all changed the DVDs for you. I used to take a break and watch an episode in here now and then after visiting hours."

Shannon tried to picture Dr. Petros's six-foot frame curled up in the recliner while she "slept." Did he muffle his laughter over the antics of the silly old characters? Did she ever stir while he was there? She suddenly felt vulnerable. But looking up at her doctor, she realized that she felt safe with him. The Draper staff and Aunt Mary seemed to respect him. Even Edmund had liked him, apparently. It occurred to her that the two men had watched over her together. She deliberately turned from the oddly unsettling thought.

"Tell the truth," she teased. "You hoped I wouldn't wake up so you could keep this as your personal TV room, right?"

He laughed, then grew serious. "At the cost of you not coming back to the people who love you? No. Not for one minute."

"Did you watch other things too, or did you stick to the A-List?"

"I watched a movie here and there, too."

"What was the last one?"

"*Breakfast at Tiffany's.*"

"You hummed along with 'Moon River,' didn't you?" she asked, and then realized she'd remembered that with no trouble at all. "Did you like it?"

"The movie, not really. But I happen to think Audrey Hepburn was possibly the most enchanting actress of her generation." Shannon's astonishment must have shown on her face because he chuckled and added, "What can I say? I'm a renaissance man."

● — ● — ●

Shannon's eyes fluttered open, her heart pounding a mile a minute.

"You were dreaming," Mary said softly from the recliner, and Shannon blinked several times until her aunt came clear.

"I was tumbling down a mountain of glittery walnuts. And Edmund didn't have any thumbs." The second it came out of her mouth, Shannon giggled. "Oh, you know what? That's an episode of *Dick Van Dyke.*"

"You remembered. That's progress, isn't it?"

"I think it is," she decided, and she noticed the large square of fabric perched on her aunt's ample lap. "What are you working on?"

Mary set a blue quilted bag on the floor next to her and groaned slightly as she pushed up from the chair. Standing over the bed, she smoothed the cloth over Shannon's blanketed thigh.

"I thought it might make a nice housewarming gift when you get to go home. We can hang it together."

Shannon inspected the cross-stitch sampler before her: a beautiful fruit tree with its branches stretched toward a bright blue sky, the words of a Scripture verse forming several of the branches. "For I know the plans I have for you," she softly read. "They are plans for good . . . to give you a future and a hope."

Tears stung her eyes, and Shannon tilted her head and smiled at her aunt. "Jeremiah."

"You remembered." She touched her hands together in silent applause.

Shannon realized then that she instinctively resisted memories of God or His Word—or anything about Him, really. Somehow she knew that thoughts of Him used to provide the comfort of a cozy old quilt. To her raw heart, the feeling was now more like the scrape of sandpaper. But she did not want to share that with Mary.

"I guess there's some stuff still in there," she said, tapping the side of her head. "A little scrunched up, but still there."

"Chapter twenty-nine, verse eleven," Mary said. "It's a promise. And the Lord always keeps His promises."

A future and a hope sounded pretty good to Shannon just then. The promise might have held more weight, however, had it come from a God she could trust to not do her in when she least expected it.

"I moved your little computer screen over to the table," Aunt Mary informed her. "When I came in, you'd dropped it to your chest and fallen fast asleep."

"Oh, right." Her head ached just a little as she recalled reading a James Patterson novel late into the night. "Dr. Petros brought it to me. It's called a Kindle, and it stores, like, a thousand books!" She hesitated, realizing how easily time had gone on without her. "Do you know about Kindles?"

"Well, I've heard of them. I don't have one, I'm afraid. Real books are good enough for me. I know that doctor of yours tried to spare me from lugging books back and forth, but I brought a couple for you anyway," she said, producing Jane Austen's *Persuasion* and one called *The Help* from the quilted bag on the floor. "I remembered how much you loved this one by Miss Jane Austen, and I had it on my shelf. And this other is a fun Southern read. They made a movie out of it. I'll just leave them here on the table."

"Thanks, Aunt Gumby."

Mary's face knotted up with joy. "You remembered! I knew you would."

The old nickname had come out without a moment's thought behind it, and Shannon wondered if perhaps all of her memories might come back in that way; in little sputtering droplets, all on their own.

"Oooh, and I spoke with your other aunties this morning," she said, shifting gears as she sat down again. "They should be standing right here in front of you before the day is out."

Lora and Lonna. Lora and Lonna. Lora and Lonna.

"Do you remember your aunties?"

"Lora and Lonna," she stated with confidence.

"Very good." Mary didn't look at her as she spoke; she simply slid the needle out of the fabric and concentrated on the sampler before her. "And if you have any trouble figuring out which one is which, you just watch me. I'll give you a little sign."

Shannon didn't pay much attention to the click of heels heading down the corridor until they shuffled to a stop and she glanced up at the young African American woman standing in the doorway.

Clamping her hand over her mouth, the woman gasped as their eyes met. Her fingers muffled her exclamation. "Shannon."

Short, glossy corkscrew curls surrounding a fresh, radiant face . . . a long, slender neck . . . dark caramel skin . . .

A rushing river of memories swept Shannon away as her heartbeat pumped hard against her chest and her palms turned clammy. She had heard that voice before. *"My mama was the product of Mississippi slaves, and Popi's family migrated from Ecuador. Mama says she's the tired and Popi is the poor, and we seven kids are the huddled masses, making us a real American family."*

"Izzy?"

Mary leapt up from her chair in a burst of pure enthusiasm. Grinning from ear to ear, she clapped her hands in swift little smacks and sang out, "Yippee!"

Shannon wondered if her aunt intended to celebrate like that every time a new memory from her past surfaced. She expected the confetti and party hats at any moment. But she felt encouraged.

"Shannon," Izzy breathed as she cautiously approached her. "I can't believe it. You're awake."

Shannon smiled at her longtime friend as Izzy took her hand and clutched it to her heart.

"Shannon, you don't look so different. Except for the fact that there's so much less of you, it's like you just woke up from a nap! Not like you've been . . ." Izzy closed her eyes and shook her head. When she opened them again, she grinned at Mary. "Can you believe she came back to us after all this time?"

Shannon eased her hand away and opened her arms. Izzy heaved a huge sigh as she sort of fell into them. After a moment, she wrapped her arms tightly around Shannon, yanking her against her body.

Shannon didn't realize Izzy had begun to cry until her slender torso trembled—and then rocked—within her embrace. "I've missed you so much," she whispered. "Thank you, Jesus."

Flashes of their friendship played across the movie screen of Shannon's muddled mind in bright, colorful scenes.

Sitting on the floor of their dorm room, surrounded by half-eaten bags of Doritos and Oreos, discarded bottles of Coke, and piles of open books as they quizzed one another for the upcoming psych exam . . . The two of them huddled up from the rainstorm in Izzy's "poo brown" Corolla with the sagging vinyl roof, sharing a bag of Twizzlers as Shannon filled her in on the new boy she'd met in the student union elevator that afternoon. Three hours with Edmund Ridgeway, and Shannon just knew that life as she'd known it had been abruptly altered . . . Izzy, clutching a bouquet of flowers, dressed in her beautiful lavender gown, ready to walk down the aisle and take her place next to Shannon as her maid of honor.

"I'm so sorry about Edmund," Izzy said as she released her, and Shannon snapped back to the moment. "Are you—how are you?"

She lifted one shoulder in a shrug and tried to smile. "I don't know yet."

Izzy pushed a chair to her bedside and sat down, resting her hand over Shannon's. "Stupid question," she said. "I'm sorry."

Shannon swallowed around the dry lump in her throat. "Tell me about you."

"Oh. Well, I'm married," she said, and she seemed to stumble over the word.

Shannon felt a pang. *I am too,* she wanted to say. Instead, she smiled. "Richard?"

"No. Richard and I split up a few months after your accident."

"Oh, wow." Her best friend had a husband now, and she probably had no idea who he was. Taking a deep breath, she asked, "So who's the lucky guy?"

"His name is Luca Rojas. He came to work at the PR firm." She hesistated. "Do you remember my job?"

Shannon nodded. "Sort of. You started right after we graduated?"

"Yeah, that's right." Izzy smiled in relief.

"Do you still work there?"

"We both still work there."

"Luca."

"Yeah. He's from Ecuador," Izzy beamed, and she giggled. "Can you believe I did the one thing Mama always told me not to do? I married an Ecuadorian like my Popi."

Shannon tried it on for size. "Isabelita Larrea Rojas."

Mary softly clapped her hands again from the chair in the corner. "Yippee," she whispered, and Shannon laughed out loud.

"She does that every time I remember something."

"And . . . we have three boys," Izzy said, and she held up a photo on a small handheld screen. Three happy, similar faces beamed back at her. "Nicolas is seven, Alberto is five, and Luis—our youngest—is three now." She began swiping her index finger across the screen, showing Shannon picture after picture of her happy family.

When she landed on the final one, she sighed. "And this is Luca."

No wonder Izzy had nearly swooned at the mere name. Luca Rojas looked a little bit like a Latin American model with his cropped dark hair, chiseled features and the fringe of dark lashes surrounding chocolate brown eyes.

"Whoa," Shannon said. "Nice going, Iz."

The two of them shared a chuckle before Shannon took the photo contraption from Izzy's hand and turned it over in her palm. "What is this, anyway?" Dropping her new terminology, she asked, "Is this your Kindle or something?"

As it sank in, Izzy's face contorted in slow motion. "You've never even seen a smartphone, have you?"

Shannon shook her head. "My phone takes pictures, but—" She broke off and took a breath. "Oh. I probably don't have that anymore."

"Probably not."

"That's cool how pictures scroll to the side that way."

"Swipe," Izzy said. "It's called swiping."

Her temple throbbed slightly. Izzy had a smartphone, and a husband—and kids. Three of them! Shannon shook her head vigorously. "It's a whole new world for me, Iz. I've missed so much." She looked down at Izzy's phone again and added, "I want one of these. Would you teach me how to use it?"

Izzy chuckled. "How about we get you up and walking around before we dive into the advancements in technology?"

"The lessons have already begun, Iz. Check this out!" she exclaimed, grabbing Dr. Petros's Kindle from the rolling table next to the bed. "This thing holds hundreds of books. Do you have one?"

"I did," she said with a grin. "When they first came out, like a hundred years ago, Rip Van Winkle. Now I read on my iPad."

"Your—?"

"iPad. We'll get to that."

Shannon sighed and fell back into the pillows behind her as she raised the bed with the remote control. "I feel like an alien."

"Well, some things never change," Izzy teased. "You've been a little alien-like ever since I've known you. Remember that costume you wore for the Halloween party at Pi Kappa?"

The memory bounded to earth. "Sexy space traveler!" she exclaimed.

In the corner of the room, Mary burst into subdued applause
and another, "Yippee!"

In the soft yellow glow, her emerald eyes
fluttered open, and the princess caught sight
of a stranger . . . and yet someone she
recognized with the eyes of her heart.
"Have we met before?" the princess asked him.
"It feels like we have," he replied.
"But I can't seem to remember where."

5

"Excuse me, Dr. Petros?"

Daniel looked up from his computer screen to find his executive assistant Eloise standing in the doorway to his office. She normally spent only one day each week with him there at Draper, dedicating the rest of her time to keeping plates spinning over at Austin-Bryant; he'd forgotten it was her day at Draper. Behind her familiar ample frame, he noticed a stylish young woman, a bright yellow leather bag slung over her shoulder.

"Doctor," Eloise began, and he raised his eyebrows. She normally only used the title with patients in earshot. "I'd like you to meet someone."

"Yes," he replied, and he pushed to his feet.

"Oh, don't get up," the young woman said, waving her hand at him as she passed through the doorway. "I just wanted to stop in for a minute, if you have the time."

He nodded her toward the chair on the other side of his walnut desk. "Please."

"You don't remember me, do you?" she asked as she sat down.

Eloise stood behind the chair, her very light brown skin contrasting with the young woman's darker coloring.

Trying to place her, he did a mental scan of patients, employees, hospital administrators, church attenders. "I'm sorry. You do look very familiar," he hedged.

"This is Izzy Rojas," Eloise stated. "She's a friend of your favorite patient."

"Edmund introduced us," Izzy reminded him. "When you

stopped into Shannon's room one night . . . before he passed away."

Realization dawned. "Oh, of course. Izzy."

"It's fine," she said. "We've only passed a few times over the years when I've come to visit Shannon."

"You were in their wedding, weren't you?" he asked.

"Maid of honor," she confirmed with a wide grin filled with perfect, polished white teeth. Her smile spread across her entire radiant face and seemed to settle right there in her light brown eyes. She glanced up at Eloise, still standing over her. "We all met at A&M."

"I imagine you're here to see Shannon now that she's awake?" Daniel asked.

"Yes, we just had a nice, long visit." She lifted one eyebrow into a high arch as she tilted her head. "It's a miracle, isn't it? She seems almost . . . unfazed. All things considered."

"Well, she has a way to go in terms of building up body strength again," he told her as he closed the laptop on the desk between them. "She's still a little hazy with memories, and I have a psychiatrist working with her on coming to terms with Edmund's death."

"That's kind of why I stopped in to see you, Daniel." She tapped the nameplate on the edge of the desk. "Or should I call you Dr. Petros?"

"Daniel is fine."

"How long do you think it will be before she's able to go home?"

"It's still too soon to say. I want to make sure she has all of the resources she needs to integrate back into her life. We're taking it one day at a time, for the moment."

"Do you think she'll be able to do that? Integrate into her life, I mean."

"She's doing remarkably well. But after we give her all the medical and emotional support we have to offer, it will ultimately be up to her on how to proceed."

"Is it okay to talk to her about the past?" she asked, concern wrinkling her smooth, bright face. "I mean, I don't want to upset her or do more harm than good. Should I steer her away from talk of things she missed, or about Edmund?"

"Not at all. I think connecting with you might be a very good bridge for Shannon to take her from the past into the present. She's going to need you, Izzy."

She sighed and turned away, staring out the window at nothing in particular for a long moment. Finally, she looked back at him with a glossy pool of moisture standing in her eyes. "I should have been here more, especially after Edmund passed away. I just never imagined she might come back to us, you know? I mean, *after all this time!* And . . . I really hate that she woke up all alone."

Eloise patted Izzy's shoulder. "She wasn't alone, honey. In fact, Dr. Petros was there when she woke up."

"You were?" she asked Daniel.

"I happened to be there, yes."

"Happened," Eloise said with a snort. "This man made a promise to that girl's husband that he never broke, not even one day."

"A promise?" Izzy looked at him expectantly.

Daniel sighed. "When Edmund realized he wasn't going to survive the cancer, he wanted a familiar voice there with her, talking to her, playing those television shows and movies that she liked so much."

"You were the one changing those DVDs? I was here a few times right after Edmund died. I wondered . . ."

"The morning she regained consciousness," Daniel explained, "I'd stopped in to check on her."

"Like just about every morning he's here," Eloise piped up.

"Okay," he said, casting a stern glance in her direction. "I think I've got it from here. Why don't you go ahead back to your office. We'll reconnect after Miss Rojas and I have finished."

She leaned over and smiled at Izzy. "He doesn't like anyone to know about his soft underbelly. But don't let him fool you. He's got one. He's spent many a lunch and dinner break in your friend's room, making sure she's got everything she needs and—"

"Thank you, Eloise," he snapped.

Once she took her leave—at last!—Izzy grinned at Daniel. "I'll bet she's a handful."

"You have no idea. But I couldn't function at two facilities without her."

"I can see that it makes you uncomfortable," she said, easing into it. "But I'd really like to hear about your time with Shannon. Especially the day she woke up."

He was going to have to have another one of those conversations about discretion with Eloise. Perhaps if he bought her a dictionary and highlighted the word . . .

"I had time for a short break that morning, and I grabbed a cup of coffee and a donut and was on my way back here to wrangle some quiet time," he explained. "I passed Shannon's room and decided to look in. *Dick Van Dyke* was on—"

"Ha! She loves that show."

"I don't think I'd ever seen more than two or three shows before Edmund brought those DVDs to her room." He shook his head. "Anyway, I thought I might as well sit down and watch it while I drank my coffee. I happened to glance over at her partway through the show, and her eyes were wide open, just staring up at the ceiling."

Daniel realized he was glad for a chance to relive the moment with someone else who knew Shannon. It had been replaying in his mind since the morning it happened. He remembered getting his first look into those green eyes. Edmund had placed photographs of the two of them around her room, and he'd checked her eyes on a routine basis, but he hadn't been prepared for the lively gaze. He recalled leaning over and giving her a smile, and how she'd wordlessly returned it.

"I'm so relieved to hear that, Daniel. Ever since Mary called me, I've felt bad, thinking she woke up all alone."

"Edmund shared those concerns." Daniel had been eager for the chance to explain himself, and here it was. "He wanted to make sure she was always taken care of, surrounded by something familiar. He asked me to do a few things to ensure that, and I did what I could."

Izzy tilted her head at him, curious. "It sounds like you and Edmund were pretty tight then."

Daniel's heart squeezed slightly, and he disguised the emotion with a smile. "I got to know him pretty well after he brought Shannon here to Draper." He chose not to share any of the details of their weekly dinners, occasional golf games, how he'd invited Edmund to join his men's group at church, how concerned he'd become when the headaches and blurred vision became unmanageable.

A moment later, Izzy rose from her chair and Daniel felt himself tugged back into the moment.

"Will you let me know when you get ready to send her home? I told Mary I'd like to stay with her for a couple of nights if she needs me."

"I think that's a great idea. Let me take your phone number."

She scribbled it quickly on the scratchpad he handed her. "Thanks again."

Several hours after she'd gone, Izzy Rojas lingered in Daniel's thoughts. It would be good for Shannon to have another loved one to help her through these confusing first weeks and months. He half expected to see her sitting with Shannon when he turned the corner and entered her room a while later. Instead, he found Shannon alone, squinting at the Kindle he'd given her, just one overhead light shining over her shoulder. The reflection of light made her hair shine. *Like a new penny in the sun,* he thought, and he gave himself a mental shake. Where had that come from? Checking up on a patient now that she was awake was unusual territory, he justified. Casting about for an opening, he focused on the Kindle.

"What are you reading?" he asked as he stepped in.

When her eyes met his, she smiled. "This biography of Abraham Lincoln you have in here."

"*Lincoln's Battle with God*," he said with a nod. "That was a good one."

"I had no idea he was once an atheist. His struggle with his faith is sort of . . . touching."

Daniel sat down in the chair next to her bed. "Especially when you consider that, at the time of his death, he was considering a trip to Israel because he wanted to walk in the Savior's footsteps."

"Was he?"

With a smirk, he told her, "Don't let me ruin the read for you. But when you finish, we can have a chat about it if you'd like. That was one of my favorite biographies I've ever read."

"I'd like that," she said, setting the Kindle on the bed beside her and leaning toward him. "Hey, Doc. It's not that this IV juice isn't completely delicious, you understand," and she tugged on the plastic tubing running from her arm. "But when do you suppose I can get a pizza or something?"

"I don't think you're ready for anything quite so tough on the digestive system. But we might try some lighter solid food for breakfast tomorrow if you're up to it."

"Really? Can I have pancakes?"

"I'll talk to Angela about pancakes."

"And tea?"

"I don't think a cup of tea would hurt you."

"If it goes well," she exclaimed with a mischievous grin, "then pizza?"

"Pizza is down the road."

Her mouth curled up into a disappointed knot and she sighed. Brightening considerably, she asked, "What about a burger and fries? I'd kill for a big juicy cheeseburger."

"You take it slow and ease into solid food," he said. "And when you're ready, I might spring for takeout from the best burger place I know. Deal?"

She nodded emphatically. "Deal!"

"But we'll start with pancakes and tea."

"And warm maple syrup."

Daniel chuckled. "You don't ask for much, do you?"

"Sorry. My empty stomach overrides courtesy. I'm hungry, Doc."

A good sign. "What do you think of a little Jell-O?"

"That depends."

"On?"

"What flavor, and with or without whipped cream?"

6

Shannon nearly lost her balance and tumbled off the huge blue ball her physical therapist insisted that she sit on while lifting her arms in one of several bodyweight-only exercises.

"Carrie, I can sit on this thing or I can do the workout," she objected, "but I don't think I can do both."

"Don't sell yourself short. I have confidence in you, Shannon. You can do it."

Something about petite, peppy Carrie Rhodes reminded Shannon of a high school cheerleader. Okay, so her blue jeans and gray polo-type shirt looked nothing like the uniform that begged to compliment her rah-rah attitude; but the bright green medicine balls she held in both hands could be mistaken for pom-poms if Shannon didn't look very hard.

"You should really dial back the enthusiasm," she suggested.

Carrie pressed down on her shoulder with one hand and wedged her elbow with the other. "Don't let your arms get loosey-goosey," she said. "And why should I do that?"

"Because. Somebody might deck you."

Carrie cackled and shook her head. "That's good. Just one more rep."

On the last lift, Shannon lost her balance again. She might have fallen to the floor except that Carrie caught her before she did.

"Whoa! I've got you."

"That's what you get when you overestimate the coordination of a patient," Shannon said, handing her the weights.

"Oh, come on. You weren't going to fall," she said, replacing them to the rack in front of the mirrored wall. "You just wanted to prove me wrong."

"Well, there's that."

Carrie stood in front of her and placed her arms in the rigid stance that told Shannon the time had come to stand up. She locked both hands on the girl's arms and groaned as she lifted up from the huge ball beneath her. Just a few seconds later, Carrie helped her lower down to it again.

"How's your lower back feel?"

"Shaky."

"Well, tomorrow it will be stiff."

"Oh, great. So much for your can-do attitude," Shannon said dryly.

"But the day after that, it will feel a little stronger. And the day after that—"

"All right. I get it."

"Tomorrow, I'd like to add some aquatic therapy to our routine," Carrie said as she handed Shannon her cane. "You up to that?"

Shannon's heart sank just a little. "Water?"

"Are you anxious about getting into the water again?"

"A little. I mean, one minute I was diving with my new husband—which I don't remember, mind you—and the next minute ten years have passed and I'm a widow with rubber legs and somebody else's memories."

Carrie rolled another exercise ball next to Shannon and straddled it. "What do you mean, somebody else's memories?"

"Well, sometimes—don't think I'm crazy, okay?" Carried nodded. "Sometimes I forget, or remember . . . Well, like the other day, I remembered myself as Laura Petrie."

Carrie squinted. "Who's that?"

Shannon groaned. "Are you really that young? Anyway, the thing is, I don't have a dog named Freeway or a butler named Max. I'm *lost*."

Carrie smiled. "I'm a little lost, too. What are you talking about?"

"Nothing," she said, waving her hand. "I guess Edmund thought it was a good idea to play DVDs in my room for ten years. I don't know why. To keep me company or something. But now those are the only voices I seem to hear when I strain to reach into my past." She hesitated, brushing a mop of red waves away from her face with a soft groan. "Anyway, can we hold off on the water aerobics? Maybe just a week or so?"

"We can do whatever works for you." Carrie touched Shannon's arm and smiled. "But I promise the water is shallow, and there are no masks or tanks."

"Still . . ." she muttered, and she turned away just in time to hide the salty droplet that escaped her eye and ambled down her cheek.

"Do you want me to walk you back?"

"I can find my way." She brushed her face with the back of her hand before reaching out for Carrie. "But if you could help me get off this ridiculous beach ball, I'd really appreciate it."

Carrie stood up and planted herself in front of Shannon. They formed a hands-over-wrists lock, and Carrie tugged Shannon to her feet before quickly retrieving the cane and wedging it under Shannon's hand.

"You're sure you don't want me to walk with you?"

"I'm fine. But thank you."

A dark feeling of hopelessness pressed down on Shannon as she struggled to put one foot in front of the other. For most of the other people on earth, the distance between the physical therapy room and the elevator probably seemed like a hop, skip, and a jump; to Shannon, it was the Serengeti. Never mind the endless corridor that awaited her on the fourth floor—that great open Sahara that stood between the elevator and her room.

When the doors slipped open and she emerged, Angela, her nurse, was there grinning at her like a desert mirage. "Look at you! Next thing, you'll be running in the marathon. How you doin'?"

"Aside from needing a six-hour nap, I'm at the top of my game."

"Can I get you a wheelchair, honey?" she asked as Shannon pushed past the circular desk.

"No, thanks. I've got a momentum going here."

She froze the wince from her face until she passed Angela and then gave into it as the charley horse in her left calf ripped through her entire leg.

"You have company waiting," the nurse called after her as she clomped down the hall.

Oh, goodie.

When she finally reached the blessed relief of her room, Shannon turned the corner to find her three aunts lined up in chairs against the windowed wall like some sort of happy firing squad.

"Shannie, look who's here!" Mary cried, and they all popped to their feet and rushed toward her.

Their three-woman embrace felt like an unexpected tsunami of relief. One of them couldn't be burdened to hold her up that way; but all three of them—with the added support of the ugly wooden cane to which she'd been remanded—made a handy collapsing point.

"We didn't think you'd ever come back to us," Lora sniffled.

Lonna chimed in, reverting to the family name. "Shannon Margaret Malone, you came back to us."

The three of them formed a clump of flabby arms and padded comfort that Shannon leaned into as tears started flowing. She dropped her cane to the floor but didn't really care as the foursome softly rocked from side to side and held her up by sheer love.

"Now everything is right with the world again," Mary exclaimed. "We're all together again."

All of us . . . besides Edmund.

7

"**I'm so glad you're** here!" Shannon blurted as Izzy appeared in the doorway of her room. Pointing at the television screen, she exclaimed, "Look at this!"

Izzy hurried in and flopped down on the unoccupied bed and peered up at it. "What is it?"

"It's a TV show where this English guy annihilates these chefs. He just grabbed a whole plate of risotto and threw it across the room!" Izzy pushed out a belly laugh, and Shannon scooted to the edge of the leather recliner and shushed her. "Seriously. Look at this guy. This woman behind him is still single, and he just told her she'll never find someone to love her if she looks like a dowdy Amish schoolteacher with the discriminating taste buds of an alpaca!"

Izzy snickered and lounged across the width of the bed, propping up on her elbow. "Yeah, he's made a whole career out of being horrible."

"And somebody gave him a show?"

"People love him. Go figure."

"I think I'll stick to my classics," she said, flipping off the television and setting the remote on the table beside her. "Guess what. I might be going home in a couple of days." She hesitated and then chuckled. "Home. That sounds strange."

"Do you feel like you're ready?"

"If by ready you mean throwing my cane on the floor and sprinting for the exit, then yes. I'd say I'm ready."

"I was thinking I might take you," she suggested. "Maybe stay with you for a couple of days while you get your feet under you."

"Izzy, you don't need to do that," she said, her hand on her heart. "But that's so sweet of you to even think of it."

"Luca will be fine with the boys. And my sister lives three blocks away if he needs any help. Do you remember Carmen?"

Shannon batted away the cobwebs between her and Izzy's family, but she couldn't quite fix on anyone named Carmen. "Sorry."

"It's okay. Sometimes I don't even remember her," she joked. Her gaze darted toward her friend. Izzy's nose wrinkled and amusement danced in her eyes. "Besides, I'd love a little mini-vacation from Luca and the kids. As long as you don't call my name every forty-five seconds, it will be like Club Med."

"Iz—"

Izzy hopped up from the bed and crossed the room, squatting in front of Shannon's chair until their faces met at the same level. "I've missed you, Shannon. I really want to spend some time with you and make sure you have everything you need. Let me do this, okay?"

Shannon's heart melted a little bit and she nodded. "'kay."

Izzy squeezed her hand and smiled. "I can help catch you up on all the reality television you've missed."

"Because I'm such a big fan," she replied dryly.

"*Giiirl!* I'm going to school you on the joys of reality TV if it's the last thing I do."

"Isn't that an oxymoron?" Daniel said as he appeared out of nowhere carrying two large white bags. "*Joys* of *reality television?*"

"Hey, Doc!" Shannon said, suddenly feeling buoyant and deciding to credit Izzy for cheering her up.

"Wait until you see what I have here," he said, dragging the wheeled table behind him.

"You don't have to tell me what you have," she exclaimed. "I can smell it!"

"The nurses tell me you've done very well on solid food for

the last few days, so I thought the time might have come for trying
a—"

"Cheeseburger!" she squealed.

"A cheeseburger," he repeated. He and Izzy exchanged grins.
"There's one for you here, too."

Izzy rubbed both hands together. "Oooh! Thank you, Daniel."

He set up the table between them and poured out a bag of fries
on a folded paper napkin, and he smacked Shannon's hand when
she reached for one. He leaned down and looked at her with stern
determination coloring his stubbled features.

"Now listen to me. I don't want you to make me sorry I did
this, all right?"

"I won't."

"You eat very slowly."

"'kay."

"And when you've had enough, stop. Izzy can always wrap up
the rest and Angela will store it in the fridge for later, all right?"

"Yes."

He raised an eyebrow and considered her answer before turning toward Izzy. "You'll make sure, right?"

"Think of me as The Cheeseburger Gestapo."

"That's what I like to hear," he said. Turning to go, he stepped
behind Izzy's back and mouthed to Shannon, "I like her."

She giggled. "Thanks for the grub, Dr. Petros."

"Have a good evening, ladies."

The moment he'd gone, Izzy sat down on the other side of the
table. "You still call him Dr. Petros?"

"I noticed you called him Daniel. That's kind of familiar, isn't
it?"

"Edmund introduced him as Daniel, and I guess . . ."

"So he really was close with Edmund," Shannon remarked.

"The two of them became great buddies, I guess. But I think
you should probably start calling him by his first name too, girl."

"Oh, I couldn't. He's my doctor."

"A little more than just your doctor, I'd say."

"No," she said, confused and shaking her head.

"I met his assistant the other day. She told me Daniel used to spend his lunch and dinner breaks sitting in here with you, watching TV and reading to your ol' comatose self. Edmund asked him to."

"Really?"

"Besides, I'm guessing he wanted to spend a little time with you now that you're awake too."

"What do you mean?"

"He didn't know I was here with you, Shannon. But he brought two cheeseburgers, didn't he?"

She gazed at the burgers and fries on the table between them, her mouth open and ready to respond; but nothing came to her.

"That's right. A little dinner with the pretty coma girl, maybe a movie afterward. I'd say Dr. Daniel thinks of you as a little more than just his patient."

Shannon didn't know what to think about that. She shook her head as if to clear it. "Hey. Don't call me a coma girl. And check that bag to see if he brought any ketchup."

● — ● — ●

Daniel leaned back into the desk chair and closed his stinging eyes. He'd lost count of how many patients he'd seen that day on hospital rounds. He only knew he'd managed to see every one of his own patients and another twelve of Josiah's so that his friend could fly to Tulsa for a conference. Thursday was always his longest day, but the added responsibilities and unavoidable delays had caused a two-hour lag in crossing town toward the Draper facility to make his usual Thursday night rounds.

Mr. Osterhaas had been languishing in a coma for nearly a year, and he'd died just half an hour before Daniel could get there to look in on him. Now came the unenviable task of calling his daughter. Daniel had long ago stopped trying to wish away that one aspect of his job at Draper. It was an unfortunate necessity when caring for long-term patients.

Once the call had been made, and the obligatory—but sincere, just the same—regrets delivered, Daniel closed his eyes again and said a prayer for the Osterhaas family. He'd had many conversations with Diana, the man's grown daughter, so Daniel felt confident that she would come to realize her father had finally reached a joyous reward; a fact that seldom cushioned the immediate blow of the loss of a loved one. But he knew, in time, Diana and her family would embrace that fact and allow it to comfort them.

In search of a happier note than the one on which his day had finally ended, Daniel removed his white cotton coat and hung it on the back of his office door. Sliding into his black suede and leather jacket, he made his way down the hall toward the elevator. Instead of pressing the lobby call button, he pushed the large number 4 and eagerly awaited.

"What are you still doing here?" Angela asked him as he passed the desk.

"I had to call Diana Richfield about her father."

Angela saw the weariness on his face. "Anything I can do for you, Dr. Petros?"

"Not a thing. I'm just looking in on Shannon Ridgeway before I head out."

The silence that followed came as a shallow relief as he left her behind him and continued down the corridor. It wasn't like he could explain exactly why Shannon came to mind immediately following the desire for something happier than a dead coma patient and his grief-stricken daughter on the other end of the phone line. He wondered if the answer resided in the fact that Shannon had been comatose for nearly ten times as long as Mr. Osterhaas with no hopeful prognosis, and yet she'd somehow still managed to awaken. He'd never had to make that phone call to Mary Winters, never had to hear the gasp of disbelief that evolved into whimpered denials, whimpers into sobs, sobs into wails of heavy-laden grief.

69

As he turned the corner and stepped into her room, his eager anticipation sank like an anvil to his feet as his eyes took in the sight before him. Shannon was curled into a ball in the recliner, a blanket clutched to her chin and tears flowing down her face.

"Shannon?" He walked softly toward her and sat down in the empty chair adjacent to the recliner she seemed to prefer to the bed. "What's wrong?"

She glanced up at him somewhat sleepily, her green eyes dark and stormy, and her freckled porcelain face covered with fresh moisture. She couldn't seem to manage a reply, but she gave him a half-hearted shrug.

"Talk to me," he insisted. "What's going on?"

When she didn't answer him, Daniel retrieved a box of tissues from the bed table and handed them to her before planting in the chair again. Instead of accepting the box, she simply pulled out one tissue and dried her entire face with it. She took another and blew her stuffy nose. He grabbed the waste can and set it on the floor beside her.

"Edmund?" he asked, just above a whisper.

She nodded again, this time gazing into his eyes so deeply that he almost felt it, as she waded into them.

"Is there anything I can do for you?"

She blew her nose again before replying, and she tossed the wadded tissues into the trash.

"I'm so *mad!*" she exclaimed. "Why did this happen? How could God do this to—" She shook her head and fell silent. Just about the time that he almost reached out and stroked her hair, she growled. "I just can't believe I'm all alone," she whimpered. "And what am I going to do now?"

Daniel sighed. "You're going to take whatever time you need to get stronger, both emotionally and physically. You'll continue working with the therapists until you're ready to ease back into life at whatever rate you feel you're able."

"No. I mean, what am I going to *do*?"

He didn't follow.

"What will I do for a living? They obviously haven't held my job for me all these years, so where will I work? How will I work? I can't imagine diving back into my career—no pun intended," she laughed bitterly. "And anyway, I don't know anything about technology in today's world. How would I go back to graphic design without knowing more? I don't even know what they're using now. I'm so clearly out of touch. I have to be able to pay my bills and—"

She stopped talking the instant Daniel's hand touched hers.

"I was going to go over all of this with you when you're discharged," he explained, "but you don't have a thing to worry about. Edmund has left all sorts of provisions for you, Shannon. You still have a home, and actually you have some money to start with. You're going to be fine until you figure out exactly what you want. My advice to you is to take it very slowly, and wait until you find something you're passionate about."

She snickered bitterly. "If *that* ever happens again."

"It will. I promise."

She blew her nose again and tossed the tissue away before she asked him, "How do you know all of this? Just how involved are you in my life, Dr. Petros?"

Good question, he thought. "You can call me Daniel."

"Oh. Okay. Daniel. Will you help me, Daniel?"

"Of course. In what way?"

She raised her hands helplessly. "In every way. I assume you've been managing the money since you even know the phone number to the cleaning service."

He hesitated, wondering if she'd find the truth off-putting. Or inappropriate. "Yes," he finally answered. "I've been the trustee."

"And Edmund's sister?"

He groaned inwardly. Millicent Ridgeway-Kearns had been a topic he'd hoped to avoid for as long as possible. "You remember her?"

She laughed. "Unfortunately, I remember her completely. And

71

I see from your expression that you've met her?" she inquired with a sardonic smile, and he nodded.

"Yes. Yes, I have."

"My apologies." Extending the box of tissues toward him, she added, "Here. You probably need these as much as I do then."

8

Mary had left a message that morning to say she had car trouble. Still waiting for the auto club mechanic to arrive, she apologized several times for the "imposition" on Shannon's big day and asked if Daniel might arrange for someone to see her home. He wasn't heartbroken about the development, he had to admit, and he phoned her back to say he'd see to it.

Daniel had loaded the last of Shannon's things into the back of his Lexus RX and headed up to her room to escort her down to the staff parking lot. Instead, he found her standing at the floor desk, surrounded by staff and patients, a cluster of a dozen colorful balloons tied around her fist and a plate of half-eaten cake in the other hand.

"Where's your cane?" he asked rhetorically, and he grabbed it from where it hung on the edge of the desk and extended it toward her. With a grimace in Carrie Rhodes's direction, he added, "And with your physical therapist standing right here, too."

"Sorry, Doc. I'm slacking on the job," Carrie said with a chuckle.

"We so seldom get to have a wonderful celebration like this around here," Angela chimed in. "We couldn't let Shannon leave without a little bit of hoopla, could we?"

He smiled at Shannon and asked, "Are you ready for the big, bad world?"

"I'm not sure," she admitted. Daniel knew that—in spite of that gleaming smile—she meant it. "But let's give it a shot."

A few final embraces and Shannon headed toward the elevator. Once they'd both stepped onboard and the doors slipped shut, she released a gravelly sigh and cringed as she looked up at him.

"Here we go, I guess."

A few minutes later, they both snapped seatbelts into place and Daniel drove them through the exit gate.

"Are you hungry?"

"Did you hear my stomach growl?" she asked. He hadn't, but she didn't pause long enough to allow him to respond. "I was too excited to eat lunch when they brought it to my room."

"I missed lunch, too. Why don't we stop for something before we head out to the house. Anything sound especially good to you? And don't say—"

"Pizza!" she exclaimed.

"Yeah. Don't say that. Or?"

Shannon chuckled. "I knew you'd be that way. How about something lighter then? I could go for soup and a sandwich. But—" She looked down at the baggy jeans and light blue sweater Izzy had brought to her the night before, and she wrinkled her nose. "—is this okay to wear out? I thought we were heading straight home."

"It's fine. We won't go black tie."

She giggled and poked his arm with her elbow.

"I know just the place."

Barely off-route between Draper and Shannon's house, Theodore's Bistro had become a new favorite of Daniel's. Ten minutes later, he pulled into the parking lot and shut off the engine.

"Shall we?"

Shannon grabbed her cane and used it to steady herself as she climbed out of the SUV. Once inside, Daniel looked around the restaurant through Shannon's fresh eyes. He admired the glossy, square cherry wood dining tables, each with four straight-backed chairs, all of them surrounding the sunken social area in the center of the bistro furnished with plush couches and overstuffed wingbacks. The entire back wall of the bistro overlooked lush greenery and blooming flower trees through an enormous plate glass window.

The hostess greeted them and led them to a table near the back.

"I know you've dined with us before," she beamed as she handed Daniel a tablet computer, "so you know how this works."

"Thanks, Gretchen."

"Your server is Kyle, and he'll be with you momentarily."

Once they'd settled at the table, Daniel swiped the menu until he reached the combination lunches and he handed it to Shannon.

"What's this?"

Her bewildered expression made him want to laugh out loud. "It's the menu," he replied.

"I don't understand."

He stood up and moved to the chair adjacent to her and leaned over the corner of the table. "The menu is broken down by groups." He demonstrated with one swipe after another. "You said you might want soup and a sandwich, so this is where the combinations start, and you can swipe between pages to look at the photographs and decide what looks good to you."

"Are you joking!" she squealed, and she snatched it from his hands excitedly. "What's this called?"

"This is an iPad."

"It's amazing!" she exclaimed, pushing the pages back and forth. "Do all restaurants have this now?"

"No," he said with a chuckle. "This is actually a little progressive still, but it probably won't be for long."

"This is so cool."

"Yeah, I guess technology has come a long way since you checked out."

"That's no joke."

"I use mine for—"

"Wait!" she interrupted. "You have one of these?"

"Yeah. You can read books on them, surf the Web, download music . . ."

"I think Izzy mentioned—" Her green eyes opened wide and she leaned toward him with the most adorable, and deadly serious, expression on her face. "Do I have enough money to get one?"

75

He wanted to laugh, but he didn't. "Yes," he said instead. "You do."

"And can I get one of those phones like Izzy has with all the pictures?"

"I'll take you shopping myself when you're up to it." It came out as a natural fact, as if it were not at all strange for him to take her shopping, and the surprising part was that it felt that way. He shot her a quick glance for some indication of how it had felt to her.

Unfazed, she swiped one more menu page before looking up at him. "Can we go after lunch?"

Daniel chuckled. "Those graphic design roots are showing. Maybe we'll get you home and see if there are other things you need. How's that?"

"Okay. But you're sure I'll be able to get one of these?"

"I'm sure."

Good grief, this girl is adorable!

"I suddenly have a flash of you as Alice, landing on the other side of the looking glass," he told her. "I wonder who that makes me. The Cheshire Cat? Or the Mad Hatter, maybe?"

Shannon giggled. "You're in the wrong fairy tale, Doc," she said without looking up from the new toy in her hands.

"Oh?"

She finally set the iPad down on the table and leaned back against the chair and smiled. "Yeah, you woke up Sleeping Beauty, remember?"

"How's that one go again?" he asked her.

"The stunningly beautiful coma patient is awakened by Dr. Charming."

Stunningly beautiful, he replayed in his mind. *That's no joke.*

It wasn't until the thought had already taken flight that the impact of it struck him.

●　—　●　—　●

"Have you had enough, or would you like dessert?" Daniel asked, and Shannon moaned contentedly.

"I'd love to order dessert," she told him. "But not because I want it. I just like playing with the menu."

"Here," he said, pulling up an image of a beautiful poached pear drizzled with a caramel sauce design. "Just stare at it instead then."

She giggled as he handed her the iPad, then winced as her back muscles pulled.

"All right?" he asked.

"Fine. Sometimes I forget how weak I am."

"Temporarily," he reassured her. "Your body just needs some time to catch up to the idea that you're up and moving around."

Daniel plucked his wallet from the inside pocket of his jacket, and Shannon noticed the set of unique bracelets he always wore. She reached out and gingerly touched one of the braided suede straps knotted at the underside of his wrist.

His curious smile acted as a catalyst, and she remarked, "I like them."

"Thanks." He handed his credit card to the waitress.

"I noticed you never take them off."

"Sometimes. But not too often."

"Do they have a special meaning for you?" Shannon suddenly realized she'd crossed over the mildly curious line and stepped right into the nosey zone. "Sorry. You don't have to answer if I'm prying."

"You're prying a little," he told her with a charming smile that fired up the spark in his chocolate brown eyes. "I happen to love the person who made them for me."

Why did those words drop inside her like a heavy stone? *Get a grip, girl,* she said to herself. *He's not really the handsome prince come to the rescue. He's just a doctor with a great smile and a warm stethescope.*

Maybe it was time for some respectable distance.

"You know, all this time you've just been my doctor and Edmund's friend," she pointed out calmly. "I guess I never thought about you having a personal life, too. So your girlfriend made them?" She paused. "Or your wife?"

He paused to sign the credit slip and slid the card back into his wallet. "A girl named Bushira."

"Interesting name." Shannon tried it out. "Boo-SHE-ruh."

"Swahili. It means *one who brings good tidings*."

She didn't quite know what to say. It wasn't hard to imagine Daniel coupled with an exotic African beauty. She imagined her with long beaded braids and a joyful, somewhat breezy disposition . . .

"After I completed my residency, and before I chose a specialty in neurology, I spent some time with an organization called Medical Mercy," he explained as he slipped the wallet into his pocket. "Sort of like a Doctors Without Borders. Part of that time, I went to East Africa, which is where I met a thirteen-year-old with AIDS."

Shannon exhaled deeply, realizing she'd been holding her breath. "Bushira," she confirmed.

"Yes. I took care of her and her mother, both of whom had contracted the disease. These bracelets were a thank-you gift Bushira gave me the day I left."

"You've worn them ever since?"

"Pretty much."

"How are they doing now? Bushira and her mother."

Daniel lowered his head for a moment before he glanced up at her and shook his head.

"I'm sorry."

He sighed. "Are you ready to go home?"

Shannon's stomach did a somersault. "I don't know. Let's give it a try."

She thanked the hostess at the door and followed Daniel out to his SUV in the parking lot.

"Are we far from the house?" she asked as she buckled the seat belt.

"Not far at all."

Shannon tapped her fingers on the door ledge as they sped along, keeping time with the music on the station Daniel had chosen. The Four Tops, Smokey Robinson, Carole King; each song seemed to bring back the distant taste of a memory that never quite made it to the surface. She knew all the words, though, she realized with satisfaction. That counted for something. She wondered if he'd chosen the station because these songs might ring familiar to her—and she felt certain he had. His thoughtfulness comforted her.

Not until they turned off the main road and passed through the stone arch announcing the Briarcliff community did any of it look even slightly familiar. The Temptations' upbeat "Ain't Too Proud to Beg" provided the soundtrack of a rush of memories that pelted her with imaginary pebbles from the sky as the Lexus carried her like a shiny white carriage around the curve of the road and into the driveway of a house that felt more familiar than anything else had in the weeks since she'd awoken.

When Daniel turned off the engine, he shifted in the driver's seat and smiled at her. "Familiar?"

"Clear as a bell," she replied, closing her eyes. "I can almost feel Edmund sitting behind the wheel next to me, telling me he just has a feeling about this house. 'This is the one,' he said when we pulled up out front that first day."

"Do you want to—"

Shannon opened her eyes, cranked open the door, and climbed out of the SUV. Had Daniel been speaking to her? It felt like the sidewalk had turned into one of those people-movers in the airport, and it carried her along toward the front door. It wasn't until she tried to turn the knob that she twisted around to look for Daniel. He stepped past her, keys at the ready.

"Thank you," she said when he pushed open the front door and allowed her to walk inside. The place smelled like fresh citrus and orange blossoms—and it looked different than she remembered. The beige carpeting she thought she remembered had transformed into light wooden floors, and the white living room walls were now painted a sweet butter cream. She felt a little disappointed.

As if reading her thoughts, Daniel spoke. "Edmund made a lot of changes with you in mind. He left the house in my care, just for basic maintenance."

She began to take in more of the changes. The new flooring wound around to the wall of glass overlooking the beautiful stone patio; it had been the selling point for them all those years ago, as she recalled. Shannon yanked the sliding glass doors open as far as they would go. The wooden pergola they'd dreamt up as they surveyed the backyard on that first day now stood in place, providing shade for several cozy couches and chairs forming a border around the fire pit in the middle.

"Edmund," she whispered. "It's just like we planned."

A tsunami of unexpected emotion crashed over her, spraying her face with hot tears as she let her cane fall to the ground before she sank to her knees, dropped her face into both hands, and wailed.

She didn't know how much time had passed before she remembered that she wasn't there alone, and she glanced up to find Daniel standing helplessly beside her.

"Oh, Daniel. I'm sorry," she said, wiping her face with the sleeve of her oversized blue sweater and struggling to get to her feet again.

"Is there anything I can do for you?" he asked in a soft voice as he helped her up. "Let me see if I can find you some Kleenex."

Wiping her face as she waited, Shannon wondered at Daniel Petros. He'd become her regular provider, hadn't he? Every time she broke down, this really handsome man turned up to make sure she had a box of Kleenex when she needed them. That handsome helper should have been Edmund. But it wasn't. She shook her head, hoping to shake loose her tangled thoughts about that. She looked up and laughed with relief to find him comically hurrying back with two boxes—one in each hand—extended toward her.

"Izzy did the shopping," he said, examining the boxes. "We've got a box of extra soft and—let's see—one with an antibacterial agent."

"They make antibacterial tissues now?" she sniffed. "What's next? Are you going to tell me they've made phones without cords?"

He grimaced, staring at her strangely.

"Ha! Kidding," she said, and Daniel groaned. "Just kidding."

The two of them sat down on one of the sofas beneath the pergola, and Shannon blew her nose.

"I seem to do this a lot around you—blow my nose. Don't I?"

"What is it they say?" he asked. "Better out than in?"

"I think they say that about gas."

"Gas? That doesn't seem right, does it? Better out than in? I mean, who's it better *for*?"

His observation struck Shannon oddly funny, and she started laughing.

"Not the person sitting next to you, that's for sure," he continued.

She cackled and snorted until she'd lost her breath, but Daniel showed no mercy.

"I think it's the snot that's better out than in, frankly. The gas? Not really so much."

"Stop!" she cried, struggling to pull herself together. She plucked one of the extra soft tissues from the box and dried her eyes as she groaned. "You have to stop."

Daniel smiled at her in triumph, and Shannon realized his thoughtfulness again. He had diverted her sadness momentarily. She felt fairly certain they would circle back around again, but for the moment, she appreciated his kindness.

"Thank you, Daniel."

"*Ce n'est rien*," he said with a wave of one hand.

"Greek?" she asked, and Daniel grinned at her.

"French."

"You're a Greek boy who speaks French."

"*Y español.*"

"Spanish, too?"

"What can I tell you, Shannon? I'm a renaissance man."

"You certainly are."

Daniel stood up before leaning over and grabbing her hand. "Izzy gets off work at five, so she should be here by six."

"Oh, I forgot."

"And your Aunt Mary will be here in the morning to stay with you during the day."

She clicked her tongue and sighed. "I don't really need a full-time staff of babysitters, do I?"

"You do not," he replied, shaking her hand playfully. "Just for the first couple of days while you get your land legs again."

"Land legs," she repeated. "For someone who nearly drowned. If that's a joke, it's not a very good one."

"It wasn't. What do you need before I go? Shall I put on a movie? Get you something to drink?"

Shannon's heart thumped a couple of times before she swallowed around the lump in her throat and asked him, "Do you have to go? Can you stay just a little while longer?"

"Sure. I'll stay with you."

● — ● — ●

"That's *chai* with a triple letter score on the C, and a triple word score besides," Shannon announced. "That makes it fifty-one points!"

"I thought your brain was compromised," Izzy grumbled. "Start acting like it."

Shannon fell backward into the sofa cushions with a soft groan. "No, thank you."

"Well, of course, I'm kidding you. But you're wiping the floor with me. I'd completely forgotten my vow to never play Scrabble with you again."

"You have to," Shannon told her with her best sad-eyed impression. "I've been in a coma for ten years. My poor little brain needs this. Would you really deny me?"

When she forced her lower lip to quiver, Izzy burst out laughing and picked up a pillow, tossing it at Shannon. "Pathetic!"

"I know. But it's all I've got."

Shaking her head, Izzy leaned on the coffee table between them and pushed up from the floor. "I'm getting more tea. Do you want some?"

"Nah," she said, her focus trained on *The Dick Van Dyke Show* episode that was playing quietly on the enormous flat television screen over the whitewashed brick fireplace.

Rolling her eyes, Izzy picked up their glasses. "Don't you ever get tired of historical white noise?"

"What do you mean?"

"You've always been like this. You'd so much rather live in that world than this one. But Shannon, there is actual *current television* to watch that is fun and entertaining instead of playing the same old thing over and over in your head until you can recite it. It's not a good thing that you can wake up ten years later and still be up to date with your favorite shows!"

"Yeah," she replied, her eyes back on Rob and Laura Petrie's living room. "But I'll bet there's no one as good as them on today, Izzy."

Shaking her head, Izzy padded off toward the kitchen. "I give up," she called over her shoulder.

"Promise?" Shannon returned.

Oddly familiar music yanked her attention back to the television, and she drew a sharp intake of breath as Mary Tyler Moore danced to *a Calypso-type beat . . .*

She fought a surge of dizziness that set her head to spinning to the rhythm of a song she somehow knew very well. *Dark leggings, a light mock-turtleneck sweater, little ballet flats, the offending ottoman moved out-of-frame.*

Shannon raked both hands into her hair and tugged on it. Had she really turned a scene from *The Dick Van Dyke Show* into her own frazzled memory? Somewhere inside the unconsciousness she'd known for the last ten years, she'd crawled deeper into the murkiness and into a pair of 1960s leggings. She'd put on her dancing shoes and felt the thump of the bongos and she'd become Laura Petrie for a moment. And then she'd become the owner of Freeway, the dog belonging to Jennifer Hart.

As much as she loved it, she suddenly knew that going back to that world wasn't helpful right now. She needed to find her own true self, as she was now. Shannon Ridgeway, coma survivor, widow . . . and what else? There was much more. She just had to find it.

"You're sure I can't get you anything?" Izzy asked as she returned with a fresh glass of iced tea.

She aimed the remote at the television and turned off the DVD player. "I think you might be right. Maybe I'm watching and listening to these old shows too much."

"Really?"

"Yeah. Tell me, what wonderful programming do they have on a Thursday night in today's world?"

"Well, for one thing, it's Monday. Not Thursday."

"Oh. Is it?"

"And if you're serious," Izzy exclaimed, snatching the remote out of Shannon's hand with a huge grin, "I'd like to introduce you to Richard Castle and friends. Girl, this is going to rock your little TV-lovin' world."

The new land frightened the beautiful princess
as she faced down so many unfamiliar people and things.

"Take my hand," the handsome stranger said.
"We'll navigate this land together."

"Can I trust you?" she asked, wide-eyed and smiling.

"From the bottom of my heart," he told her,
"I pledge you my loyalty and protection against
the inhabitants of this peculiar place."

9

The days had started running together for Shannon, and she'd hardly noticed when the weekend came and went.

Ten minutes into that first episode of *Castle*, she'd been hooked, just as Izzy had predicted. When TNT aired a marathon of past shows that weekend, she'd hunkered down for nine straight hours with a ruggedly handsome novelist and his crime-fighting friends.

"After ten years flat on my back, you wouldn't think I'd still spend so much time on my duff, would you?" she asked her aunt when she'd awakened Shannon from her Sunday afternoon nap.

She took several minutes to stretch out her legs and back before commuting to the kitchen for a meal of the favorite childhood comfort foods that awaited: beef stew, hand-tossed biscuits, and sweet tea. *Heaven!*

On Friday morning, her aunt propped herself up with stacks of pillows behind her on the bed to embroider while Shannon inventoried her clothes hanging in the closet and folded in the bureau.

She finally plopped down on the corner of the bed and fell backward with a thump. "I'm losing my mind, Aunt Mary. Let's do something."

"All right, dearie. Would you like to stitch a while?"

Oh, bless her heart. Needlework was one activity Shannon had no trouble remembering she didn't like. Other memory lapses were already much fewer and farther between than in those first stressful days after her coma. All her doctors and therapists were pleased with her progress in general. What she needed most now was purpose.

"No. Thank you, though. I just feel like getting out and about. Do you want to go for a ride or something?"

Mary secured the needle in the corner of the fabric and lovingly folded it around the wooden hoop. As she tucked it into a quilted floral bag, she asked, "Where would you like to go?"

"I have no idea," she admitted, and she hurled herself upright and grinned at her aunt. "But Edmund's car is just sitting in that garage out there waiting to be driven. Let's crank 'er up and see where she takes us."

"Whatever you say, Shannie. I'm game if you are."

A flash of a memory tickled the back of her brain just then. A summer long ago, sipping lemonade on the front porch of Mary's sprawling home in the suburbs.

"Nothing ever happens out here in the boonies," Shannon had whined. "Why do I have to spend all of my summers here with you in the middle of nowhere? Can't we go have an adventure?"

"What would you like to do, Shannie? I'm game for it if you are."

Shannon blinked back to the present and smiled at her so-much-older aunt. She leaned forward and took her fragile, wrinkled hand and kissed it. "I love you so much, Aunt Mary. Just give me five minutes, and we'll fly."

"Ready when you are," Mary said as Shannon hobbled into the bathroom, her trusty cane firmly in hand.

Edmund's blue BMW started up with one turn of the key, purring like a happy cat. The two women had gone for a few short test drives in the neighborhood earlier in the week, and for her first time driving after a decade asleep, Shannon considered the couple of slight jerks on acceleration to be nothing more than a relearning curve. Now as she slid behind the wheel, she felt confident. Her aunt, however, exhibited distinctly less confidence as she clung to the door handle and stared through the windshield with wide, glassy eyes.

"It's just a matter of getting used to this again," Shannon reassured her.

"I wonder," Aunt Mary said through gritted teeth. "Are you sure you wouldn't like *me* to drive today?"

"It's fine," Shannon promised. "See, I'm already getting the hang of it again."

With only a vague idea where they were headed, she steered the touchy car around the curve, out through the Briarcliff arch, and along with the flow of traffic toward town. At the intersection, she tapped the brake at the stoplight, and the car lurched forward with a screech.

"Sorry," Shannon said as she opened the sunroof and the driver's side window, allowing the buttery Texas sunshine to melt over her.

At a stoplight she glanced at her aunt and watched her for a moment. Mary's eyes were softly closed, her pudgy face turned upward into the breeze. Shannon realized she would have preferred a more solitary exploration on her first full day at the wheel. She was feeling good physically after a week at home, and though she knew her use of a cane and her upcoming appointments at Draper would be necessary for awhile, she had grown weary of so many eyes fixed on her, waiting for she didn't know what. It was as if they expected her to nod off for another decade or two at any given moment.

"Green," Mary murmured from beneath mostly closed eyelids.

Shannon checked the light and eased her foot onto the gas pedal, driving on with a chuckle of relief. She shook her head at the realization that her aunt had probably been monitoring every move she'd made since leaving Draper. She guessed Aunt Mary had been on guard even while she napped, one ear trained on her breathing and a compact mirror handy to hold under her nose at regular intervals.

It wasn't that she didn't appreciate having her aunt close by. After all, ten years was a long time—and what would she have done if she'd awakened to find her father's older sister gone too? But she found herself longing for those first few days, when Izzy gave her more relaxed company . . . or that very first evening, alone with Daniel.

With cash in her wallet that Izzy made sure she had on hand, Shannon enjoyed a full morning of idle shopping with her aunt, reacquainting herself with the area. It had certainly seen some changes—a few new buildings, new strip malls, some storefront turnover—but it still held enough familiarity to give her confidence in her next move.

"You know," she said as they lingered over lunch at a new café in town, "I've really appreciated you staying with me the way you have, Aunt Mary."

"It's my pleasure, Shannie. You know that."

"I do know. But I was thinking, I'm feeling so good now. Maybe it's time you go home."

Mary froze with a forkful of salad halfway to her mouth, her face suddenly a mask of fright and worry.

"It's not that I don't love having you around," Shannon continued. "I just think it's time that I start figuring it all out on my own, you know?"

Mary said nothing. Just kept staring at her with those wide, confused eyes.

"Please understand, I'm not kicking you out here. I'm just— you know . . ."

Mary obviously did *not* know.

"Please don't look at me like that, Aunt Mary. It's just that I don't want everyone walking on eggshells and feeling like they need to staff this tight babysitting schedule for me. I know I was out of it for a long time, but I'm better now. I'm a grown woman, and I can do this."

Her aunt sighed, setting her fork down and sitting back in her chair. "Of course you can."

"So do you understand?"

"Of course."

Shannon spotted the waitress nearing their table with the bill, and she quickly seized the opportunity. With a confident smile she reached out for the padded folder before Mary could see it coming.

"I'm navigating a whole new world," she said as she tucked some cash into the folder. "I need you all so much; you and Izzy, Aunt Lora and Aunt Lonna. I just don't want to use you all as crutches when it's time that I took a few steps on my own. I hope that makes sense."

Mary turned toward her, a volatile puddle of tears standing in her eyes. "It does."

"Why are you crying then?"

"I don't want you to ever," Mary took Shannon's hand and shook it briskly, "*ever* feel like you're alone."

Emotion tightened her throat and Shannon felt like she might start to cry too.

"After my mom died," she said softly, "you became my mother, Aunt Mary. And when Dad passed away, you opened your doors to me and took in your brother's orphan, no questions asked. In all those years, I've never felt alone even once because I always had you."

The dam broke and Mary's tears tumbled down her rosy cheeks in bumpy streams. "And you always will."

"I know." Mary opened her arms and Shannon lunged into them. "How about we celebrate our last overnight tonight? We'll wear our favorite pajamas and work on your embroidery together, and you can make me some of that warm cider before bedtime. What do you think?"

"A nice send-off before you put the old girl out to pasture?" her aunt teased. "I'd like that very much."

"There's not a pasture that could hold you, Aunt Mary. And besides, it's not like we won't talk every day," Shannon promised. "And remember those Sunday dinners we used to make together after church? Maybe we should start doing that again. What do you think?"

Mary's smile lit up her face. "You remember?"

"I do," she replied with a nod. "I woke up last night thinking about your roast chicken with rosemary potatoes."

She expected a response like, "Then that will be the first meal we make," or "You always loved those little potatoes." Instead, her aunt happily lifted her hands in front of her chin and clapped them.

"You remember. Yippee!"

Shannon giggled. "Yippee."

She hugged her aunt and planted a warm kiss on her cheek as they rose from the table.

"So where are we headed now?" Mary asked as Shannon led the way toward the car.

"Well . . . Hey! How about some ice cream?"

"Whatever you want, dearie."

"Over near Draper, there's a little shop with a big jar of candy toppings painted on the front window," she said. "I could see it from the physical therapy room."

"Let's go there then."

After ten minutes of inner debate over the wide array of ice cream flavors, toppings, and cone varieties, Shannon sensed the clerk's goodwill waning. "This is my first ice cream in—in a really long time," she explained lamely. How could she adequately communicate how remarkable it was for her to be alive, to be well and walking, to be doing something as normal as getting an ice cream cone? She couldn't. So she just ordered a coffee ice cream with crushed Oreo cookies and caramel sprinkles in an oversized waffle cone. Her aunt requested a simple frozen fudge bar while Shannon leaned on her cane and navigated to the white iron bistro table by the window where they could enjoy the treats.

"You know," Shannon said, and she paused and closed her eyes long enough to let the flavors sink in for a moment. "Aunt Mary, this is unbelievable."

Mary chuckled. "If we listen very closely, do you suppose we'll hear your taste buds singing after ten years without sweets?"

Shannon hesitated. "I think I do hear them." She grinned at her aunt and continued with her interrupted train of thought. "I'd like to head into the bakery next door and pick up something nice for the staff at Draper. Would you mind if we did that?"

"Not a bit."

Shannon wiped off her sticky fingers and threw away her napkin. Mary continued to take demure little swipes at her fudge bar as they walked to Hannah's Bakery.

Shannon chose a dozen cupcakes in a variety of flavors—from red velvet to orange citrus to espresso fudge—and the bakery attendant quickly wrote letters atop eight of them, spelling out THANK YOU, before placing them in the white box. She tied the box with bakery string and placed a neon pink HANNAH's label on the front.

Shannon hadn't even sneaked a glimpse of the Draper facility across the street when they'd pulled into the parking lot and climbed out of the car. But now, waiting for the light to turn green to signal their welcome into the entrance, she faced it head-on.

From the inside—and behind closed eyes for most of her time there—Shannon had never been able to enjoy the cheerful terracotta façade or the lively yellow and red flowers bordering the entire front of the building. She pulled into guest parking and turned off the engine before leaning back with a rumbling sigh.

"It must be strange to come back here," Mary remarked.

"Well, I have a running PT appointment with Carrie and a few other checkups for the next couple months, so I'll get used to it. Good thing I have you to help me get the first time over with, right?"

"We'll battle the nerves together," she replied, squeezing Shannon's wrist.

A security guard sat posted behind a small desk angled into the corner of the lobby, and he smiled at Mary as they walked through the glass doors.

"Miss Mary, I sure didn't think I'd see you again," he exclaimed.

"Curtis, I'm not sure you ever met my niece. Shannon was the patient I came to see all those years when you took such good care of me."

He removed his hat to show short, kinky salt-and-pepper hair underneath. He planted the cap on the desk as he sang, "Ooh-weee, it's good to know you're up and around, Miss Shannon."

"It's good to be back among the living, Curtis," she answered him with a smile. "I just brought along some thank-you cupcakes for the staff on the fourth floor. Is it okay if I take them up?"

"I'll have to call to clear you first. Give me two quick snaps, and I'll see if I can get them on the horn."

When the elevator doors slipped open on the fourth floor, they were immediately greeted by Angela's grinning face as she stood there behind the circular desk.

"Now what in the world are you doing back here?" she beamed. "You didn't get enough of us already?"

"What can I say? I'm a glutton for punishment."

Angela rounded the desk, her arms outstretched, and Shannon had just enough time to hand the bakery box to her aunt and steady herself against the wooden cane before she was tugged into an embrace. "Shannon Ridgeway! You're a sight for sore eyes."

"She certainly is."

Shannon reeled at the sound of Daniel's voice, and the sight of him sent an unexpected surge of joy straight through her.

"Daniel. How are you?" Before he could answer her, Shannon took the cupcakes from her aunt and held them out in front of her. "Look! I brought cupcakes."

"Now it's definitely good to see you," he teased.

A couple of other nurses and an orderly seemed to descend upon them all at once, greeting Shannon and Mary, and Angela lifted the bakery box out of her hands and set it on the desk to open it for them all.

"How are you doing?" Daniel asked her as the others gathered around the desk behind them.

"All right," she said with a shrug. "Trying to get my bearings."

"Want to walk with me? I have something in my office for you."

"Angela, will you take care of my aunt for a few minutes?"

94

Shannon asked. "I'll be right back, okay, Aunt Mary?"

"I'm not going anywhere. Come back when you come back."

As they stepped into the elevator, Shannon heard her aunt turn down the offer of one of the cupcakes. "We just came from the ice creamery across the street. I've had my allotment of sugar for one day."

On the way down the corridor toward Daniel's office, Shannon updated him on her latest adventure. "So guess who drove here today."

He looked down at her cane and winced. "Your aunt, I hope."

"No! Me. I drove."

"Have you been to the DMV to renew your license?"

She stopped in her tracks and gawked at him. "You're kidding. I really have to do that?"

● ⋯ ● ⋯ ●

Daniel shook his head and grinned as he opened the door to his office. Eloise greeted them with perfectly-rounded eyebrows arched over her wide, surprised eyes.

"Well, look at you!" she exclaimed.

"Hi," Shannon returned shyly, and she followed Daniel into his office.

He closed the door behind her and motioned to the chair on the other side of his desk. "Have a seat."

The moment they'd both settled, he leaned forward. "By the way, yes. You do need to renew your license before you go driving around Austin."

"Do I have to take the test again and everything?" she asked him, concern staining her cheeks with a flush of pink. "I'm not sure I could still parallel park."

"Tell you what," he said as he reached into the deepest desk drawer and pulled out the bag nestled into it. "We'll go online and check it out."

"All right," she said, and he saw that she was delightfully clueless about what was about to come next.

He'd been imagining her surprised delight for two days, and his heart pounded at the realization that the moment had arrived. Brushing away the momentarily nagging thought that perhaps he'd crossed a line, he grinned at her.

"I got you a little waking-up gift," he said, and he slid the flat package across the desk toward her.

Her gemstone eyes sparkled as she smiled at him. "A present?"

He nodded. "Open it."

She inched forward in her chair and leaned over the desk. He watched her excitement flare up as she tore into the bag. Then she gasped.

"Oooh, it's the menu thingie!" she cried, and Daniel laughed out loud.

"Well, that was an iPad. This is an Android tablet, like mine."

"You bought this for me? Why did you do that?" she asked as she fumbled with the box and slid the tablet and the packing material out across his desk. "Will you help me make it work?"

"Happy to. I was—well, actually, I'd planned to call and ask if you'd like to have dinner, which is when I was going to give it to you."

"Oh, I'd like that!" she exclaimed. "When?"

"How do you feel about Chinese takeout?"

She gasped again and closed her eyes. "Cashew chicken with white rice, an order of crab rangoon, and two eggrolls with plum sauce!"

"Wow! A woman who knows what she likes—and remembers it!" he joked, scribbling down her order on the notepad next to his phone. "Are you free tonight?"

She started to agree, but he watched as she caught herself. "Oh. I made plans with Aunt Mary for tonight. Can we make it tomorrow?"

"Absolutely."

She didn't bother packing up the box again. She just pushed it all toward him. "You better keep this until you can teach me how to work it. I can't be trusted."

"What big plans did you ladies make for tonight?"

"Embroidery," she replied, her little button nose wrinkling up until the dusting of freckles across the bridge gathered into one uniform splotch. "I told her she and Izzy need to stop babysitting me, and tonight is my effort at making her realize it doesn't mean I don't love and appreciate her. I'm just ready to ride a few yards without the training wheels, you know?"

"And she understood?"

"No. But she agreed," she said, and she tossed her long hair over her slender shoulder with a laugh. "Speaking of Aunt Mary, I'd better go and find her again before she thinks I left without her."

"I have two more patients to look in on, so I'll walk with you."

When they reached the door, Shannon hesitated, her hand resting on the knob. Suddenly, she spun around and faced him. He paused for a beat, waiting for her to speak, before she reached up and threw her arms around his neck in a friendly embrace.

"Thank you, Daniel," she blurted as she hugged him. "For the—the menu thing, and the promise of cashew chicken, and . . . you know, everything."

"It's my pleasure."

Her arms lay gently around his neck and the sweet citrus fragrance of her hair wafted up his nostrils. Instinctively, he leaned down to nuzzle the side of her head.

What are you doing, man? he asked himself, and he jerked away from her.

"Okay!" he said brightly, clearing his throat. "So let's get you to the fourth floor to retrieve your aunt."

10

Reliving the moment at Draper, Shannon chastised herself. It had seemed like the most natural thing in the world to thank Daniel with a friendly embrace, but she had ended up feeling completely flustered. It had taken her three tries to grasp the doorknob, for one thing. She rationalized that she probably just felt lightheaded or something. It had been a long day for her first big outing, after all. She shook her head to clear the memory and focused on the cross-stitch project on her aunt's lap next to her on the sofa.

"It's so pretty," Shannon said truthfully. The idea of basing her new life on a Scripture verse about a future and a hope left her heart a little cold at the moment, considering that the Originator of that Scripture had been the One to take away the old one. She decided on a softer place to land than those particular thoughts. "I love the colors."

"I thought we could frame it in a nice light wood like your floors," Mary said without looking up from her work, "and hang it right over there on the wall behind the dining table."

Her aunt grasped the large round wooden hoop and held up the fabric to inspect her work. The colors of the fruit on the tree caught Shannon's eye, and she noticed that the first line of words of the scripture that comprised the flawless branches had been completed.

"You're really making headway on it, Aunt Mary."

"A labor of love, dearie," she replied, and she handed the hoop to Shannon. "Why don't you stitch while I make us some warm cider."

"Me?" She pulled back and raised her hands as if the fabric and thread might take a bite out of her. "I don't know how. I'll ruin it."

"I've told you before, Shannie. There's no such thing as a permanent stitch. If it's not right, we just pull it out. This is one of your Aunt Lonna's patterns."

"She designed this?"

"Yes. She made it just for you."

Her aunts had gone to such extraordinary trouble to give her something that might renew her faith when she privately doubted there were enough embers of it left to stoke back into a flame.

Setting the fabric and hoop on Shannon's leg, Mary set the pattern on top of it. "It's all counted out in x's. See here? The row we're on now starts right here."

Shannon fluttered. "So I would just . . . start making x's there?"

"Yes. Half an x, then half an x, just like that until you reach the end of this row. Then you go back in the opposite direction and complete the other side of each x."

Shannon watched after her as Mary toddled into the kitchen. As her aunt's clear voice sang from the other room, Shannon inspected the pattern closely, counting x's in one row, and then comparing them to the stitches on the fruit tree. When it started to make sense to her, she unpinned the needle and began cautiously sewing in half-x's to the row that followed.

The doorbell rang just as she turned around to complete the first row. She jumped slightly at the sound of it, and the needle poked through the fabric and pierced the skin of her index finger.

"Ouch!"

"Shannon? What happened?" Mary asked as she passed her and headed for the door. "Are you all right, dearie?"

"Fine. I just pricked my finger."

The creak of the opening door preceded Mary's surprised exclamation. "Oh my. Hello. . . ."

Shannon dabbed her bleeding finger with a tissue as she asked, "Who is it, Aunt Mary?" But when she glanced up to find Edmund's sister standing in the middle of the living room, the question was regrettably answered for her.

Millicent Ridgeway-Kearns sneered down at her, condescending without speaking a word, and a flood of memories washed over Shannon in a few seconds' time. Millicent had aged with a fair amount of grace, Shannon thought as she looked into the woman's dark, piercing eyes—and then she wanted to shield her own from the intensity of Millicent's glare. Dressed in an impeccably tailored black suit and standing atop several inches of straps and buckles, the woman grimaced.

"So it's true," she said in that unforgettable elocution that screamed Texas Money and was uniquely Millicent. "You're actually alive, are you?"

"Hello, Millicent. Good to see you, too."

●　—　●　—　●

Daniel sat on the bench and tightened the laces on his shoes, wondering how Josiah had managed to rope him into this. The two of them used to play amateur lacrosse together some weekends, and he'd opened with a reminder of how many shifts he'd covered for Daniel lately before asking him to come out to help demonstrate the sport to a group of teenage boys.

"All right, listen up!" Josiah called out, and nearly a dozen kids gathered around them. "This is my buddy, Daniel. He's gonna help me give you ladies a crash course out on the field. Lacrosse 101 for Dummies. You got it?"

Daniel suppressed a grin over Josiah's phony tough guy act. The dude loved working with the kids from the youth center.

"Yes, sir, Doc," one of the boys replied, and several other less enthusiastic voices echoed the response.

"Yes, sir."

"Now that I've laid out the basics for you on the blackboard, you think you're ready to throw some balls around?"

The enthusiasm quotient kicked up a few dozen notches. "Yes, sir!"

"Ready, Doc!"

"Let's go!"

Daniel watched as the boys accosted the cardboard boxes leaning against the dingy gray wall by the door, plucking out sticks and gloves and helmets as they scurried out of the makeshift gym. Josiah slapped his shoulder with his large gloved hand as he passed.

"Let's go, old man," he said. "Let's show 'em how it's done."

Only a couple of the boys showed any real talent for the game, but their concentrated efforts impressed Daniel just the same. They paid focused attention as he and Josiah demonstrated the different ways to handle a lacrosse stick, and they cheered when the ball passed smoothly between the two of them.

"It's ideal to hold the stick around halfway up, like this." Josiah showed them. "But as beginners, don't be afraid to choke up on the throat if you need to. When you go to throw, keep your elbow up with the stick behind your head. When you catch—look at Daniel—the stick is straight up and down, in front of his face. Once he catches it, he drops his hand and tosses it back, overhanded."

They exchanged a few passes before one of the teens called out, "That's cool. Can we try it now, Doc?"

"Not until I see a helmet over every thick skull here. And that means you, Brandon. We're gonna see what it does to that pretty hair you've got there."

Daniel's friend had been mentoring the boys at the youth center for more than a year, and he'd regaled Daniel with amusing tales of the varied activities they'd tackled. Josiah was one of the most athletic guys he knew, so lending his talents to a group of wayward teens would naturally gravitate toward physical activities whenever he could manage it. Basketball, bowling, baseball, even golf, and his friend seemed to love every minute of it.

Brandon—who bore a striking resemblance to a certain teen idol—dropped the helmet from his hand and tossed his well-trained hair to one side as he raced to cut between them, stealing the ball from in front of Josiah before he could cradle it. The other boys oohed and aahed at the strike, and Josiah's laughter resonated across the field.

"All right, all right," he called. "Get the helmets on and break up into pairs to practice throwing and catching. Do it the way we've shown you."

After about an hour of walking around and tutoring the boys on tightening up their shoulders, improving stances, and keeping their eyes on the ball, Josiah tossed his car keys to one of the boys and sent him and a friend to retrieve a cooler from the trunk. When they returned, the whole group of them found spots on the rickety wooden bleachers to throw back bottles of juice and munch on trail mix.

Daniel's cell phone rang, and he pulled it from the pocket of his jeans.

"Dr. Petros."

"Daniel?"

The timbre of Shannon's voice pricked his ear. "Shannon? Are you all right?"

"Not really."

"What is it?"

"I—can you come over to the house?" she asked him. "I wouldn't ask, but it's really important."

"What's going on?" he asked, and then he covered the phone with his hand and nodded to Josiah. "I've gotta take off. Call you later."

"Everybody thank Daniel, huh?" Josiah said, and the roar of appreciation drowned out Shannon's reply.

"I'm sorry," he said, jogging toward his car. "Say that again?"

"Edmund's sister. She's here. And I think I have a problem."

"I'll be right there."

● — ● — ●

He'd only met Millicent on three occasions—all of them unpleasant—but Daniel easily imagined the stark contrast characterizing

103

a face-off between Shannon and her. Good versus evil. A fresh-faced angel confronted by a villain.

He remembered the woman as a well-dressed, updated version of a wicked witch from a fairy tale with her raven-black hair and dark lined eyes and unearthly pale skin. Every time he'd seen her, she'd been clad in black from head to toe, and each time he'd wondered how she and Edmund could have emerged from the same DNA.

He pulled into the driveway and had to park two tires on the grass as he squeezed his white SUV in next to Millicent's sleek black Porsche. *Of course she drives a Boxster,* he thought. *Her broomstick.* Before he reached the front door, it opened, and Shannon's aunt stood there waiting for him, fidgeting and wringing her hands. He gave her arm a reassuring squeeze before he walked inside and found Shannon and Millicent squared off and silent on opposite sides of the dining room table.

The instant she saw him, Shannon stood up and leaned against the rim of the table. "Daniel. Good. You're here."

Millicent's gaze shot upward, and it was as if he physically felt something sharp as her dark eyes met his. He knew the polite thing to say—something akin to "Good to see you again"—but he couldn't manage it. Instead, he took Shannon's arm and asked, "So what's going on?"

"Well . . ."

Mary didn't let Shannon's hesitation stand. "Millicent says Shannon has to turn over the house to her."

Daniel immediately felt his blood begin to simmer. He paused and took a deep, cleansing breath as he led Shannon to the table where they sat opposite Millicent.

"Coffee, Daniel?" Mary asked. "Or tea?"

Sending Mary into the kitchen with something to do besides fret seemed like a good move. "Coffee would be great, Mary. Thank you."

As an afterthought, she surrendered to courtesy over distaste. "Millicent?"

"No."

Once Mary had gone, Daniel drew a deep breath and sighed. Turning to Millicent, he asked, "So what's this about the house? This was all settled in court last year."

"Court?" Shannon muttered, her head low as she leaned toward him slightly.

"Yes. After Edmund's death, Millicent initiated court proceedings to untie Ridgeway family money from the arrangements he'd made. After eight months circling the mountain, the judge gave a final ruling that she wasn't entitled to counteract any of it. She inherited most of Edmund's share of the Ridgeway estate as stipulated in his will anyway, but it didn't seem to be enough for her and she wanted everything else."

"Millicent?" Shannon said through tight emotion caught in the base of her throat. "You really did that?"

"Come on," she condescended. "No one ever believed you'd actually wake up again, Shannon—"

"Edmund did," Daniel reminded her.

"—and the truth is you were only a member of our family for less than a week before your accident. Does that entitle you to anything, really?"

"Three days or thirty years," Daniel pointed out evenly, "it was still up to Edmund, and he had several years to make his choices, which were very clear."

"What do you want with this house anyway?" Shannon asked her. "We only bought it a couple of months before the wedding. It has nothing to do with you or—"

"It has everything to do with Ridgeway money," she cut in. "It's lovely that you woke up again after ten years, Shannon. Really. I'm not heartless—"

Shannon sniffed in response.

"—but you had very little when you met up with my brother.

What, a car? That ridiculous job at a print shop?"

"I was a graphic designer for a large corporation, Millicent. Not a copy clerk someplace."

With a nod toward her aunt in the kitchen, she added, "No family, to speak of."

"Hey!" Daniel exclaimed. "That's enough."

"And I think, after only a few days of marriage before you went missing—"

"Missing?"

"—surely you can see you're not entitled to anything that came from Edmund. What would you have done if you hadn't met him?"

"But she did," Daniel interjected, working hard to defuse Shannon's obvious tension.

"You'd have had to find your own way," Millicent continued as if he hadn't broken in. "I think you need to find your own way now, without the help of all that convenient Ridgeway money."

Shannon dropped her head and a few seconds went by before Daniel noticed her trembling, another few seconds before soft sniffles betrayed the fact that she'd begun to cry.

Daniel pushed up from the chair and leaned over the table, propping up his anger with both hands. "You're out of line here. First, I suggest you rethink your *I'm not heartless* bit, because I'd say you're way over the edge in that direction. Next, if you want to pursue this, you know how to reach Beverly Rivera, the attorney representing Shannon's interests. If you set foot on this property again without an invitation, Beverly will be happy to counsel Shannon on how to obtain an order of restraint."

Millicent didn't even flinch. She didn't move a muscle except for her cat eyes, which rose slowly and glared at him. Seeing she didn't intend to move, he raised his eyebrows.

"I'm trying to be a gentleman here, but I'm not above physically removing you. So let's avoid that, why don't we, and just head for the door on your own."

From the corner of his eye, he couldn't miss Mary's shape

standing at the sink in the kitchen. He blinked and glanced over at her to find her beaming from one ear to the other, silently clapping her hands in front of her chin. Suddenly, it was just about all he could do to keep from laughing, both from amusement and from relief. The little woman had taken a big chunk out of his tension.

Millicent rose from the chair with the grace of a starched shirt unfolding and transferred her withering gaze to Shannon. For a moment she just stood there glowering down at Shannon, who lifted her head and dared to look straight into the eyes of an enemy she hadn't even known she had.

"There is jewelry," Millicent said. "My mother's ruby pendant, my grandmother's pearls. They are Ridgeway heirlooms that you have no right to keep, Shannon."

"I'll look for them," Shannon said simply. "They belong to you, not me."

"I'm glad you can see reason."

Shannon stood up and folded her arms. "Of course I can. But this house was ours; mine and Edmund's. You can't have it."

"We'll see about that."

Without another word, Millicent turned and slithered straight out the front door.

Neither of them made a move; Shannon and Daniel both just stood there watching the black cloud of evil she'd left in her path. After a moment, Mary toddled toward them. Rubbing her arms briskly, she rumbled out a shiver. "Brrrr!"

Daniel shook his head. "You said it."

● — ● — ●

Shannon peeled back the comforter and top sheet so that she could fluff the pillows before her aunt crawled into bed.

"Do you need anything, Aunt Mary? A glass of water?"

"Certainly not, dearie," she said with a chuckle as she climbed up. "Never offer a woman over fifty a glass of water before bedtime."

Shannon giggled. "Good to know."

Once Mary settled in, Shannon pulled up the blanket and kissed her aunt on the cheek.

"He's quite dashing, your Dr. Daniel. Don't you think so, Shannie?"

"Dashing?" she said with a laugh. "I don't know about that. But he was pretty spectacular, the way he handled Millicent."

"If ever there was a dragon to be slain . . ."

"She's still pretty horrible, isn't she?"

Mary nodded and smiled. "You know, that's not the first time Daniel has had to draw a sword against Millicent."

"You mean all that stuff he mentioned about going to court?"

"Yes, that . . ." Her aunt couldn't hide anything with that face of hers.

"Was there more?"

"There was also the matter of her wanting to flip the switch on you."

"Flip . . ." Shannon didn't understand. "What switch?"

"Is that the wrong term?"

"For?"

"Pull the plug? Maybe that's it."

"Pull—" Realization dawned with an icy tingle on the back of Shannon's scalp. "Oh. You mean pull *my* plug."

"Mm-hmm." Mary nodded, her eyes wide and glistening. "Daniel drew his sword on your behalf then, too."

"He did?"

"He's quite a valiant defender, your Dr. Daniel."

Shannon sighed. "Okay, Aunt Mary, you have to stop calling him *my* Daniel. He's been a good friend to me, and to Edmund."

"Yes, but—"

"Put that thought right out of your head, Aunt Mary. I mean it. Right now."

Mary pressed her lips together so tightly that they disappeared into a straight slit.

"Sleep well," Shannon said, and she kissed her forehead before flipping off the lamp on the night table.

"You know—"

"Uh-uh," she warned from the doorway. "Out of your head this minute."

Without another word, Shannon eased the door shut until it clicked. Approaching the kitchen, she saw Daniel standing at the counter dunking tea bags in a small porcelain pot. She watched him for a moment, then shook her head when she drifted off into a blank canvas of indiscernible thoughts.

What was I thinking? she asked herself. *Oh, right! Daniel.*

She liked the way his dark hair matched his deep, dark eyes.

"Mary said you like English Breakfast, even when it's not time for breakfast."

Shannon tried to remember, but it didn't ring any bells. "Do I?"

"That's what she said. With a little sugar and milk."

"If she says so," she replied with a grin. "She's usually right about everything." With a second thought, she emphasized, "Usually."

Daniel handed her a couple of empty cups. "Why don't you take these to the table, and I'll follow with the tea. I have your tablet all set up there and ready to give you a tour, if you're up to it."

"It sounds like a great diversion, Daniel. Thank you."

He arrived at the table with the teapot in one hand, balancing the milk and sugar with the other. They sat down side by side, just where they'd been seated across from Millicent.

"I see you're walking without your cane," he observed as he poured the tea.

"Sometimes it's more trouble than it's worth," she replied.

"Have you talked to Carrie about that?"

"Yes, *Doctor*," she said. "We're working together to get me ready to shove the thing into retirement as soon as possible."

"Just don't do it too soon."

"Couldn't be soon enough for me," she muttered. Shifting gears, she added, "You know, Aunt Mary told me how you came to my rescue more than once while I was sleeping."

He darted a glance at her before returning to the tea.

"I guess Millicent wanted to hand me over to her flying monkeys or evil goblins or whatever?"

He chuckled. "It's scary how easy that visual is."

"Well, thank you, Daniel," she said. "Truly. I guess I'm here at all because of you, on so many levels."

"You're here for a lot of reasons," he told her. "Not the least of which is Edmund, but also because of all those prayers circling around you. Millicent the Malevolent is no match for that."

Shannon giggled. "That just rolled right off your tongue. Tell the truth. You've been calling her that for a long time, haven't you?"

Daniel grinned, placing a small silver spoon in one of the cups and sliding it toward her. "I'll let you doctor it up how you like it."

Shannon stared down into the cup, wondering for the hundredth time why she remembered some preferences clearly but not others. The fragrance triggered no familiar feeling at all.

"I wish I knew how I like it."

After a beat, Daniel joked, "I know. Let's wake Mary and ask her."

Shannon shook her head and smiled. "How is it that I can remember this house, but I can't for the life of me recall how I like my tea? I remember old TV shows so well that I get confused and think I'm a character in one of them, but something as important as Edmund's mother's jewelry and I can't even remember having it."

"It's just going to take some time to—"

"You know how I told Millicent my old job had been doing graphic design for a big corporation?"

"Sure."

"I had to call it 'a big corporation' because I can't remember the name of the company I worked for, Daniel. I remember the cubicle I sat in, but not whether I liked it there. Did I have work friends? And did they come and visit me after the accident, or did they just forget about me—out of sight, out of mind? And what about my church? I remember fragments of conversations with Edmund about attending a marriage class, but where did we go? Did anyone from there visit me in the hospital? Were they there for Edmund when he got sick? There's just so much that's missing," she finished with a frustrated sigh.

"I can tell you that they didn't come to the hospital for you the way Edmund thought they should, which is why he stopped going there without you."

"So then he went to church with you?"

He nodded. "I think it started as just somewhere to go, with no real heart behind it. But you know, your accident made him think about God in a way that he hadn't before. He ended up pretty entrenched. He volunteered for several big projects—and he was baptized just a few months before his diagnosis."

"Edmund was baptized?"

"He was. And our pastor was there at his bedside, praying for him with your aunts when he passed away."

Thankful emotion and guilty resentment tangled up in her throat, nearly choking her. Her accident had driven them apart yet finally brought him to God. It was all so hard to take in. When she could trust her voice, she said, "I'm really happy to hear that he wasn't alone. I just wish I could remember the church we went to before, so I'd know who to be mad at."

Daniel chuckled. "Shannon," he said, and he took her hand between both of his as he looked into her eyes. "There are no hard and fast rules about these things, but I feel pretty certain it will come back to you, a little at a time."

She closed her eyes and groaned. She didn't know why, but she instinctively let the heart of the matter tumble right out of her.

"I can't even remember . . . the wedding."

"Yours?"

"Yes. I can't remember my dress or the flowers. I can't remember Edmund in his tuxedo, presumably standing at the end of the aisle waiting for me." With a chuckle, she added, "If he was even

111

wearing a tux. Maybe he wore jeans and his UT sweatshirt. He loved that ridiculous thing; wore it every weekend, rain or shine."

"Hey! You remember that."

Joy surged inside her, and she grinned. "You're right! I do. Edmund got his graduate degree in architecture from the University of Texas!"

"See what I mean? Bits and pieces."

Daniel got up from his chair and headed into the living room without a word. She heard the cabinet door on the bottom of the built-ins scrape before he returned with a large white book cradled on his arm.

"You might want to have a look through this sometime," he said, setting the book down on the table before sinking into the chair beside her. "Maybe by yourself."

But now she had to look inside. Her wedding album. This time she had a reason not to remember something—she had never seen the book before. It was a quilted white leather album adorned with small iridescent pearls, and it was bound with a strip of stiff white lace tied at the side in a large bow. Shannon reached for the album slowly, her heartbeat pounding against her chest, and she sighed as her eyes landed on an 8 x 10 inch portrait of the happy bride and groom.

"I never saw my wedding pictures, did I?" she remarked, gingerly tracing Edmund's face with the tip of her index finger. His fair good looks, his boyish grin. So different from her in so many ways.

"He had it made after the honeymoon."

"Of course."

She moved from Edmund's picture to her own. How could she have forgotten that beautiful dress? Form-fitting, French lace, illusion sweetheart neckline, and that pretty little ribbon and rhinestone belt.

"Edmund took me to a party once with an island theme, and I wore my hair like this," she said, pointing to a picture. "Parted on the side with soft waves and a big magnolia behind my ear. I didn't wear a veil for our wedding because he asked me to wear it like this, the way I wore it when we went to that party."

"Pretty."

"He was so laid-back. Well, you know that, I guess. If he hadn't been tied down to the Ridgeway name and all of the responsibilities that came with it, I think he would have lived alone on a beach somewhere, surfing all day and sipping coconut drinks at night."

He chuckled softly. "It's a bit of a stretch, but I could see that."

She leaned back and rested her head against the back of the chair. Daniel's shoulder was right next to hers, and she found herself tempted to lean into it. Confused, she closed her eyes. He and Edmund had been good friends, apparently. She and Edmund had been married—but they had been together for such a short time even before then. Suddenly, she realized Daniel might have known her husband better than she had.

Her husband.

She reminded herself that she was no longer married. Edmund had dissolved with hardly a trace, and the realization scorched the edges of her heart. Daniel's clean, soapy scent lulled her somehow, and she let her tumble of emotions go for the moment. "Thank you," she whispered.

He patted the back of her head. "Anytime."

"I understand why Edmund wanted to be your friend."

"You're my friend too, Shannon. Anything you need."

She felt a strange tug at her heart at his words. Straightening, she moved away from him. "You know what I really need?"

"What's that?"

"I need to do something I've never done before, or go somewhere I haven't been. Something completely new to me. Something I can discover now, as I am now. Does that make any sense?"

"A bit. What do you have in mind?"

She sighed and curled her leg underneath her as she lifted the cup of tea to her lips. "I don't have a clue."

After a few beats, Daniel asked, "Would you like to come and meet the folks who knew Edmund best when he died? There's a baptism service tomorrow night out at Barton Springs—do you remember that place?"

She nodded, remembering the natural springs and pools built around them. But a baptism. She wondered if she could bear it. Baptisms were joyful, celebratory events. She'd been giving God the cold shoulder since waking up out of the coma. The thought of celebrating with a group of new Christians, with their enthusiasm and trust and joy . . .

Tears crested and sprang from her eyes. She didn't even know why, but she nodded. "I—I think I'd like that."

"I'll bring over that Chinese takeout I promised you, and we'll drive out to the Springs together."

"It's a date!"

The moment the words came out, Shannon regretted them. She peeked at him out of the corner of her eye. He didn't seem to have noticed.

I'm so glad Aunt Mary didn't hear that.

Covering quickly, she said, "Now! Show me how to work this menu thingie."

"Tablet," he corrected. "Say it with me. It's called a . . ."

In unison, they sang, *"Taaaaa-blet."*

11

By the time he arrived at Shannon's house, his arms laden with fragrant plastic bags of food containers, she'd already set the table out on the patio with festive plates, colorful linen napkins, and frosted glasses of water. She'd dressed casually in a bright-colored, embellished tee shirt tucked into black capris—her nod to Laura Petrie, no doubt—and she grinned at him, both hands in her pockets as he stepped through the glass doors to the patio. To his relief, he could already see that her mood seemed lighter than it had been when he left her the night before.

The day had been a rough one for him, filled with unexpected schedule changes and several emergencies. Something about seeing Shannon standing there like that, looking so adorable, made him wish they could light up the fire pit, prop up their feet, and just stay put for the evening. But taking her out to meet some of the folks from United Point of Grace Church took precedence.

"So how was your first day with no babysitters or nannies?" he asked as they dug into the meal.

"Kind of great," she told him with a grin. He wondered why he hadn't noticed the subtly charming little gap between her two front teeth before. "I wanted to know about the shape of my finances, so I went through those folders of paperwork in the office. I found the debit and credit cards, and the bank statements. I feel much more informed."

"Always a good start."

"And I went to the DMV this morning and renewed my license. No parallel parking involved."

"Excellent."

"And then I had my first outpatient session with Dr. Benedict."

"You were at the hospital?"

"Yes."

"And?"

She hesitated, and he watched her green eyes narrow as she weighed her words. "It was strange to be meeting with a psychiatrist. But I think it's going to be good once we get comfortable with one another."

"Outstanding."

"But this afternoon while I was doing my stretches, I got so caught up in one of those cooking shows on television that I almost didn't get changed before you arrived."

"Do you like to cook?" he asked, heaping a chopstick load of cashew chicken into his mouth.

"Well, I didn't think so. I mean, I don't remember enjoying it or even thinking much about it one way or the other. But this afternoon, I suddenly found myself so involved in what they were doing on the show that I was riveted."

"What were they making?"

"Spinach Fandango."

"Which is?"

"Fascinating!" she exclaimed. "Beef, mushrooms, spinach, sour cream . . . all these ingredients that combine into one big pan of deliciousness. It just grabbed me by the taste buds and wouldn't let go. And you'd be so proud of me, Daniel. I used my *tablet* to go to their website and get the recipe."

"You don't say."

"I do say!" As she tossed her copper mane over the shoulder of her bright teal tee shirt, he noticed the sunlight glinted off the rhinestones scattered around the neckline. "I'm going to the market in the morning and getting all the stuff I need to make it. If it works out, I'll save you some."

As Daniel paid the fee to enter the park, Shannon realized the spot did look completely familiar to her, especially when they passed an area with a mini-train and several signs pointing toward the botanical garden.

"I've been here before," she told Daniel as she fidgeted with her seat belt. "A long time ago, when I was in high school maybe."

"Probably. Just about everyone in Austin has made it out here more than a few times."

As they approached the Barton Springs Pool area, Shannon perked up. "Is this where Edmund was baptized, too?"

"The very same."

"Funny that they're having this thing on a Wednesday night. I thought most churches did their baptisms on Sunday afternoons after services."

"Wednesday is the church's night of fellowship, and during the summer we sometimes have outdoor movie nights in the park, or a concert, and the occasional baptismal ceremony here at the springs."

Someone waved at Daniel as they pulled into the parking spot, and Shannon's stomach tumbled over into a couple of quick somersaults. A mist of cool perspiration developed on her palms.

"Oooh," she blurted. "I feel so nervous all of a sudden."

"If you find you're not comfortable, or you just want to leave, say the word. There's no pressure here," he reassured her. "Okay? Ready to do this?"

Shannon tried to appear more behind the nod than she actually was, and they both pushed open their doors at the same time.

"Good to see you, man," a tall—*kind of gorgeous*—dark-skinned man said, and he and Daniel exchanged a complicated fist-bumping handshake.

"Shannon, this is my buddy Dr. Josiah Rush. We actually work together at the hospital, so he's familiar with you even though you haven't met before. Josiah, meet Shannon Ridgeway."

"It's a real pleasure," Josiah said with a sincere smile and a nod. "I've heard a lot about you over the years."

Well, try not to believe it until I can remember if any of it's true, she thought.

"I'm afraid to ask," she teased instead.

"Happy you're back with us."

"Happy to be back."

Daniel placed his hand on her shoulder blade and guided her along with them as they headed toward the edge of the water where a small group had gathered, apart from others dotting the landscape.

A tall bald man with wire-rimmed glasses smiled as he approached. "Shannon Ridgeway," he said. "You look just like your pictures."

"This is our pastor, Rich Blevins," Daniel told her.

The man who prayed at Edmund's bedside.

Despite her irritation with God, the thought warmed her heart. "Daniel told me you were really good to Edmund. Thank you so much."

"It was my pleasure, Shannon. He was a remarkable man."

She'd no sooner shaken the man's hand before the others began to circle, repeating her name and telling about how much they'd cared for Edmund. It was difficult to grasp—strangers who had known her husband in a way that she never had. And because he had been attending the church longer than he'd dated her, these people had probably known him better than she had too. Their voices created a sort of strange hum that droned in her ears, and she hadn't been onsite more than twenty minutes before she began to feel overwhelmed, wishing she hadn't come.

Once they all settled on blankets on the grassy hill and the half dozen or so people being baptized followed the pastor and Josiah to the water's edge, she felt like she could breathe again.

Daniel touched her arm and asked, "Are you good?"

"Fine," she said with a nod. "It's just that all these strangers who knew Edmund as a faithful believer, who seem to know me, too, but I've never met them . . . It's disorienting. I'm feeling a little left out." She gave a short laugh. "I guess I *was* out, wasn't I?"

"I'm sorry," he said softly.

She shook her head. "No. I'll be all right. Really. It's just—" she shrugged. "It'll take time, like you said."

They fell silent as the pastor told the story of Jesus's baptism by John the Baptist. "It's an act of obedience, Jesus taught us," he said. "And let's pray for these that have come to the water in obedience, in that same way that Jesus came."

Shannon couldn't help herself. She wondered how long it might be before those bright, shiny new Christians felt the disillusionment she had come to know. She regretted the thought, but she lingered on it just the same. Her faith had felt so simple before, so natural, so lacking the complications it possessed now.

A young woman with a headful of short blonde curls, probably in her mid-twenties, lowered to the grass next to Shannon and touched her hand. "Hi, Shannon. I'm Emily Dawson. I knew your husband."

"Hi, Emily."

"I just wanted to tell you what a good man he was," she said, her golden hair glistening under the last rays of the day's sun. "I mean, I'm sure you already know that. I just mean . . . I met him at Draper. My gramps was there when you were. I was pregnant and unmarried, no insurance and jobless. I was a complete mess, and he was so kind to me. He actually paid my medical bills when my son was born, and he called my folks and brought us all to the church for counseling. We're a real family again now, and I just wanted to tell you . . . I won't ever forget what he did for us."

Shannon stared at the young woman. The corner of her eye began to twitch. She didn't know what to say. She didn't recognize the Edmund about whom the woman spoke. But she had to say something. "Thank you for telling me that, Emily."

The girl narrowed her eyes and stared at the grass for a long moment before she chirped, "He loved you very much." And with that, she popped up to her feet and hurried away.

Shannon turned toward Daniel, and their eyes locked together for a frozen block of time before she finally blinked and a fresh fall of tears tumbled down her face.

"Shannon," he said, and he touched her hand. "I am so sorry. You said you wanted a new experience, and I brought you to a place where new and old come in the same box. Look, do you want to get out of here?"

She hoped it wouldn't hurt his feelings, so she treaded softly, wincing as she replied, "I really do."

Without a word, Daniel hopped to his feet and offered her his hand. He pulled her up in one swift motion, and she groaned at the pain running down her leg from hip to heel. Daniel offered his arm, and the two of them walked straight back to his Lexus.

"Where would you like to go? Your choice this time."

Shannon wondered what he would think of the answer that came to mind.

"An appliance store."

"An *appliance store?* Like ovens and refrigerators?"

"Yes," she declared. "Just like that."

"You were struck with a sudden need for a new microwave?"

"No. Freezer."

"Freezer. Okay."

Shannon laughed at his expression of amazement, and she jabbed his arm with her elbow. "I want to cook some things and freeze them. On one of the shows I watched today, the woman had a two-sided freezer in her garage, and when she opened it, it was filled with all of these neatly stacked and labeled plastic containers."

Daniel pulled his phone out of his shirt pocket and handed it to her without a word.

"What's this for?" she asked.

"To call Izzy."

"Why?"

120

"Inquiring minds want to know. We have to find out if you had this penchant for cooking before the accident, or if it crept up on you while you were unconscious."

She giggled, staring down at the small screened phone in her hand. "Yeah. I don't know how to use this."

He took it from her, swiped the screen a few times, tapped it twice, and handed it back to her. Ringing on the line blared through the speaker.

"Can I get one of *these* at the appliance store?" she asked just before Izzy answered.

"Hello?"

"Iz?" she exclaimed.

"Shannon?"

She grinned at Daniel. "You have Izzy on speed dial?" she asked, and he shrugged. "Izzy, before my accident, did I enjoy cooking?"

Silence.

"Iz?"

"Is this a trick question?"

"No. I really want to know. I don't remember ever giving the idea of cooking a second or third thought. Do you know if it was something that appealed to me?"

"Ah, well, I don't think you ever got any closer to cooking than heating up doggie-bag leftovers in the microwave."

"Oh." Perplexed, she asked, "Didn't I cook for Edmund?"

Izzy clucked out one severe "Ha!" before she explained. "No, honey. You did not cook for Edmund or anyone else. Why are you asking me this?"

"Because I suddenly feel really warmed up to the idea of cooking." A long pause followed, and Shannon asked, "Izzy, are you still there?"

"Yeah, I'm still here. I'm just trying to imagine it."

●　—　●　—　●

121

"This one might be a good selection for you. It's our eighteen-point-six cubic foot model in stainless steel. Three adjustable glass shelves, two wire baskets, and electronic controls."

Shannon stood back looking at it with the most adorably serious expression on her face, her arms folded loosely.

"How much is it?" she asked the clerk with a tag on his company shirt that read, *Hi, my name is Dominic.*

"Fifteen ninety-nine."

"Sixteen hundred dollars?" she repeated. "For a garage freezer?"

"It's top of the line."

"How about we see something at the middle of the line then," she suggested.

"We have one over here for six ninety-nine."

They followed him across the aisle. Daniel was certainly no expert on freezers, but it looked pretty much the same as the expensive one to him.

"It's only seventeen-seven cubic feet with two shelves," Dominic said in monotone as he tugged open the door. "It's serviceable for your purposes, I think."

Shannon poked her head inside and inspected it like a used car. When she emerged again, her emerald eyes twinkled at Daniel. "I like the other one. It's bigger, and it makes ice."

He tried to suppress the chuckle, to no avail. "It's your freezer. I'm just the driver who brought you here."

Shannon pointed a finger at the other one and smiled at Dominic. "I want the first one."

The boy brightened considerably. "I'll write it up for you."

"Do you deliver? I live over in Briarcliff."

"We can make delivery between noon and four tomorrow afternoon."

She looked as if she'd just won the lottery. "Okay!"

"Is there anything else I can show you?"

Shannon turned to Daniel and held out her hand. "Can I see your phone?"

He handed it to her and she displayed it to the boy like Vanna after turning some key letters. "Do you have one of these?"

"Yes we do! Right this way!"

It might have been Dominic who'd won the lottery.

As they followed the clerk to the front of the store, Shannon slowed to look at a display of label-makers. As she stood there inspecting them, she sang along with the piped-in music. Not only did she know all the words, but her clear voice rang out exquisitely. When she plucked one of the devices from the wall and caught Daniel looking at her, she smiled.

"What?"

"Your voice. It's beautiful."

"Oh." She paused and thought it over. "Is it really?"

"Stunning."

"I always liked that song."

"And you remembered that you liked it," he pointed out.

"Progress, right?" She grabbed his wrist, pressing the beads of his bracelets under her fingertips. "Let's go get me one of those phones! I'm feeling good."

"I can tell." He worked to keep up with her as she reached the long glass cases of smartphones, cameras, and tablets.

"After this, I want to see your line of transporters," she told Dominic.

"I'm sorry, ma'am. Our transporters?"

"Yeah, like you're in one place now, and a few seconds later you're in Arizona."

Daniel felt almost as confused as Dominic looked until Shannon turned to him and widened her eyes in mock amazement.

"Like the ones in *Star Trek*. You don't have those yet? Sheesh, what have you people been doing while I was asleep?"

⚬ — ⚬ — ⚬

Daniel had stayed late as they played with all of Shannon's new toys. She didn't have many important contacts these days, but

123

the ones she did have had been safely programmed into her new phone. She'd typed in Daniel's name and created a test label with her new labeler, sticking it on the back of his hand; and they'd used her brand new laptop with the teal-blue cover to set up an email account and to check out the software package that had come with the computer. Despite the fact that she'd never been much of a shopper, she had enjoyed their excursion immensely. She probably wouldn't do much of it again—but for now, getting up to speed on gadgets was just what she needed.

It was just after midnight, each of them with their iPhone in hand—he'd annihilated her at Words with Friends for the second time, from the opposite end of her sofa—before Daniel said goodnight and made his way home. After he got there, however, Shannon sat up in bed playing another game remotely with him before turning out the lights and trying to get some sleep. When she awoke that morning, she checked the final score of that last game. He'd won that one too, but at least she'd come a lot closer to catching up to him.

In fact, she'd come a lot closer to him in general. She wasn't sure what she thought about that, but she certainly did enjoy his friendship. She didn't want to dig any deeper than that into her feelings at the moment. Just realizing she'd enjoyed their time together was enough for one day.

The next morning, Shannon hopped out of bed and grabbed her new phone before hurrying down the hall in bare feet and the long tee shirt she'd worn to bed. She put the kettle on the stove and rummaged through the cabinet to decide on a tea flavor that looked interesting.

English Breakfast. She crinkled her nose and shook her head. *I know I'm supposed to prefer it, but it really didn't do much for me. Cinnamon plum? Yikes. Chamomile? No, thanks.*

She suddenly wondered why a confirmed tea-drinker might crave a strong cup of coffee right out of the blue this way, but that's what she wanted. Checking the cabinet and finding everything she needed, Shannon yanked the kettle off the stove and pressed a filter into the coffeepot on the counter instead. A few minutes later, she padded out to the patio with a steaming cup of coffee, her laptop, and her phone. An idea had been brewing, too, and she felt anxious to get to it.

"I feel brand-new," the princess confided.
"How long was I asleep?"

"Long enough," her friend replied.

"Do you suppose I'll ever return to the girl I was before?"

"Do you want to?"

"I'm not sure. Ask me again tomorrow."

12

"**Shannon? Are** you here?"

Shannon had been leaning down to place a tray of cranberry-orange scones into the oven, and when she straightened again, Izzy screeched.

"You scared me half to death!"

"Sorry."

"What are you doing in there?"

"I'm making scones."

Izzy snorted. "Scones."

"Yeah. I found a recipe online. They look really good."

"Are you serious?"

"Yes."

"*You*. Are *baking*."

"Well, don't look so horrified," Shannon said with a chuckle. "I went to the market this morning and I've been cooking and baking ever since." She opened the refrigerator door and waved her arm with a flourish. "Check me out!"

Izzy took two short little steps toward the refrigerator, her mouth gaping open and her brown eyes round as shiny quarters before she planted there and stared at the contents. "Are you kidding me with this?"

Shannon looked inside in an effort to find what might have been so shocking a sight. The bottom three shelves were tightly stocked with tidy, labeled plastic containers.

Spinach Fandango

Salmon w/Ginger Glaze

CHILI RELLENOS CASSEROLE
CORN SALSA

Izzy glanced around the room strangely. "Am I being punked?"

Shannon frowned, confused. "What do you mean?"

"You did not make all of this. Do you even know what corn salsa is?"

"Of course I do, I just made it. It has cilantro and black beans and—"

"Stop it!" Izzy cried. "What's really going on here?"

Shannon giggled. "I don't know, Iz. I just . . . like to cook!"

"Since when?"

"Since I woke up, I guess. It's crazy, right?"

"Little bit," she replied with a spark of crazy all her own glinting in her eyes.

Izzy tucked a hand on her hip and surveyed the battalion of new techno-toys across the dining room table, and she shook her head and clicked her tongue.

"Help me get some of these containers out to the freezer, will you?" Shannon asked. "It should be good and cold by now."

"What freezer? Out where?"

"Oh! Come and see! It was just delivered today."

She piled Izzy's arms with as many containers as she could hold before taking on a load of her own and leading her friend out to the garage. "Check it out. I give you . . . *Freezasaurus*."

Izzy remained silent while Shannon carefully lined up the containers on the shelves, adjusting them with precision so that the labels could be easily read. When she felt satisfied with the order of things, she closed the freezer door and turned toward her friend with a grin.

Without any forewarning at all, Izzy grabbed Shannon and pulled her into an embrace so tight that an expelled groan rumbled out of her. "What's going on with you, honey? Talk to me."

"I . . . can't . . ." she said, and Izzy pushed her back, clutching both of her shoulders.

"Of course you can. Talk to me."

"No, I meant I *couldn't*. You were holding me so tight I couldn't breathe, much less talk to you about—"

Izzy released her, reeled around, and puffed out an exasperated sigh as she went back inside, leaving Shannon standing there next to her beautiful new freezer. When she followed, Izzy had already reached the sofa in the living room and flopped down on it.

"Can I get you something?" she asked her friend just as the oven timer sounded. "Oooh, my scones. How about some coffee to go with them?"

"You don't drink coffee."

"Oh, I know. But suddenly I do. You want some?"

Izzy's mouth opened, but she didn't—or couldn't—reply. She just sat there staring at her.

"Okay. I'll be right back."

While she poured coffee and placed the warm scones on a plate, Shannon mulled over Izzy's reactions. Surely she hadn't expected Shannon to wake up in a new decade and just remain stuck back in the old one. So she'd changed a little. So she'd developed a new appreciation for interesting cuisine and a taste for strong coffee. So what?

She drizzled honey over two scones and dusted them slightly with cinnamon, twirling the plate as she did to make sure they lined up just the way she thought—

Shannon froze into a sudden statue, her thoughts shimmering around her like ice crystals.

"Iz?"

"Yeah?"

She set down the cinnamon and backed up until her fanny touched the edge of the sink behind her.

"Yeah?" Izzy repeated.

"Have I had a psychotic break?"

She waited for a reply.

Finally, Izzy stepped up to the counter and leaned against it. "I'm not sure."

Shannon turned around, looking at her friend through a haze of stunned panic. "Do I need to call someone? Or check myself into Betty Crocker Rehab for Coma Patients?"

"If they had one of those, I'd drive you myself." Barely missing a beat, Izzy shifted gears. "Hold on just one hot second now! *These are your scones?*"

Shannon chuckled as Izzy floated around the counter seemingly led by her nose until she hovered over the plate and breathed in so hard that she almost expected one of the scones to levitate straight to her mouth.

"Honey, whatever you've caught, I don't think you should be too hasty about searching for a cure."

"Grab the plate," Shannon said. "I'll bring the coffee."

Once they'd settled out on the patio, Shannon strained to pull her stiff legs up and tucked them underneath her. Holding the coffee with both hands, she inhaled its fragrance before taking a long draw of it and closing her eyes. Izzy's strange moaning inspired her to open them again, and she watched as her friend indulged in a second bite of the cranberry-orange scone clutched greedily in her hand.

"Good?"

"Nope," Izzy replied, her eyes gently closed. "There isn't a word in the English language yet to describe this. It's . . . celestial."

Shannon leaned forward and took one for herself. After she licked the warm honey from her finger, she bit into the scone and understood precisely what Izzy had meant.

"Wow," she breathed.

"I know." After several beats—and another couple of bites— Izzy asked her, "What happened to you while you were sleeping, girl?"

"I don't know. But something."

"Listen. Tell me how you're doing with all these changes, Shannon," she said seriously. "Do you feel like you're adjusting?"

"Well, I'm not sure what's normal here." She sighed deeply. "One year for Christmas—I think I was about five years old—someone gave me this beautiful bride doll in a glass case. She wore this amazing tulle and satin dress and long gloves, and she had these thick, beautiful eyelashes. I loved that doll so much, and all I wanted to do was take her out of the glass case and play with her, but my mom wouldn't let me. She said that the doll had to stay in the case and live up on the shelf in my bedroom, that she was only for looking at and not for playing with."

Izzy's awkward smile indicated her confusion about where the story might be headed.

"Edmund feels a little like that doll to me now. I want to touch him and talk to him, not leave him up on the memory shelf behind a wall of glass. You know?"

Izzy leaned forward and clutched Shannon's hand, giving it a tight squeeze. When their eyes met, Shannon noted the veil of moisture in her friend's pretty eyes.

"You're going to get through this," she said, and she blinked a thin stream of tears down the slope of her cheek. "I promise you."

"How?" Shannon asked with raspy, emotional sincerity.

"I have no idea. But I know you will. We'll get through it together."

Her friend's confidence buoyed her, and Shannon sighed.

● — ● — ●

Daniel had just completed patient rounds when he'd been paged back to the ER for a consult that had put him into proximity for a couple more emergencies and distractions. He'd returned to his office two hours later than planned, and he hadn't even reached his desk yet when another unplanned delay crossed his path.

"Thanks for stopping by, Dr. Benedict," Daniel said, motioning his colleague toward a chair on the opposite side of his desk. "Can Eloise get you some coffee?"

"No, thanks," she replied with the wave of her thin hand. "I exceeded my two-cup limit about three cups ago." She sat down across from him and folded her hands over one knee. "I met with your patient, Shannon Ridgeway, yesterday."

"Yes, she mentioned that."

"Did she?"

Daniel didn't know Cynthia Benedict very well, but her reputation had convinced him that she might be a good fit for Shannon's particular challenges.

"You asked me to circle back and let you know if I thought I might be able to help her acclimate to her life again," she said.

She adjusted her glasses, the roundness of which relieved an otherwise severe picture: hair pulled into a tight bun at the back of her small, narrow head, exceptional slenderness. He noticed that her wrist bone protruded in a way that looked like it might burst through her skin.

"What did she say to you about our meeting, if I may ask?"

He leaned back in his chair until it creaked and sighed. "Not a lot. Just that she'd met with you and thought your sessions might prove helpful once you get comfortable with one another."

Dr. Benedict nodded slowly, considering his words. "Good. I think that's a helpful attitude. I did note that she's unusually tethered to you, Dr. Petros. She seems to be inordinately reliant on your relationship and on your role in her life, post hospitalization."

Daniel narrowed his eyes and wondered where she might be headed. "I think she's very concerned about where she fits in today's environment," he told her. "Because I knew her late husband, I think I'm a strange mixture of her old and new lives. And when she's feeling very much trapped in a fish bowl where the people around her are watching and waiting to see that person they knew ten years ago, it could be that I'm just a welcome buffer."

"It's a good observation," she replied. "She's clearly somewhat removed from her old life before the accident and has a real desire to discover who she is now, and where she's going. I think it's a somewhat typical reaction to losing so much time."

"Are you concerned about her bouts of confusion?" he asked.

"It's still early yet, but I'm not too worried. Her memories are like blocks floating around in her head, and depending on the angle of them at any given moment, she can only access them in intervals. I would estimate that, as more time passes, she'll start to line them up and make sense of the information contained in each of the blocks."

"You mentioned that she seems reliant on me." He hesitated. "Do you think I'm a detriment to her recovery in any way?"

"Not as long as you don't take on a replacement role. Her late husband was apparently quite a figure of leadership in her life ten years ago. If she resorts to the submissive position in an effort to move you into the dominant one that he once filled, that would be another story."

Her concern struck him slightly funny, but Daniel didn't let on. He thought back to Shannon leading him around the store, comparing label makers, choosing a laptop, buying a more expensive freezer than the one he suggested. *Submissive* and *Shannon* weren't terms that really seemed to match up. He wondered about her relationship with Edmund. Just how different had she been then from the headstrong girl he knew now?

"You'll just have to keep a watchful eye," she added, and he suppressed the smile threatening to give him away.

"I'll do that, Dr. Benedict. Thank you."

●　—　●　—　●

"I like the way you always kept everything clean, Aunt Mary. There was never any processed, packaged stuff on the Sunday table—was there?"

Mary shook her head in confirmation.

"And very seldom was there anything too rich or heavy or creamed. I think I was more influenced by that than I'd realized."

"Thank you for saying so, Shannie."

Shannon held the small basket while Mary cut sprigs of rosemary from the herb garden thriving under her kitchen window and placed them into it.

Another surge of excitement coursed through Shannon. She'd been feeling them ever since she'd stepped foot out of bed that morning. She could hardly wait for Izzy's arrival, with Luca and the boys in tow.

"Thank you so much for inviting Izzy and her family today."

Her aunt made a little sound of acknowledgment before asking, "Shall we cut some mint for the tea?"

"Perfect!" Shannon replied with a wide grin. "Hey, do you think you could teach me how to care for a small garden like this in my yard? I've really been getting into cooking lately, and it would be so nice to grow my own herbs."

"Let's make a plan to do that, why don't we," her aunt said, picking up the large basket overflowing with ripe red tomatoes and cucumbers.

When she groaned, Shannon took the basket from her. "Your crop of veggies is really lovely this year."

"It's done me proud. Ready to poke some rosemary under the skin of a couple of roasting chickens?"

"More than!"

Mary looped her arm through Shannon's and leaned heavily on her as they ascended the three short steps to her back door. Once inside, Shannon pulled a stool around the island and helped her aunt onto it.

"This will be more comfortable," she told her.

"Thank you, dearie."

Shannon loved the smells of her aunt's kitchen on a Sunday afternoon. There were still many things she was discovering that she'd forgotten, but that sensation wasn't one of them. She closed her eyes for a moment and breathed it in.

"What do you think about alternating Sundays, Aunt Mary? Next weekend, you come to my house and we'll cook in my kitchen."

"Whatever inflates your sails, Shannie. I'm just happy to be cooking alongside my little girl again."

As Mary scrubbed tomatoes, cucumbers and bright green scallions in the deep porcelain sink, Shannon opened the oven door and peered inside. She salivated at the sight of the large chickens bubbling in their golden juices. Surrounding the birds, a small mountain of quartered Yukons turned toasty gold. Using the pointy end of a long meat fork, she carefully lifted the birds' skin in several places, poking sprigs of rosemary inside. She dropped a few more sprigs next to the sizzling chunks of garlic cloves and potatoes.

As she secured the oven door again, Dean Martin crooned from the old phonograph in the front room, and Mary belted it out right along with him in a warbly, high-pitched rendition. Shannon stood next to her aunt, peeling the skin from the cucumbers. Before long, she found herself singing too.

"You remember the words to this old-fogy song?" Mary teased.

"I know," Shannon said with a shrug. "I don't know where they're stored, but here they are."

With her hands buried in water and tomatoes, Mary wasn't able to clap them; but her wide grin and soft *yippee* made Shannon laugh before she started singing again. "My someplace is *here . . .*"

Another lilting voice chimed in: "Hellooooooo!"

Shannon's heart lifted at the familiar, sing-song greeting of her other two aunts.

"Look who we found, Sissy!" Lora called.

Lora and Lonna waddled into the kitchen, each of them with a guest on their arm. Izzy kissed Mary's cheek when she entered, and Shannon was astonished when Daniel paused behind her, leaning against the doorway to the wide open room, smiling at her.

"Daniel!" Shannon exclaimed. "I didn't know you were joining us."

"I phoned him," Mary announced. "I thought it might be a nice way to thank him for everything he's done for the Malone family."

"I hope it's all right," Daniel said with a smile.

"Of course! Are you kidding? This is great."

"What can we do to help, Mary?" Izzy asked.

"Iz, where's—?" A sudden roar from the front of the house answered Shannon's question before she could finish asking it.

"Ladies and gentlemen, the human explosion that is my family," Izzy annouced dryly.

Two young boys stampeded into the kitchen, and their mother snatched them by the arms with expert aim. "You are in someone else's home," she chastised, leaning down to their level. "What did I tell you about today?"

"O-kaaay," the eldest of the two boys said, shaking his mop of dark hair. "We got it, we got it."

Izzy straightened and smiled at Shannon. "This is Nicolas. And this—" she ran her fingers through the younger boy's equally unruly thatch of hair— "is Alberto. Boys, this is my good friend Shannon."

"You were asleep for longer than I been alive," Alberto blurted out.

Shannon grinned. "How old are you?"

"He's five," Nicolas chimed in. "And I'm seven, and you been sleeping longer than since I was born too."

"That's true!" she said, chuckling. She decided she liked these two.

"I bet you got enough sleep stored up that you don't gotta take a nap for about twenty years," the younger one observed.

"Well," she replied, acting as if she needed to think that over, "I happen to think naps are pretty great. So I think I'd like to take them whether I need them or not."

Both boys looked as if she'd fed them a lemon, and Shannon laughed.

Luca trailed in just then, carrying the smallest of the children on one arm. Unlike the older boys, who she now saw were mirror images of their handsome Ecuadorian father, the baby of the group had inherited Izzy's darker skin and kinky black hair. His wide, sparkling eyes boasted a fringe of enviable dark lashes as he surveyed the room.

"You must be Luis," Shannon said, and the three-year-old retreated into the shelter of his father's neck.

Luca reached out and touched Shannon's arm, nearly blinding her with his dazzling smile. "Shannon, I'm Luca," he said, and she detected the slight Hispanic melody in it.

"Are you?" she teased. "I thought you were Izzy's *manny.*"

"I'm that, too," he laughed.

"Pool boy, housekeeper, sometimes-cook," Izzy added. "I'm the luckiest woman in Austin. Good help is hard to find."

"It's good to finally meet you," Luca said. "And to welcome you back to us."

"Thank you. I'm so glad to meet you, too. Although I admit I'm still getting over the fact that my best friend suddenly has a husband and family," she said, shaking her head good-naturedly and turning to the children. "Now you met my aunts Lora and Lonna outside, right?" When they nodded, she added, "This is my other aunt, Mary—"

"Are you guys sisters?" Nicolas cut in.

"We certainly are," Lonna replied.

"And this is Dr. Daniel Petros," Shannon told them, and Luca reached around the child in his arms to shake Daniel's hand.

"Pleasure."

"Why don't we break up the logjam," Mary suggested. "Sisters, you can pour everyone some iced tea from the pitchers in the icebox. There's fresh mint in the basket on the counter."

"What about us?" Luca asked.

"If you can do it one-handed, perhaps you can get that leaf into the dining table so your wife can set it? Everything's out there."

"We're on it," Izzy returned. "Come on, boys."

Once they'd all moved along, Daniel stepped up next to Shannon. Their arms touched, and her flesh there tingled slightly. "What about me?" he asked.

"Ooh, Shannie!" Mary piped up. "Why don't you take Daniel out to the garden and cut some more mint. I don't think we'll have enough for the dinner tea."

Shannon nodded Daniel to follow her through the back door.

The late afternoon sun darted behind some clouds, and a cool breeze caressed the warmth of Mary's kitchen from Shannon's cheeks and slightly lifted her thick hair. "Oh, that feels so good," she said as she dropped down and nested in front of the mint. "It's such a gorgeous day, isn't it?"

Nicolas and Alberto exploded through the back door, the younger one screeching as his brother chased him. They flew past Daniel and Shannon, and then Nicolas stopped to tighten his grip on a makeshift plastic slingshot with a large rubber band hanging from it. He plucked a ping-pong ball from his pocket that bulged with more of them, loaded it, and aimed, flinging a direct hit at the back of his little brother's head.

"I got you!" he cried.

"Whoa, whoa, wait a minute!" Daniel said, snatching it out of the boy's hand. "What do you have here?"

"I'm David, and Albie's Goliath, and this is my slingshot so I can take him down."

"Where did you get these?"

"We made them in Sunday school today," Alberto clucked in his high-pitched little voice as he scurried back to them. "Wanna see mine?"

Shannon finished breaking off sprigs of mint, enjoying the scene unfolding before her.

"It don't hurt," Nicolas insisted.

"It *doesn't* hurt," Daniel said playfully. "And let's make sure. You two load up your slings and I'll be your Goliath."

"For real?" Alberto cried, eyes widening.

Daniel wiggled his fingers at them as an invitation. "C'mon. Hit me with your best shot!" And with that, he lifted both arms like a bear and roared, inciting them to screech as he chased them around the garden path past the tomatoes and toward the zucchini.

Shannon straightened and stretched, enjoying the sound of Izzy's boys playing with Daniel. Sliding open the back door, Izzy joined her outside.

"You look happy today."

"You know, I feel sort of happy. Is that weird?"

"Why would that be weird?"

"Sometimes," she admitted, "I almost feel guilty about it."

"Why?"

"I don't know. Feeling so much joy . . . It was only a few days ago that I was married to Edmund and we were starting our lives together; but it was almost ten years ago as well. I feel like I should still be grieving, and then—at the same time—like I should have gotten over it and moved on. Does that make any sense?"

"I can see what you mean," she replied. "But either way, you have nothing to feel guilty about. Seems to me whatever you're feeling is what you should be feeling. You know?"

"I know that here," she said, tapping on her temple. "But here—" she thumped her hand a couple of times over her heart—"I don't know."

Izzy reached over and gave her friend a quick hug. "You're gonna be okay," she said, squeezing her tightly. "Come on. I think your aunts are brewing up a storm in there," she said, returning to the kitchen. Before Shannon could follow, Daniel returned from battle with the boys in tow.

He brushed his layered mane of dark brown hair away from his face and glanced around them. Adjusting the beaded strands of cord on his wrist, he observed, "This is quite a garden your aunt has going here."

She peered up at him. He was backlit in the bright yellow sunshine and she wanted to tuck a stray dark lock behind his ear. She turned to survey the garden. "Aunt Mary has a gift. I've asked her to teach me in hopes that it's in the genes. I'm going to start with an herb garden and see how it goes."

"My mother had a garden like this when I was a boy," he told her. "In fact, we didn't live too far from here."

"Really? I wonder if it's still there," she mused. "Wouldn't it be great if the next owners tended it over the years?"

"I'd like to think the seeds she planted led to something lovely, something that lasted."

She sensed a certain melancholy in his voice, and she looked up at him. "Hey," she said with a grin. "You're a seed she planted. And you grew into something really lovely that lasted. I, for one, am really grateful to her for that. Is she still alive?"

The back door creaked open, and Shannon spotted Luca standing on the steps, little Luis still in his arms. He spoke softly to his grinning son as he grabbed the metal beater hanging by a leather strap from the porch overhang, and he placed it into Luis's tiny hand. With a little more coaching from his papa, the boy used it to bang the metal triangle hanging there, and he laughed wildly.

"The universal call to supper," Shannon told Daniel with a little smile.

She hadn't even realized she remembered those words, spoken to her so many dozens of times in her formative years. Mary's voice sang it back to her from inside the fog of her memory.

"When you hear this bell, no matter where you are or what game you're playing," she'd explained, "you come running home that instant. This lovely sound is known worldwide by children and parents alike as the universal call to supper."

Luis's howls and snorts of merriment reached straight across the garden and grabbed both corners of Shannon's mouth, lifting and stretching her lips into a broad grin. Luca allowed him to strike the triangle several more times before he smiled at Shannon and Daniel apologetically.

"Your aunt said you'd know what it means."

Shannon chuckled. "Yes. I know what it means."

Shannon looped her arm through Daniel's, and the two of them moseyed back toward the house. Between the tomato plants and the back door, years of memories flowed through her. Bike rides and jumping rope . . . hopscotch on the driveway . . . games of hide-and-seek among the trees that formed a makeshift border beyond the garden.

At the door, she paused and looked back at those trees, and at the half acre of woods beyond them at the edge of Mary's property. She'd spent so many carefree days with her neighborhood friends back there.

The honey-blonde curls and crystal blue eyes of her young friend came to mind—Caitlyn Morrisey. And with her, the clear vision of the two of them—the best of friends, maybe six years old—acting out their favorite fairy tales. Maid Marian saved by a sword-wielding Robin Hood . . . Cinderella hiding in the trees from her wicked stepsisters . . . Snow White frolicking with seven tiny imaginary men who whistled while they worked.

The neighborhood boys crash-landed on their fairy tale endings every time, and Shannon and Caitlyn finally surrendered to the less predictable and more adventurous games that the boys wanted to play as well. The memory of tucking away her fairy tale dreams squeezed her heart slightly, but the joy of those new adventures almost made up for the discomfort. With the neighborhood boys as their new playmates, she and Caitlyn had perceived that small patch of wooded land as some great and dangerous setting for pirate adventures and Robinson Crusoe survivalist expeditions.

Over the years, she'd lost touch with those kids who had shared her passion for such fantastic imagined ventures. They'd moved on to tenured teaching jobs and corporate raiding and the like, while she'd studied graphic design and found a secure little spot for herself at . . .

"*Weston Designs!*" she shouted, and she slapped the doorway with her fist.

Daniel raised his eyebrows.

"The name of the company where I worked, Daniel. It's called Weston Designs."

"Very good," he congratulated her.

"Oh, you must have known that already. Well, it's such a relief to remember," she groaned. "It was like this horrible itch under my brain that I couldn't quite scratch. And it just came to me out of nowhere. *Weston. Designs.*"

From inside, Shannon barely heard her aunt's spontaneous applause. But the exclamation that followed sounded as clear as the clang of that triangle calling her to dinner.

"Yippee!"

13

"Daniel, would you like to say grace?"

"Happy to."

Everyone joined hands around the massive food-laden table. Izzy, Luca, and their two boys on one side—with a portable booster chair that they'd brought along for Luis angled next to Izzy at the foot of the table. Lora, Lonna, Daniel, and Shannon occupied the opposite side, and Mary surveyed her kingdom from the head.

"Lord, we thank You for bringing us all together today under Mary's lovely roof," Daniel prayed, and Shannon glanced over to find his eyes closed, his head bowed reverently. "In particular, we thank You for restoring Shannon to her family and friends. Bless this amazing spread of food and those of us enjoying it. And most of all bless the hands that prepared it. In Jesus's name we pray. Amen."

As a chorus of *amens* followed, something contracted just beneath Shannon's ribcage. Above the melodic activity of conversations and plates of food moving from one spot to another, intense emotion surged through her. She didn't know exactly what she felt, but she knew what had triggered it.

Something about Daniel's prayer over the meal . . .

"Oh, it wasn't just me, dearies. Shannon and I worked together," Mary's voice cut in to her turbulent thoughts. "You can thank her as well."

Shannon pushed her lips into a smile, and her eyes met Izzy's, then Luca's. They'd clearly been talking about her.

"I just can't get over Shannon's sudden accomplishments in the kitchen!" Izzy exclaimed. "The Shannon I used to know had no interest whatsoever. It's just amazing. You should see what she's been cooking up and stocking in that new freezer of hers. I had one of her scones the other day with a cup of coffee. Can you believe she's drinking coffee now?"

Shannon gave a courteous nod and half a smile then set about the business of transferring a few potatoes from platter to plate. That strange electrical buzz inside just wouldn't set her free, and she had no desire at all to fight it in order to talk about scones or indulge in the great coffee versus tea debate.

"Excuse me," she muttered, pushing her chair from the table. "I'll be right back."

"Are you all right?" Daniel asked softly as she passed him, and she gave one firm nod.

"I'll be right back."

Once the bathroom door clicked behind her, Shannon leaned against the pedestal sink and stared at herself in the beveled oval mirror, wondering about the conflict within her over Daniel's prayer.

The instant it hit her, she groaned out loud. How on earth could she have missed it?

She closed the lid over the toilet and sat down on it, propping her feet on the ledge of the claw-footed bathtub and burying her face against her knees. The verse from Jeremiah, the one promising the reader a future and a hope, tripped clumsily through her emotions. There was a time when she'd known that verse of Scripture and its reference by heart. Now, though, it simply waved at her from a distance through the rustling leaves of the embroidered tree on her aunt's lovingly made sampler.

One corner of Shannon's mouth lifted in an odd little smile as Abraham Lincoln stalked deliberately across her mind next, with seemingly no discernible purpose. But then she remembered reading the biography on Daniel's Kindle, learning that the president had endured his own faith struggles. She imagined how he had knelt before God, repentant and broken. So much like her.

"I'm so sorry," she whispered, her eyes clamped shut. "Can you ever forgive me? I don't know why . . ."

● — ● — ●

Daniel finished drying the last crystal glass and he draped the hand towel over the handle on the oven door. He walked over to where Mary stood in front of the sink and planted a kiss on her cheek.

"What else can I do?"

"Oh, dearie, you've done more than enough. Why don't you go find Shannie and take her for a walk. She always used to love going for a walk after a meal."

He strolled through the dining room as Luca removed the leaf from the table and into the front room where the three boys played quietly on the floor. Through the large plate glass window, he saw Izzy, Lonna, and Lora rocking in chairs on the wraparound porch, chatting casually.

He turned back toward Luca and asked, "Have you seen Shannon?"

Luca shook his head at Daniel as he passed, the bulky table leaf in his arms. "Mary, does this go upstairs?" he called out.

"Yes. You'll see the attic pull directly over your head at the top of the stairs," Mary replied.

Luca plodded upward to store the leaf for Mary, but he suddenly backtracked. From the middle of the staircase, he called out to Daniel, nodding toward the second floor. "I think she's in the attic."

When he reached Luca, Daniel took the leaf from his arms. "Thanks. I've got this."

Beyond the landing, a narrow wooden ladder extended from the ceiling, and a yellow glow of light escaped the opening above it. He climbed the ladder, which turned out to be far sturdier than it appeared, and spotted Shannon seated on a wooden chest in the corner of the A-frame attic. With her focus on a small box in front

145

of her, she leaned against the wooden frame of a large antique wheel, idly spinning it with one hand.

"What are you doing up here?" he asked, and Shannon nodded him over to the elaborate carved chest with the name *Malone* burnt into the wood. They both sat down on it and Daniel noticed an open round box decorated in paper that looked like vintage photographs. Shannon lifted it to her lap.

"It belonged to my grandmother on my father's side," she said, producing a stack of yellowed handwritten cards.

"What are they?" he asked.

"Pictures and recipes and records of birthdates, random thoughts or quotes she liked. Daddy said she tended to write everything down on these cards and just toss them into this box."

He chuckled. "That's a new one."

"It was her way of keeping things in one central place so she could pass them on, I guess." She picked up the lid to the box where she'd tossed five or six of the cards. "This one says, 'Grandchild born today. Shannon Margaret Malone. Seven pounds, twelve ounces. Nineteen and a half inches.'" She chuckled. "She wrote down how long I was but forgot to record my birthdate."

Daniel laughed as he took the card and inspected it more closely. "Shannon Margaret Malone," he repeated. "With red hair and green eyes. You're as Irish as I am Greek."

In her best Irish brogue, she replied, "Sure and begorrah, that I am."

They shared a chuckle that ushered in a few moments of comfortable silence before Daniel asked, "What happened to you at dinner, Shannon?"

"You mean when I left the table for a bit?"

"Yes."

Shannon brushed the hair away from her face and sighed. "It was your prayer," she admitted. "It got me."

Confused, he asked, "Why?"

"I realized when I heard it that . . ." She let her words trail off before completing the thought. "You know," she said, changing gears, "I used to pray all the time. I worried, in fact, that Edmund seemed to never pray. Here, he was supposed to be the spiritual head of the family we were forming, but he hardly had anything to back it up. I was always the one pushing him, insisting we go to church."

"He came around in the end though," Daniel pointed out, and he hoped that the reminder encouraged her in some way.

"Yeah. I wish I'd been there to see it."

"So my praying over the meal brought up those memories?"

"No. That's not really . . ." He waited a few beats for her to complete the thought. "The thing is, Daniel, I've been—so angry. And so lost. I used to feel so close to Him, you know?"

Daniel nodded.

"I never imagined something like this could happen to me . . . that God would *even let* something like this happen." Her eyes and face contorted with the pain. "I haven't prayed even once since I came out of the coma."

The silence that followed was dense between them.

Finally Shannon uttered, "I feel awful about it, too. But I can't seem to muster up the . . . I don't know. It's not like I don't still believe. I do. But . . ." She shook her head and fell silent again.

After another few beats, Daniel asked, "Would you like to pray now? With me?"

"I don't think I'd even know what to say."

"What's in your heart?"

"Loneliness . . . and worry. I mean, what's next? Who am I now? I'm not the wife of Edmund, or a designer, or even a tea drinker! I don't know where I belong in the world. What good can I possibly be to anyone?" She sniffed before adding, "What if I draw close to God again and then *something else happens*?" A single tear fell from her chin and dropped onto her clenched hands in her lap.

"You're asking the wrong guy," he said. Daniel squeezed Shannon's hand. She looked up, confused, and he gazed back into her emerald eyes. "Let's ask the right one."

Shannon had sat motionless with her eyes clamped shut as Daniel prayed, letting him hold her hand, hoping that his line to God was a clear and open one, because hers felt clogged these days. He'd asked God to give her a fresh direction for her life as she rebuilt it. He'd asked that she might be able to rest in the knowledge that, even if bad things happen, He would help her; He would somehow turn it to good.

"There are so many things we don't understand, Lord," he had prayed. "But we take comfort in the knowledge that Your thoughts are higher than ours. Help Shannon find her joy and purpose again."

Driving home to her empty Briarcliff home had been difficult, but she'd managed it. She sat there motionless inside the closed garage for a while—she didn't know how long—listening to the muffled chirp of crickets on the other side of the metal door. Something had changed, but Shannon couldn't quite put her finger on it. She pondered it for several more minutes before finally dragging herself from the car and heading inside.

She thought she might give tea another stab, so she put on the kettle while she changed into the drawstring knit pants she'd been wearing around the house lately, and an oversized pink tee shirt with a swarm of colorful butterflies screened across the front. She didn't remember ever buying such a thing, but there it was in the drawer, so she put it on and stood in front of the bathroom mirror as she piled her hair into a messy nest atop her head.

After securing the mop with a clip, she looked down at the front of the oddly happy shirt and frowned. Butterflies and rhinestones might have suited her once upon a time, but they certainly didn't now. "I've got to get myself some new clothes."

Shannon steeped a cup of the tea she supposedly preferred to all others and took it, along with a small throw and her phone, out to the patio. She stoked up a nice little fire in the pit and settled into the corner of one of the couches. The first sip of tea was a little hard to swallow. The second one nearly gagged her.

"What happened to my taste buds?" she asked no one at all. She leaned forward and emptied the cup into the edge of the fire pit with a noisy "Blech."

Shannon tilted her head back to the cushion and gazed through the rungs of the pergola at the shimmering stars in the night sky overhead. A velvet blanket of midnight blue dotted with thousands of tiny silver miracles glistening from somewhere far away. The house, at least, was just as she wanted it to be.

An odd noise caught her attention, and Shannon lowered her head and scanned the patio area for its origin.

"Rutt." There it was again.

She set down her phone and padded across the flagstone to the grass. The cold blades touched her bare feet, and she stood there for several minutes, peering into the border of plants and flowers.

"R-rutt."

She jerked toward it, then let out a shriek as her eyes landed on a short, stout little creature with wide, glassy eyes.

"Hello . . . dog," she nervously greeted the thing, making no move to approach. "How did you get into my backyard, huh?"

"Ruh-ruh-ruh-ruh!"

The emboldened creature moved out of the shadows toward her, and Shannon giggled when she got a good look. "You're a basset hound," she said. "My goodness, that's quite a bark for such a short little guy. Why don't you come closer?"

She leaned over slightly and snapped her fingers, but the dog backed up into the shadows again, barking as he went. She checked behind him, but the gate appeared to be closed tight.

"How did you get in here?" she asked him, but he just continued the noisy tirade.

"Okay," she said, shaking her head. "You can be that way if you want to. I'm just going to go back to what I was doing. You can just think about it for a minute or two, but then we'll have to discuss what we're going to do with you."

She ambled back to the couch and sat down, curling her legs under her and covering them with the cotton throw. She risked a quick look at the dog as she picked up her phone and sent an invitation to Daniel to play a word game. When she glanced back, the basset hound had stretched out at the very edge of the patio, its front paws on the flagstone and its back on the grass. The thing's giant ears looked far too big for its head.

With a sniff, the dog rolled over on its side and pointed its head directly at Shannon, watching her like a nervous hawk. He nearly flew up again when the alert sounded from Daniel that he'd accepted her invitation.

"Words with Friends," she told the dog. "I'm playing with Daniel. He's my friend. Well, he's my doctor. And my friend."

The dog dropped its large fanny to the grass and sat there, alert and watching her closely.

"Ohhh," she announced. "Look at this. He played *script* for a double word score. Nicely done, Dr. Petros."

As she added *ure* to it, the hound stood up and walked over to the couch and stood at her feet, panting.

"Are you thirsty?" she asked him. "Me, too."

Shannon set down her phone and used caution as she stood up and inched toward the house. "I tried some tea," she continued as she went inside and hurried to the refrigerator. She grabbed a bottle of cold water and tucked it under her arm so that she could fill a ceramic bowl with filtered water from the sink. When she rushed back to the door, the dog had moved to the edge of the doorway. "I used to like tea, but I don't anymore," she told the dog as she sauntered back to the couch and set down the bowl of water. "I seem to like coffee more these days. But water is always good to take care of thirst, don't you think?"

The hound walked right up to the bowl and started to drink. And drink. And drink some more.

"Wow. You really were thirsty, weren't you?" she remarked.

Daniel had played the next word—*stint*, built from his original *s*

—and Shannon figured out how to send him a message through the chat window.

It seems I have a guest.

Really, he returned.

Kinda unattractive, short, sad droopy eyes.

Old boyfriend?

Shannon howled with laughter and shook her head as she typed in her reply.

Does look a little like my HS prom date but no.

Who then?

Shannon leaned down and gingerly rubbed the dog's head, and he stopped drinking just long enough to graze her with his bloodshot hound dog eyes. She took the chance and felt for a non-existent collar.

Don't know his name, but he seems to want to stay. She thought she'd let him think about that for a while.

After a long and silent pause in communication, she grinned and took pity on the guy.

Basset hound wandered into my yard somehow. Not tall enough to open the gate.

I'm gonna have to meet this guy. Tomorrow night?

After agreeing to the date, Shannon turned her attention to her visitor. "How *did* you get in here, anyway?" she asked him, but he just shook the water from his mouth in a powerful spray and sat down next to the empty bowl and stared up at her. "What? You want more? I'm not sure how much it's safe for you to drink in one sitting. Wait a little bit and maybe I'll make us both a snack."

She wondered what kind of snack she might have on hand that a long, low-to-the-ground dog might enjoy. Switching over to the browser, she typed in *basset hound* and spent some time reading about the breed's propensity for hip dysplasia and weight issues.

"We might have to avoid the scones," she told him. "A second on the lips might make for a lifetime on the hips, and neither of us wants any of that. I think I have some lean ham, though."

When Shannon's next-door neighbor popped over the following morning to introduce herself, Shannon had the feeling it was really more about getting the scoop on the coma patient who woke up than just spotting some activity at the house that had been dormant for so long. But she had taken the opportunity to introduce the woman to the stinky dog napping on the patio. She'd never seen the dog before, but suggested Shannon post a picture on the Briarcliff community Facebook page. She didn't know how to do that, but Izzy or Daniel could likely help her. She decided to call Daniel.

After his arrival, Shannon waited for Daniel to snap a photo of the dog with her phone.

"He really is unattractive, isn't he? Try to make him look . . . perky. Or something."

"Or something," Daniel muttered.

"Maybe if we don't get a bite on where he belongs, someone will want to adopt him."

Daniel turned and grinned at her. "If I ventured a guess, I'd say he's already chosen his adopted home."

"Oh no!" she exclaimed. "He smells. And I don't need a dog."

"Everyone needs a dog."

"Then you take him home."

"Can't. I'm a doctor. We have very hectic schedules, you know. Despite the fact that I managed to rearrange it for you, I still have rounds to make later."

"Well, I'm unemployed with no prospects. That's hectic, too."

"Come on," he said, nodding toward the glass doors. "I'll show you how to do this. Then after that, we'll find out where we can take him for a scrub-down. He reeks!"

Shannon went inside, followed by Daniel, followed by a stench.

"Oh no!" she cried at the basset. "You get back out there, mister. You belong downwind from the inside of my house."

Daniel had connected a small wire between her phone and her laptop. "Come here and watch so you'll know how to do it next time."

"Next time," she muttered.

With just a few motions, he saved the image of the dog to her desktop.

"What's his name?" he asked.

"He didn't mention."

"Well, what do you call him?"

"Mostly, *Ewww*."

"Well, what would you like me to name the file?"

"Dog?"

Daniel laughed and typed *dog* as the title for the image. "Okay, let's hook you up to the world of Facebook!"

A few minutes later, she had an account with one friend—Daniel—and was about to join the community group.

Shannon pulled a chair close to his and sat down. "What are we going to say?"

He began to type, reading it aloud as he did. "Do you know this dog? Found in Briarcliff last night. Please PM me if you know him."

"What's PM?"

"Private message." In another instant, he'd attached the picture and it showed on the page. "Voila!"

"You're scary good with technology," she commented.

Shannon glanced through the door and spotted the basset standing there atop his stubby little legs, his massive ears nearly drooping to the ground as he stared at them.

"You really need to name him," Daniel said. "Even just so you have something to call him while he's here."

She considered it. "Well, he looks a little like Rodney Danger-field. Remember him?"

Daniel chortled in reply. "Rodney it is then."

"I was actually thinking of trying to give him a bath."

"There are people who do that sort of thing," he said.

"But then I have to put him in my car and get it all stinky."

"Better the car than you."

Shannon tilted her head to one side and thought that over. "I need a leash or something."

"Do you have any rope?"

"You probably know better than I do," she joked, and they went off to search.

An hour later, Shannon and Daniel sauntered through the doors of the groomer, Shannon leading Rodney along behind her, knotted at the neck with the three-foot sash that normally kept her bathrobe shut.

Shannon and Daniel moseyed around the store while they waited, squeezing plush toys until they squeaked, investigating jingling balls, and trying to figure out what purpose a two-foot robot might serve in the life of a dog.

"Go long," Daniel exclaimed, and Shannon backed down the aisle until the Frisbee he tossed at her sailed right into her hands.

"One shot at catching this thing might do Rodney in," she surmised. "Do you think he'd like a soft little pillow shaped like a bone?"

She picked up a pastel blue one and squeaked it at Daniel.

"What guy wouldn't like that?" Daniel returned.

"And I guess I better look at a collar and leash, don't you think so?"

"If you intend on wearing your bathrobe any time soon."

Shannon made her way to the correct aisle and chose a blue polka-dot collar with a matching eight-foot leash.

"Polka-dots?" Daniel observed.

"Rodney seems like he has a good sense of humor."

"He does?"

"Well . . . Like he needs one. And polka-dots seem funny to me."

"Whatever you say. But be sure and tell him I had nothing to do with your choice."

Shannon hung the leash around her neck and slipped the collar over her hand like an oversized bracelet.

"And I was thinking I might as well get some dog food. I'm

already out of ham, and there's no telling how long he might have to stay, right?"

"That's a good idea."

The two of them strolled over to the dog food aisle—and stopped, gaping. There appeared to be at least two dozen varieties. They stood there, side by side and wide-eyed.

"I had no idea," Daniel muttered.

"How does a person know which kind?"

After a few minutes of reading packaging labels aloud, Shannon finally landed on one and tugged an eight-pound bag down from the shelf.

"Weight management," she said as she wrapped both arms around it. "I think this is the one for Rodney."

"I saw some dog treats in that variety," Daniel said. He scanned the aisle until he found a box and pulled it down, too. "These. Dogs twenty-to-thirty pounds . . . That's him, right?"

Shannon shrugged.

"I think so. He can have up to four of them a day."

"Oh, that's nice," she said with a nod. "He won't feel so much like he's dieting if he has a little treat in the afternoons."

"Here. You carry the treat box. Give me the bag of food."

They switched and lumbered down the aisle with the intended purchases in tow.

"I better get him some of these," Shannon said when they reached a display of food and water bowls. "Frankly, I don't like sharing my bowls with him."

As she chose a festive set of matching bowls that might easily double for serving guacamole and salsa, Daniel continued on down the aisle.

"Shannon, check this out," he called out to her a moment later.

When she turned toward him, she burst into laughter at the sight of Daniel holding up a large velvety dog chair in the shape of a puffy throne.

14

"**I have to be** over at Draper by two," Daniel told her as they coaxed a bright and shiny new Rodney into the back seat of her BMW. "Do you want to stop for lunch somewhere?"

"What about Rodney?"

"I know just the place."

Daniel hadn't felt the need to hang out on Congress Street in six months or more, but the idea of wandering around the SoCo District of Austin with Shannon and her wobbly little friend filled him with unexpected eagerness. The problem arose when they arrived to find that the downtown population of outdoor food trucks he'd frequented so often in the past had thinned considerably since his last visit.

"What happened?" he asked Jody when he spotted her sitting atop a picnic table in front of one of the last trailers left behind. "Where is everybody?"

Jody's trailer had some of the best fish tacos he'd ever tasted. She grinned at him and scratched the side of her mousy brown, slicked back ponytail. "Don't you read your newspaper, Dr. Petros? We got our walkin' papers. They're buildin' a big ole hotel on this parcel o'land."

"When did this happen?"

"Spring."

Jody leaned down and clicked her fingers, to which Rodney immediately responded.

"It took me hours to get him to come to me like that," Shannon joked. "You must have the mojo. Do you still say that? Mojo?"

Daniel laughed. "Well, some people do. " Turning to Jody, he asked,

"How much longer will you and George be around then?"

"Ah, we're shut down already. Just gettin' a last look before we move out. Prob'ly move north toward Dallas for a while. We're a dying breed, least around these parts of Austin. Who's your friend?"

"Sorry," he replied, and he guided Shannon by the arm toward the table. "This is Shannon Ridgeway. Shannon, Jody Conklin. Jody's husband is a former patient of mine. And so is Shannon," he added for Jody's sake. The women exchanged greetings.

"We were looking for somewhere we could grab some lunch with Rodney in tow."

Jody chuckled. "Rodney, huh?" She scratched the back of the dog's floppy ear. "You could try downtown. I heard some folks relocated down there."

"Thanks, Jody. Best of luck in Dallas."

Once they returned to the car, Daniel shook his head and sighed. "That's a shame," he said. "The food trucks gave the area such character."

"I don't know if I'd ever heard of them before," Shannon commented as she pulled out into traffic. "But I have to admit I'm a little surprised to hear that you come down to a bunch of food trucks to grab a meal."

"Hey, don't knock it until you've tried it. There's nothing you could be hungry for that you couldn't find down here south of Congress."

"So where to?"

After some discussion, they agreed to return to Shannon's house for a little sampling out of her refrigerator. When she clammed up for most of the drive back, Daniel couldn't help inquire about the silence.

"What's on your mind? Anything you want to share?"

"I was thinking about those food trucks, actually. It kind of gives me an idea."

"Ready to buy a motor home and hit the road?" he teased.

"That's not entirely wrong," she answered with a chuckle. "I've been thinking about this newfound culinary talent I seem to have developed in my sleep, wondering if there's anything I can do with it rather than going back to the corporate life of graphic design."

"So you're going to start a food truck."

"No, silly . . . Well, maybe . . . But what if I took my food on the road?"

"I don't understand."

"Well, when Edmund and I were first dating, we were both professionals, always working. We had restaurant meals two or three times a day. I don't know for sure, of course, but I don't think I cooked us a meal in all the time I knew him."

"I think that's pretty typical in this town. It's filled with young professionals, artists, musicians, and politicians. We keep the food industry pretty well thriving."

"But what if there had been someone who would come to our house and cook good, healthy meals for us, stock the freezer and the fridge, and make it so easy and enticing to eat at home that frequenting a restaurant for every meal wasn't necessary? Or even preferable."

"So you're thinking about becoming . . . a mobile . . ."

"Personal chef," she finished for him. "What do you think?"

He mulled it over for a minute. "I don't know what to think. I know there's a lot of legalities involved in something like that. Not just the business licensing, but also the permits you would need."

"Isn't that what I have Betty Rivera for?"

"Beverly."

"Beverly Rivera. For things like this?"

"I think it's worth a phone call. Beverly is contract law and the like, but if she can't help you, she'll know someone who can. So what would you call your business?"

"I'm not sure yet. It's just the germ of an idea inspired by our food truck excursion."

"All right," he said, nodding. "Here's hoping your germ spreads."

After another silence, she thought of something else. "Speaking of icky things, when I was in my closet looking for a belt to leash up Rodney, I came across the jewelry Millicent wanted. I saw the box on the shelf of the walk-in, and I remembered it. There are several pieces in there that belonged to Edmund's mother and grandmother. I'd like to take it over to her and I was wondering—"

"Why don't you talk to Beverly about that, too."

"They are her family heirlooms, Daniel. Now that Edmund's gone, they belong to Millicent, not me. I'm not going to fight her for any of them. I really want to return them to her. But I thought maybe you might—well, go with me."

"Oh, sure. You decide to climb the mountain to the dragon's castle, but you want me to go along as your shield!"

"Sorta. Would you?"

Daniel wondered if they'd have time to make a run to Lake Austin before his rounds at Draper.

"I will. But not today. Give her a call and set up a time this week, and I'll polish my shield and sword. Will I need wading boots?" he asked with a mock frown.

"Wading boots?"

"I assume there's a moat." He'd actually been to the house once before, and there wasn't a moat in sight. But there should have been.

Shannon giggled. "No. No moat." Pushing her nose straight into the air, she put on her most condescending voice as she added, "Just the one dragon in the *fahmal* living room, *dahling*."

● — ● — ●

"You know the way to Millicent's," Shannon observed as he drove. "Why is that?"

"I went out there once. Early on, after Edmund passed away." Daniel stared directly out the windshield, avoiding her gaze, as he turned the car into the gated community where Millicent lived.

"For?"

The corner of Daniel's mouth twitched slightly. The girl didn't know how to let anything pass.

"She'd just filed the first papers with the court. A transfer of Edmund's power of attorney. A petition for medical guardianship—"

Shannon tossed her head back against the headrest with a thump and laughed out loud. "You're joking! Guardianship implies looking out for my best interests. She just wanted to pull the plug and be done with me so she could take the money and run."

"I thought I could talk some sense into her, try to get her to see things from Edmund's perspective."

"How'd that work out?" she asked dryly.

Daniel chuckled. "Once I pulled up this driveway to her lair, I kind of got a glimpse at what was ahead."

The iron gates stood open this time around, and Daniel steered down the long driveway bordered on both sides by a short wall of whitewashed brick and stone. Tall, thin Italian cyprus trees groomed to a sharp point at the top led the way around a bend where the massive two-story home loomed beneath a gloomy gray sky.

"Yep," Daniel said as he pulled up out front. "Put this place at the top of a hill in the middle of a thunderstorm, and we've got the makings of a really scary movie."

Shannon giggled. "The first time Edmund brought me here, I wanted to turn around and run through the front gate."

"It's hard to imagine him coming from this kind of place."

"I know what you mean," she said, leaning forward and glaring up at the house. "He was just a kid when they moved into The Point. I think he looked past the ghastly castle aspects and actually loved the place with its big Spanish front doors and the dock out back. You know he was the one who inherited it when their mother died, right? Even though she got a different house—the one up in Napa—and a sizeable chunk of the family business, it was always a bone of contention for Millicent. But I couldn't even imagine living in this house, so as you probably know, Edmund gave it to his sister and we bought the place in Briarcliff."

"You could fit that house into this one about twelve times."

"Yep," she said, still gazing at the house through the front windshield. She shuddered. "Of all the things my brain decided to forget, why couldn't this place have been one of them?"

The hundred-year-old front door creaked open. A stiff-lipped sentinel, with black hair and a suit to match, stood in the doorway staring at them.

"Lurch or Alfred?" Daniel cracked, and Shannon giggled.

"I can't remember. But he's the son of the man who worked for them for a couple of centuries. That was Reginald."

"You're joking."

Snickering as she cranked open the door, Shannon stepped out of the SUV and grabbed the antique box from the floor. Tucking it under her arm, she joined Daniel and they walked toward the front door together.

"How is your father?" she asked him, and the uniformed sentry glanced at his polished shoes before he replied.

"He passed away five years ago, Miss."

"I am so sorry," she told him as she touched his sleeve. "Reginald was always so good to me."

He tilted forward and softly added, "He would have been so happy to see you've recovered, Miss."

"Thank you so much. I'm sorry that you lost your father. Is Millicent around?"

"In the library."

Daniel followed Shannon over the stone tiled floor, between marble columns and across thick Persian rugs until they reached ten-foot double doors. Despite the fact that they stood wide open, no trace perception of welcome beckoned.

"Got that sword and shield at the ready?" Shannon muttered.

"I thought you brought them."

She snorted softly before stepping into the library, shrouded on two sides by floor-to-twelve-foot-ceiling bookcases. When the doorman had called it a library, he sure wasn't kidding.

"Millicent?"

They heard a clipped voice say, "What do you want, Shannon?" as a dark figure emerged from the shadows, several leather-bound books in her hands. Daniel could almost hear the cued organ music setting the stage. *Dun-dun-duuuuuun.*

Shannon walked straight up to Millicent and set the antique box on the nearby table. "I found the jewelry you asked about. At least I think I did. Is this it?"

Millicent levitated over to the box and opened it. The upturn of her catlike eyes allowed Daniel to deduce that Shannon had found the heirlooms. He couldn't help himself, and he moved in for a closer look as the woman removed a dazzling strand of milk-white pearls and held it up to the light from the arched window.

With just a barely perceptible sigh, she replaced the pearls and plucked out an eye-popping emerald choker, an opal ring encrusted with diamonds and a ruby pendant the size of a large prune. Edmund had left a fortune worth of jewels just sitting in an antique box in the closet? Daniel knew nothing about gemstones or karats or stone quality, but he didn't have to be a jeweler to know that one small antique box probably rang up to half a million dollars or more.

"They're the ones, right?" Shannon asked.

Millicent looked for a moment like she hadn't even heard her. "Of course they are," she finally snapped. "Where else would the likes of you come by them?"

Daniel swallowed his sudden urge to intervene, waiting instead for Shannon's reply.

"Well, that's the truth," she said, surprising him with the sincere little chuckle that followed.

"So what's it going to cost me?"

Shannon glanced at Daniel before looking back at Millicent with the quirk of her head. "I don't understand the question."

"Well, surely this isn't just a goodwill visit, Shannon. What do you want in return?"

Daniel took note of the subtle change in stance as Shannon straightened, planting herself equally on both rigid jeans-clad legs.

"Edmund would have wanted you to have them."

"Yes." She drew the one syllable out into a slow slither.

"Take care of yourself, Millicent."

And with that, she turned around and stalked out of the room.

Millicent stared at him, narrowing her black eyes until her gaze poked him in the gut. "You are her new Edmund, I take it."

"I don't think she needs one," he said. "She seems to do pretty well on her own."

He shot her a smile before he turned and caught up to Shannon, following her straight out the front door.

"If you think you've seen the end of me, you're mistaken," Millicent called after them, but neither of them bothered to press pause. They simply climbed into the Lexus and left the evil queen to her own devices, whatever they were—probably cackling maniacally and counting her millions.

●　–　●　–　●

Shannon leaned hard against the straight-backed dining room chair and stretched, groaning loudly. Rodney followed suit from the floor beside her chair, his little groan followed by an unceremonious belch.

"If you're going to be rude while you're living here," she told him, "I'm just going to have to go and check that Facebook page and find out if anyone wants to claim you."

She realized she was hesitant to do so, however. The little guy had started to grow on her.

Several Briarcliff residents had commented about not knowing him, and one even bothered to say he looked "used up."

"That picture was taken before his bath," she spoke back to the guy, clicking off Facebook with a snort. "He's the picture of beauty now, mister." One glance at the floor to find a fat basset on his side, struggling to get back to his feet, and Shannon shrugged. "Work with me here, Rodney."

When the phone rang, she picked up her cell phone first. "Hello?"

Then, realizing it had been the land line, she snatched the cordless.

"Hello?"

"What are you doing?" Izzy blurted instead of a greeting.

"Fine, and how are you?"

"Good. Whatever. What are you doing?"

Shannon chuckled. "I'm working on a business plan."

"For what business? Are you going back to design?"

"Well, I'm using my design skills right now," she rationalized. "But no, I'm not going back into design."

"Then what are you going to do?"

"I'm putting together a possible brochure and some specs for a new business altogether. How does the name *Dine-1-1* strike you? You know, like culinary 911?"

Izzy laughed. "Details, please. Exactly what kind of business are we talking about here?"

"Hot meals for urban professionals, delivered straight to their door. No more fast food or restaurants five nights a week. Just hot, healthy food prepared by me. Whatcha think?"

Izzy remained silent, and Shannon tapped the phone. "Hello? Is this thing on?"

"Shannon, you've been cooking for about fifteen minutes. Now you want to do it as a business?"

"How about *Fresh Solutions*?"

"Shannon—"

"Okay, I get it, Iz. You think it's a bad idea. Let's skip it."

"It's not that I think—"

"So why'd you call? What's up?"

"Well, would you like to come over and join me and the kids for a swim?"

"You hate to swim."

165

"Yeah, well, Luca loves it, and he passed that gene to our children, which is why we have a swimming pool outside the back door. So now I'm out there so much I realize it's actually a *good* idea to be cool when you're outside in Austin."

"Ohhh, I get it. You mean people can *change* over time?" Her voice dripped with sarcasm. "They might take up unlikely things like swimming or cooking? Imagine that."

"Nice try. Listen, come and swim. We're grilling later, after Luca gets home."

"Oh, Iz. I don't think so . . ." A current of nausea washed over Shannon in prickly, cold perspiration, and her temples tapped out the opening chorus of a building crescendo.

"Why not? It'll be fun."

"I don't really—I guess I'm the one who doesn't swim now." She closed her eyes and massaged her left temple with two fingers. "Truthfully, I can't even take a swim in the tub these days, Izzy. It's all I can do to stand in the tub for a shower."

"Are you serious?"

"It's like I panic whenever I think about water any deeper than a puddle. My new therapist says it's a circuit breaker in my brain that jolts me with the feeling that water took away everything I had. I know it sounds nuts, but—"

"Honey, that's not nuts. It's your truth, until another one takes its place."

"Thanks, Iz," she said with a sigh. "I didn't think you'd understand."

"Look, I don't pretend to understand all of the changes in you since you woke up, but I am so happy to have you back that I don't even care. Come over. We'll make it very chill. We'll barbecue and let the kids and Luca splash around as much as they want to. You can tell me more about this business idea you've been dreaming up."

"Really?"

"Really."

As an afterthought, Shannon asked her, "Where do you live, anyway?"

They both laughed at the question, and Izzy promised to email the directions.

"Do you mind if we invite Daniel? Luca really liked him."

"Oh. You can, I guess. I think he's at the hospital on Wednesday nights though. Do you mind if I bring Rodney?"

"I'm sorry, did you say Rodney?"

"Oh, that's right. You don't know about him, do you?"

"Shannon, have you met someone?"

"Well, he's kind of homely, but I've been able to overlook that because he's really quite charming. He's got these huge ears though—"

"Aw, that's cute. Like Will Smith?"

"Oh, much bigger than Will's."

"Uh. Oh. Okay."

"He could stand to lose a few pounds, and his eyes are kind of droopy and tired. Probably because his life hasn't been easy lately. He was homeless when we met . . ."

"Shannon?"

"He's a basset hound, Iz." She chuckled.

"You have a dog?"

"I have a dog! He wandered into my backyard, and we kind of fell in love."

"Rodney."

"Yeah. He looks like that old comedian, Rodney Dangerfield."

Izzy heaved out an exasperated sigh. "Lovely."

"I was only joking about bringing him."

"Good. But you know what, I'm glad it's a dog you're talking about, 'cause I was about to be disappointed that you'd met some guy. I kind of like to see you with Doctor Daniel. Just sayin.'"

Shannon plopped down on the padded bench and stared at the clothes still hanging from metal rods in her closet. So many of the pieces she'd bought before her honeymoon—several with tags still dangling from them—seemed to jump off the hangers at her every time she paid a visit to that bench. Finally, she yanked down a pair of dark pink capris pants with white enamel buttons positioned over the little v-slits at the cuff, and the pink and white checkered sleeveless peasant blouse. Scanning the rows of shoe cabinets on the opposite wall, she landed on a pair of bejeweled silver sandals, and she grabbed them on her way out of the closet.

"Come on," she urged Rodney, and she shut the door after him when he finally waddled out. "I think I'll wear this outfit while I still think it's cute. Izzy will tell me soon enough what I can get away with from my old wardrobe and what's miserably out of style."

Shannon slipped into the pants and stood before the full-length beveled mirror on the back of the bathroom door and nibbled the corner of her lip as she inspected her reflection. She dropped the checkered blouse over her head, and it fell past her shoulders and down both arms until she tightened the drawstring ribbon around the top and brought it back into place.

Pale skin, an abundance of poorly placed freckles, and an outfit two sizes too big. How attractive.

She'd lost a good bit of weight in the ten years she'd been inactive. Her muscle tone was still suffering, but she had no more serious side effects than that. She figured the staff at Draper must have—thankfully!—known what they were doing. She padded back into the closet and rummaged through the cedar drawers until she found two oversized safety pins which she used to gather the waist of her pants.

"That should at least keep them up," she mumbled. Turning to Rodney where he collapsed to the floor at the corner of the bed, she added, "I don't know why it matters so much. It's just Izzy and her family . . . and maybe Daniel."

Her stomach gave a sudden anxious lurch.

"Oh, he's not coming," she assured the dog whose breathing resembled snoring despite his wide-open eyes. "And even if he does . . ." She couldn't manage to complete the thought.

If he does, what then? He already knows I'm pasty white. He was my doctor while I languished away in a hospital bed for ten years, for crying out loud. She tied the hem of her shirt into a knot that rested low on one hip, and she shifted to one foot and then the other.

"Like this even matters," she said aloud. "He's not coming. And if he does, what do I care what he thinks of how I look? I'm being ridiculous." Rodney yawned noisily and flipped to his other side. "Oh, what do you know? You have one fur coat, and you wear it all the time."

She inspected her reflection for another minute or more before groaning and rushing over to flop down to the bed.

"I've got to get some new clothes!" she exclaimed.

"What do you think of this one?" the princess inquired,
and she twirled in front of the large oval mirror before her,
the skirt of the ball gown rustling as she did.

"Too plain," her friend replied. "Try the other one."

It took both their efforts to get the princess into the sparkling gown,
but after the buttons were clasped and the ribbons tied,
they both stared at the reflection before them, mesmerized.

"I'm . . . transformed," the princess said with a sigh.

15

"I just wanted to let you know I'm running a little late."

"I was starting to get worried," Izzy told her, and Shannon covered the speaker on her phone as she handed several cash bills to the sales clerk. "Where are you?"

"I had to safety pin my pants up, and that broke the last straw. I was almost to your street when I noticed a sale sign on the marquis over that little boutique around the corner."

"You went clothes shopping without me," Izzy accused.

"Just making up for lost time! I only bought a few things. I didn't want to come over looking like I did."

"Bring everything in with you so I can see what you got."

"I changed into the sweetest little dress. There were a lot of long ones on the rack, so I'm guessing really long dresses are popular?"

"You're right on trend; they're called maxis."

"Good to know. Okay, I should see you in about ten minutes."

She disconnected the call and looked down at the color burst of blue, pink, and lavender. It fit just right in the waist, and the strands of beaded spaghetti straps actually stayed on her shoulders without any amount of prodding necessary.

After paying the clerk, Shannon picked up her two shopping bags and resisted the urge to skip out the front door and to her car. Clothes that fit made her feel like a new woman.

What was she talking about? Ask anyone who knew her before the accident, she realized, and they would surely report that Shannon actually *had* become a new woman. But now she'd started to catch up to the feeling.

● — ● — ●

Daniel ran by the Greek café Opa! and had them make up a plate of hummus with pita and cucumber slices on his way out to Izzy's place. His day had been a long one, but for some reason he hadn't really been looking forward to going home, so her invitation to dinner came as a welcome surprise. He really liked her and Luca, and he relished the idea of getting to know them better. Josiah's involvement with the youth center and his plans for a mission trip to Haiti in the fall had been overshadowing everything else, and it seemed like the only time they saw one another anymore was at church or in the cafeteria line at the hospital.

"Turn left in one-half mile," his robotic GPS navigator instructed.

Shannon skittered across his thoughts, her long reddish curls dancing around his brain, and her creamy skin, dotted with cinnamon freckles. He'd been thinking about her like that more and more lately as she'd made the transition from patient to friend.

He'd never mentioned it to anyone, but he'd had the oddest experience at the end of Edmund's life. So sure that his wife would one day awaken from her coma, he'd all but chosen Daniel to replace him when Shannon faced the news that he was gone, and it made Daniel uncomfortable. Living up to that kind of romance— the one where the man sat lovingly by the woman's bed for endless hours, just waiting to look into her eyes one more time—well, that was as intimidating as it got. As a medical professional, he had given Shannon Ridgeway all the attention she deserved, but he didn't really expect it to happen the way Edmund seemed to. Now that she was awake, however, and so lovely, inside and out . . .

He pulled into the driveway and parked. Shannon's blue BMW carved a patriotic notch into the sprawling white Colonial with its border of blooming red flowers.

Luca answered the door wearing long swim shorts and an open Hawaiian shirt, his youngest perched on his arm. The boy's chubby face brightened at the first sight of Daniel, and he extended both arms toward him. Luca chortled and shook his head as Daniel traded his hummus platter for the boy's enthusiastic, spontaneous welcome.

"He's never done that before!" Luca exclaimed as Daniel took Luis into his arms. "Look how he's taken to you."

Luis tapped Daniel's stubbly cheeks several times with both hands and giggled when he opened his eyes extra wide.

"Good to see you, too, young man. How have you been? Anything new with the toddler set?"

Luis replied. "Uh-uh."

"Look at this!" Luca proclaimed as they joined the others on the caged patio. "Baby, Luis went straight to him."

Izzy grinned at him before slipping into a pair of sandals and adjusting her modest blue bathing suit. As she ambled toward him, she tightened the sarong knotted just above one hip.

"Do you have bacon in your pocket?" Izzy asked, and she gave Daniel a casual hug and smiled at him, taking Luis. "My children are like dogs. They can be bribed with food."

"I did walk in the door with a platter in my hands."

She laughed. "Welcome, Daniel."

"Thanks for inviting me."

He glanced over Izzy's shoulder and nodded at Shannon where she sat at a large rectangular table playing a board game with Nicolas and Alberto. She scraped her chair away from the table and stood up.

"You look exquisite," he said as she floated toward him.

She diverted her eyes to the ground, flustered as her face and neck took on pink blotches of embarrassment. He reached out for a hug, and he thought they must have resembled a couple of pecking hens as they made two awkward attempts.

She thanked him for the compliment and pulled away, fiddling with one of her large hoop earrings and brushing away curly wisps that had escaped the nest of hair piled at the top of her head.

"Daniel brought appetizers," Luca announced, and he pulled the plastic dome from the platter and set it out on top of a bamboo bar angled into the corner of the patio. "What can I get you to drink, man? How do you feel about fruit punch? It's a family favorite today."

"Sounds good."

Shannon wandered away just as Nicolas, the eldest of the boys, climbed up on the barstool next to him and thumped his fist on the bar. Luca wiped the bar with an imaginary towel and asked, "Welcome to our tiki bar, young man. What'll ya have?"

"I'd like a large tiki, please," his son replied in a deepened voice.

Daniel laughed, and Izzy shook her head. "It's the family comedy routine, Daniel. If you encourage them, I might have to hear it over and over again for the next twenty years."

Luca handed him a frosty mug of red liquid, and Daniel took a sip.

"I wanna tiki," Alberto cried as he rushed toward them, and Daniel lifted his drink in the air and navigated out of his path before a collision resulted.

"Albie, watch where you're going," Izzy warned him. "Go get Luis's water wings from the cabinet."

Daniel made his way over to Shannon where she cleared the game pieces from the table. "Good to see you," he said as he sat down next to her.

"You, too." She placed the lid on the box and slid it to the corner of the table. "Thanks again for going with me to see—" For a moment, her brain sort of fogged over and she struggled to produce the name, though it lingered right on the tip of her tongue. "*Millicent!* Thank you for going with me to see Millicent."

"You've already escaped death once, young lady. I can't have you wandering into her realm all alone, can I?" He spotted the teal laptop on the chair beside him. "Is that yours?"

"Oh. Yeah. I was sharing some of my ideas with Izzy."

"Ideas?"

The pink stained her cheeks again and she shook her head. "It's nothing yet, really. I'm just thinking about things, that's all."

Nicolas's laughter waylaid their conversation, and they watched as Izzy dove into the pool after him. Luca slowly descended the concrete stairs into the water with Luis in his arms.

"What kind of things?" Daniel finally asked.

"The future, I guess."

"Show me?"

She hesitated. "I'm just doodling at this point. I don't have any cohesive ideas just yet."

"Don't let her snow you," Izzy chimed in, poolside. "She's charting out a whole new path, Daniel. Show him, Shannon."

"Iz, stop it."

"Oh, and you know what? If you decide to go forward with this," Izzy added, "Luca could build you a website. That's what he does. My husband is a techie. Did I tell you that?"

Shannon looked at Daniel seriously. "I don't really know what I'm doing yet. I only know I don't want to go back to a cubicle, you know?"

"Sure." When she didn't continue, Daniel suggested, "Why don't you show me what you're thinking."

She gave it a moment's thought, and then shot a questioning look in Izzy's direction before she shrugged and reached for the laptop. While it fired up, she warned, "These are really just notes, and I don't even know what it might shape up into, if anything. So don't expect—"

"Shannon, just show me."

She opened a desktop file, and a sketch of a logo filled the screen.

"Dine-1-1," he read aloud. A vertical knife and fork formed the double ones. Script letters beneath the logo read, *For all your culinary emergencies.*

"It's a play on words," she explained. "Like 911."

175

"Yeah, I get it," he said with a grin. "It's catchy."

She closed the file and produced another one in its place.

"This one appeals more to the anti-fast food clientele," she said, and Daniel examined the colorful round logo where the title—*Fresh Solutions*—offset an abundance of vegetables, from lettuce and tomatoes to a zucchini and a few small onions.

"What's the concept?" he asked. "You're considering catering?"

"Remember our discussion the other day?" she asked him. "I can't let go of the idea that sometimes people just need a warm meal. How to apply that, though, I don't know."

"Professionals in the workplace spend a really large portion of their salaries on eating out," he chimed in.

"Right. Fast food and restaurants and stuff like that. There's just no time for grocery shopping and meal planning and cooking, you know?"

He grinned. "Preachin' to the choir, sistuh."

"So I thought maybe I could do all the work, and deliver healthy meals to people's refrigerators where all they'd have to do is heat it up and eat."

With another few clicks, she brought up a working layout of a brochure still in progress.

"You've obviously retained your graphic skills," he told her. "This is really good work."

She lifted one shoulder in a halfhearted shrug. "This is all I could come up with using the program we bought with the laptop; I'll have to get up-to-date with design software again. I just . . . I don't know. The idea really stemmed from those food trucks of yours, the ones downtown. After you took me there, it just started churning around in me about taking healthy meals mobile, you know? That's the only part of it all that keeps resonating. It's still just the beginning of an idea. Something's still missing, but I don't know what it is yet. I'm in the process of pulling it together."

"I'd say you're off to a good start."

"You know when you prayed for me up in my aunt's attic on Sunday?" she asked timidly.

"Sure."

"You prayed that I'd find my sense of purpose. Find my joy again."

He nodded.

"Well, I feel like I'm on the right track, but I'm not quite there yet. I can't help feeling this is all part of—I don't know, a plan. Does that make any sense?"

He nodded and smiled. "Yes. It does."

"I was thinking maybe—I mean, not right now or anything—but I wondered if maybe you'd consider . . ."

"Would you like us to pray together again?"

She nodded and puffed out a sigh of relief. "Really a lot."

"I'll do that, and more. Why don't you come to church with me on Sunday."

"Oh."

"You don't have to. But I'd really like it if you'd come, Shannon."

"Well, it's just that my aunts are coming to Sunday dinner at my house, and I have so much to do to prepare . . ."

"So we'll go to church, and then I'll come back and help you. What do you say?"

"Well . . . okay." The idea seemed to settle in, and she brightened. "Okay. Thank you. That sounds nice, actually."

"Can somebody give me a hand with the burgers?" Luca called out.

Soaking wet, Izzy wrapped a large flowered towel around her body and sank into the chair across from Daniel.

"Shannon, can you help my husband? I want to have a chat with your doctor."

"About what?" she asked with clear trepidation.

"Go on," she prodded, and Shannon reluctantly stood up and went to help Luca.

"Can you believe this girl is starting a business centered around

177

cooking?" Izzy asked. "Daniel, I've known her since college, and I never saw her cook one solid meal in all those years. And now she says she has a dog!"

"Oh, yeah," he laughed. "Rodney."

"You've seen him? Is he awful?"

"No." He caught himself and shrugged. "Well, he's nothing much to look at, but he's all right. Not awful at all."

"Shannon never cared about dogs. What do you suppose happened to her? Have you ever seen this kind of thing before where a coma patient wakes up with a whole other personality?"

"Comas change their victims, there's no question about that," he replied. "Memories, personalities, preferences—they're all unpredictable."

"I just don't know if this whole catering thing is a good idea," she said softly. "I mean, starting a new business can be overwhelming, and I don't want her to get in over her head. How do I support her when—"

Daniel touched Izzy's hand and smiled. "I think the best way to support her is to *support her*. She's trying to find her ground again, and she needs to do that in a way that seems right to her."

The resonant sound of Shannon's laughter silenced them both as they watched her interact with three-year-old Luis in order to distract him from the hot grill.

● ⸺ ● ⸺ ●

The boys had been safely tucked into bed for about half an hour, and the adults sat around the patio table, chatting casually. Shannon had just started on her second cup of coffee, wondering if such a bold French roast might be a bad idea so late in the day. But it tasted like heaven, and she just couldn't resist.

She heard the glass slider slip open with a *whoosh!* and looked up at Albie, the middle boy, standing there in cowboy pajamas, his wavy hair mussed.

Izzy straightened when she spotted her son. "What are you doing up, young man?"

"I can't sleep."

Luca opened his arms, and the boy moved into them, standing beside his father's chair but leaning full-force against him. "What do you suppose would help you sleep?"

"A story?" the five-year-old suggested with a sheepish grin.

Luca chuckled. "You want me to read you a story."

"Well, we were thinking—"

"We?" Izzy demanded playfully. "So your brother is in on this, too. As I suspected."

"Yeah, Nicolas is still up too, and we were thinking maybe Daniel would come and tell us a story."

"Daniel?" Luca repeated, one eyebrow lifted into an arch as he smiled.

"Yeah, he played Goliath when we went over there for supper," he explained. "And he made all the noises. You don't make the noises, Popi."

"Albie, Daniel is a guest tonight and—"

Daniel interrupted Luca with a soft chuckle. "I really wouldn't mind."

Alberto immediately pushed off and scampered around the table, grabbing Daniel's hand. "I'll show you our room."

The moment they disappeared through the glass door, Luca let out a hearty laugh and looked at Izzy. "I've been replaced, baby."

"Only temporarily," she pointed out. "You can't expect them to overlook the fact that Daniel *makes the noises*, honey."

He shrugged. "So true."

Shannon admired the lighthearted camaraderie between them. It resonated beyond the obvious spark of attraction, and she wondered if she and Edmund had come across that way to outside observers.

"Daniel is very good with children," Izzy remarked. "He'll make a wonderful father, don't you think?"

179

Shannon's face puckered and she grimaced at her friend.

"Subtle much, baby?" Luca asked.

"I'm just saying, he seems like good father material. Good husband material too, for that matter."

"Iz!" Shannon exclaimed at the same time that Luca echoed her reaction. "Izzy."

"Simmer down, you two. It's just an observation. He's a good guy. That's all I'm saying."

● … ● … ●

That French roast had certainly done its job. Ten o'clock had come and gone, and there Shannon sat in an oversized tee shirt and thick, nubby socks, propped up by several pillows as she watched a DVD—wide awake and forcing down sips of supposedly soothing chamomile tea. She curled her legs under the blanket, and Rodney outlined them on top of it as Rob and Laura Petrie led the way on yet another comedic adventure; her third of the night.

She paused the show when her phone buzzed and she saw Daniel's number showing on the screen.

"Admit it. You miss me," she answered.

"Is your tablet nearby?"

"You mean the menu thingie?" she teased.

"Yeah, the menu thingie."

"It's right here next to me."

"Good. Do exactly what I tell you to do."

Ten minutes later, a program had been installed, and a virtual Daniel sat there smiling at her.

"I can see you!" she cried. With a second thought, she gasped. "Oh no! Can you see me?"

Before he answered, she plopped the tablet screen side down on top of Rodney.

"Shannon. Is that the dog's butt?"

She picked it up and held it to her face momentarily. "Sorry." And she lowered it to the blanket beside her.

"Hey."

She lifted one corner of the tablet and told him, "I don't want you to see me. You should have warned me."

"Why not? You look fine."

"I do not. What do you want?"

"I want to see you. Pick up the tablet, Shannon."

She sat there staring at it, as if it might roll right over and bite her.

"Pick it up, Shannon."

"No."

After a long silence, she barely heard him say, "Okay, then. Goodnight, Shannon."

She tipped it up slightly and replied, "Goodnight." Then, "Wait! Are you still there?"

"Yes."

"How do I turn this thing off so people can't look at me all night?"

"No one can look at you except me."

"Who died and made you Big Brother?" *Poor choice of words.* "Let me put that another way."

"Goodnight, Shannon."

A strange tone sounded, and she flopped forward with her face to the surface of the bed, lifting the tablet only high enough to peek at the screen and confirm that he had disappeared. She tossed the tablet aside and hopped from the bed, scurrying to the bathroom mirror. With a groan at the sight of her reflection, Shannon yanked the bright red scrunchie from the mop of hair on top of her head and ran a wide-toothed comb through it. She quickly snatched a tissue from the box on the counter and wiped the smeared mascara from underneath her eyes before rummaging through the make-up drawer until she found a tinted lip balm and dipped her finger into it. One last fluff to her hair, and Shannon flew back to the bed and covered her bare legs with the comforter.

"How do I . . . how do I do this?" she mumbled as she stared at the tablet screen again. "Okay. Let's try . . . this."

A moment later, the weird little space-age tone sounded, and soon Daniel looked back at her again.

"Yes?" he said dryly.

"Hi. It's me."

"I can see that. And this is me."

Shannon giggled.

"Your hair looked fine before, by the way."

"Okay, so you could have pretended not to notice that."

"You're right. I apologize."

"Well, why did you beam me up before anyway?" she asked.

"Beam you up?"

"Yeah. Why did you want me to put this on my screen and everything?"

"So I could see you."

"Oh." She chewed on the corner of her lip as she thought that over. "How come?"

"I don't know. I wanted to see what you were doing."

"Watching *Dick Van Dyke*. What are you doing?"

"Thinking about you," he admitted somewhat timidly. "Don't ask me why. Which episode?"

She glanced at the frozen television screen in relief, unsure how to respond to his confession. "Oh, right. It's the one where Rob calls Laura and pretends to be a flirtatious wrong number. Right now he's trying to convince Buddy and Sally that she knew it was him all along."

"Turn the tablet around to face the screen," he suggested. "I'll watch it with you."

A few minutes later, it struck Shannon how truly strange it was to watch something so hilariously funny and share guffaws and hysterical laughter with someone who wasn't even in the room with her.

"This is weird," she said, but when she turned the tablet toward her so she could see his face, Daniel wailed.

"Hey, wait a minute! Let me see the ending first."

"Okay," and she faced the tablet toward the screen. Pulling it back for just an instant, she added, "But it's weird, right?"

"Nothing weird about watching TV together. Now turn me around."

16

Daniel plucked a fruit and cheese plate from the display case and grabbed a cold bottle of water from the refrigerator next to the register.

"That's what you're eating?" Josiah said as he stepped up behind him while Daniel paid.

"Why, what are you having?"

"They've got those chili burritos again this week. I just ordered two of them with rice and beans."

"Nice." Daniel winced. "I hope you've finished your surgeries for the day."

His buddy slapped him on the shoulder. "I'm waiting on my order. I'll join you in a sec."

Daniel carried his food to a table across from the window. He found himself sitting there alone, grinning like an idiot, thinking about his interaction with Shannon the night before.

"So how are things with Sleeping Beauty?" Josiah asked as he dropped a plate of burritos and rice to the tabletop and scraped his chair closer.

"I think she's starting to adjust to her surroundings, little by little."

"And what about you? Is she adjusting to you?"

"What?"

"Oh, come on, Daniel. I've always known by the way you went all doe-eyed when you spoke about her that there was a spark there, even while she was still out cold. But after seeing you together at Barton Springs—"

Daniel waved his hand and silenced him. "Enough."

Eyebrows raised pointedly, Josiah picked up the paper-wrapped burrito and took a huge, sloppy bite out of it.

"Ah, man, that's disgusting."

"Don't let Paco hear you say that. He's pretty sure he's the finest Mexican chef on the planet. And I'm not entirely sure he's wrong."

Daniel shook his head and looked away, tossing a chunk of cheddar cheese into his mouth as he did.

"Seriously, man. What's happening between you and Shannon? Is it going anywhere?"

Daniel considered his words carefully. "I'm not going to lie to you. I really like spending time with her."

"And what about her?"

"I don't know. I think so. It might be just a little too soon for her, you know?"

"It's been ten years."

"Right," he said, popping a grape into his mouth. "But in her world, it's a few weeks. She's working with Cynthia Benedict to try and work through the trauma."

Josiah set down his food and looked at Daniel seriously for a moment before speaking. "Well, there's no one better than Cynthia with TBI," he said, referring to her specialty of traumatic brain injury. "But who's helping you work through it?"

One side of Daniel's mouth twisted upward in a lopsided grin. With half a shrug, he raised his index finger and pointed upward.

"Well, there's that," Josiah replied.

Daniel's phone announced an incoming text, and he plucked it from the pocket of his lab coat.

Eloise wrote: *Banfield cld. Needs u 1 hr early at Draper for mtg. LMK to confirm.*

"Patient?" Josiah asked when Daniel sighed.

"Nah. They need me early at Draper today."

"I thought your days of jumping and running for Draper might thin out once Shannon was released."

"No, are you kidding? I still have patients over there. Families that are counting on me, just the way Edmund and Shannon counted on me. What I do there means something to me. Like your work with the youth center means something to you."

"Speaking of which—"

"How did I know?" Daniel grimaced. "Roping me into another practice?"

"Nah, I just wanted to tell you the boys really enjoyed having you come out for them. You've got an open invitation to come back any time you want to get the blood flowing. Looks like we may start a junior lacrosse team and join a small league the city has going."

"That's great," he replied. "I enjoyed it. Maybe I'll check them out again soon."

Go ahead and confirm, he typed into a reply text to Eloise.

Will do. Also Davis from Medical Mercy cld again.

Thx. Will phone him back later.

"I better get it in gear if I'm going to get there by three," he told Josiah, and he stood up and grabbed the last couple chunks of cheese. "Catch you later."

By the time he finished up with labs and test results, Daniel barely made it to Draper by three-thirty.

"I'm sorry, Dr. Banfield. I got tied up at the hospital."

"It's fine, Dr. Petros," Banfield told him. "Come on in and take a seat."

He glanced around the conference room, surprised to find nearly every board member in attendance. Cyrus Banfield sat at the head of the long table. No mistaking that he ran the place.

"Have you enjoyed your time at Draper?" Banfield asked the moment he sat down, and Daniel's gut stirred with nervous reaction to the question.

"Absolutely, sir."

"Good, good. We're all glad to hear that." Banfield opened a file folder and hesitated as he looked over the contents.

"Is there something wrong?" Daniel asked, looking around the table.

A couple of them smiled at him, but out of deference to Banfield, no one else took the floor.

"Quite the opposite," he finally replied. "In fact, the board is very pleased with your role here."

"Oh." *And?* "Thank you."

A few more moments spent gazing down at the paperwork in the file folder in front of him before he finally said, "Did you know that Dr. Okata is retiring this month?"

He glanced over at the older Asian gentleman and smiled. "I did hear something about that."

"We are in the position of looking for a replacement to fill his seat on the board," Banfield stated. "And your name has been bandied about, Daniel. Would that be something that might interest you?"

Of all the topics of conversation Daniel had considered, this one hadn't even been in the neighborhood.

"You're asking me to take a seat on the Draper governing board, sir?"

"This is what we're asking you, yes."

"I'm . . . honored."

And astonished, shocked, in disbelief.

"We're very happy to hear that, Daniel. No other name we've considered has received the unanimous support that you have received from this board. In fact, Dr. Okata told us all just before you arrived that if he alone could pick his replacement, you would be in that seat before it ever had the chance to grow cold."

"Really." Turning toward Okata, he shook the man's hand. "Thank you so much for that confidence, Doctor."

"Good," Banfield said, putting the period at the end of the sentence of their meeting. "That's settled then."

Daniel grazed the faces around the conference table.

Not one of them under fifty.

And yet they'd chosen a forty-one-year-old neurologist to join them.

He wanted to inquire about a catch, but he resisted. Daniel had come to realize over the years that he'd developed an innate tendency to question every good thing that came his way, and he'd determined to cease and desist with the skepticism.

"You'll start right away," Banfield announced. "Regular board meetings are held in this room on the first Tuesday of every month at nine o'clock. That means we meet next week, and we'll see you then."

He almost expected the rap of a gavel as his attendance had been written into law. Instead, the hum of several conversations raised a backdrop for handshakes and offerings of congratulation.

●　—　●　—　●

Shannon set a plate in front of Daniel. "It's grilled salmon and lemon-vegetable risotto with asparagus, yellow squash, snap peas, and lemons. I think it turned out pretty great, but you tell me."

With his Greek heritage, Daniel was accustomed to lemon juice in his rice, but he tried not to betray his thoughts about eating grilled lemon. He maintained a neutral expression as he scooped a small forkful and took a taste.

"Whoa." He felt as surprised as Shannon looked relieved. "Shannon, this is really good."

"Really?"

"Really." He sent his fork back into the mound of rice for a more liberal serving this time. The fresh vegetables partnered perfectly with the grilled lemons. "I admit I wasn't sure, but this is truly amazing."

Shannon beamed and shook out her napkin, placing it on her lap before she picked up her own fork. "I'm so glad."

"So what were you saying about Bon Jovi?"

"Oh!" she exclaimed, and she set down her unused fork again and leaned forward. "First of all, can you believe he's still rocking after all these years?"

Daniel chuckled. "I saw them live in the late eighties when they still had all the hair."

"I know. He's aged pretty gracefully, huh? I mean . . ." She drifted off, losing her train of thought again.

"You read about something he did," he prodded.

"Oh, right. He's from New Jersey, did you know that?"

He nodded, continuing to enjoy the meal she'd placed before him.

"Well, he started this restaurant there called Soul Kitchen. Do you know about this?"

"Yeah," he said, wiping the corner of his mouth. "I think I caught a segment about it on one of those morning shows. It's a charity thing, isn't it?"

"Well, that's the beauty of it. It's a regular restaurant with good, healthy food on the menu. They use organic preparations when they can, and it looked like they have a pretty wide array of dishes. There are no prices on the menu, and the patrons who eat there just donate ten bucks—or more, if they have it—to pay for their meal. And if a person can't pay, then they volunteer by cooking or bussing tables or whatever they can do."

"That's a pretty spectacular idea," he acknowledged. "Rock star and philanthropist."

"I know! I think the concept is really a good one. But it got me to thinking."

Shannon's enthusiasm was contagious, and it got Daniel's own wheels turning.

"What if I had one of those mobile trailers like the ones that used to be on Congress Street? And maybe I could go around to different places where there are office buildings, for instance, where professionals can come and grab some lunch during the day—but in a location that would also invite needier people who might not have a healthy, hot meal that day. I thought I could use the Soul Kitchen as my roadmap, and try to combine my new thing for cooking with something bigger, something where I could make a difference, you know?"

The idea that had begun to form in his mind grabbed ahold of him, and Daniel could hardly contain his eagerness to spill it out on the table between them. But he didn't want to get her hopes up before he talked to—

"You're thinking I'm crazy, right?"

"Not at all."

"No?"

"No. I'm thinking you have a heart to do something bigger than yourself. I relate to that desire, Shannon. I've had that in me for as long as I can remember."

"You understand then." She sat back in her chair and smiled at him. "I guess that's why you joined up with the Medical Mercy group and went to Africa." Leaning forward, she reached across the table and tentatively touched one of the beads on his cord bracelets. "Do you think you'll ever go back?"

"I don't know," he admitted. "I can't say I haven't thought about it. In fact, they've called a couple of times recently about a specific need they have for doctors in Sudan. But I've found something satisfying here in my work, and I tend to feel more led to think about settling, about planting some roots."

Shannon grinned at him before she withdrew and focused on her meal again. "When I saw you with Izzy's boys . . . Izzy said she thought you'd make a great dad someday. Do you ever think about marrying and having kids?"

The bite of salmon in his mouth suddenly expanded, and he forced it down his throat. In the next moment, Shannon looked as if a shot of electricity had jolted through her.

"I'm so sorry. I mean, that's really intrusive, isn't it?"

"No," he fibbed. "Not at all."

A bubbling chuckle rolled out of her, and she shook her head. "Don't be so polite, Daniel. You're under no obligation—"

"I think about it sometimes," he cut in. "When I hit the big four-oh, I started to wonder. I mean, I've dated, of course, but I guess it just hasn't happened for me yet for some reason. What about you? Obviously it's a lot to think about just yet. But do you think you could—you would ever want to commit to someone again after all you've been through?"

She appeared to take a gulp of air before leaning into an awkward shrug. "I hope so," she said, wide-eyed. "I mean, I'd like to think there's someone who can see me through all this nonsense."

"Nonsense," he repeated. "What are you talking about?"

"Daniel," she said with a sweet grin, "I was pretty out there *before* the accident. I don't remember everything about my life back then, but I think I've recently figured out this much: I spent my time sort of stuck in the past, trying to force Edmund into becoming a born-again Rob Petrie. I was opinionated and stubborn."

He chuckled and shook his head. "Shannon."

"And then I'm out of commission for ten years, my poor husband is gone, I have no interest in or memory of so much of my former life, and now I have the audacity—this person who never prepared a full meal in her entire life feels like she can change the world with . . . with . . . some salmon and *risotto with lemons in it!*"

She pushed her plate away and jumped from her chair like a jack-in-the-box.

"Who am I kidding here?" she cried, massaging her temple roughly. "I'm just running around taking stabs in the dark, hoping I hit something. I'm—I'm—"

Daniel tossed his napkin to the table and crossed the room. With one thrust, he pulled her into his arms. She pressed against him with both hands for a moment and then succumbed, wrapping her arms around his neck and giving in to the embrace. When she lifted her face from his shoulder, tears had moistened the firestorm in her eyes.

"Daniel," she whispered.

He raked his fingers into the mass of hair at the nape of her neck and held her there, wading into those eyes as far as he could safely go without drowning.

"Run for your life," she muttered. "Save yourself while you still can."

Daniel tightened his grip on her hair and leaned his face toward hers until their cheeks touched.

"Did you think I was joking?" she asked in a low, raspy whisper. "Run like the wind."

Daniel swallowed around the lump in his throat and hesitated, his eyes closed. They suddenly parted, seemingly stunned by the undercurrent still rushing between them, and stared silently into one another's eyes.

"Daniel," Shannon said softly, and her sweet, soft utterance of his name pinched his throat.

With a sharp intake of breath—the kind that usually marked something sudden and painful—he stepped away from her.

●——●——●

"Then what?"

"I'm not sure."

Josiah twisted the cap off a bottle of Snapple and handed it to Daniel. "What do you mean you're not sure?" he asked.

"I think I said something ridiculous," Daniel surmised. "Made some quick excuses and got out of there."

His buddy cackled with laughter. "What are you, in high school? So you didn't kiss her?"

He swallowed half the bottle of tea before replying. "Nah."

"Oh, man. You got it good, dontcha?"

"Afraid so."

"What are your plans from here?" Josiah asked, and Daniel glared at him.

"I have no clue. That's why I came over here."

Daniel's eyes stayed trained on his friend. Josiah leaned back on the kitchen counter and shook his head, running his hand over the surface of his short, cropped hair. He clicked his tongue as he clenched one side of his square jaw and shot one of those gleaming smiles of his across the counter at Daniel.

"Yeah. You've got a real dilemma there."

"When it comes to assessing a situation, you're king," Daniel said dryly. "Have I ever told you that?"

"Simmer down now. Give a brother a chance to think."

Daniel waited about thirty seconds before he slapped both hands against the counter and groaned. "All right then. I'll see ya later."

"Hang on," Josiah exclaimed. "I'm just weighing the options. Give me a minute to think it through, 'cause I don't want to shoot you in the chest with a round of bad advice."

Daniel stood there feeling like an idiot for another half a minute. Nothing.

"This is a big old case of role reversal," Josiah observed. "You're usually the sensible one, and I bring my lady troubles to your doorstep, not the other way around. But we can work this out. I can do this. Just give me another minute to think it over."

"Let me help you out," he said. "I did the right thing. In fact, given Shannon's vulnerability, I was considerate with her frayed relationship nerves and I'm a man among men for doing so. Isn't that what you were going to say?"

Josiah cocked his head and lifted one eyebrow. Finally, "Uh, okay. Let's go with that."

Daniel laughed as he rounded the counter and smacked Josiah firmly on the back. "Call me if you come up with anything else. Thanks, buddy."

● ― ● ― ●

Shannon had tried on six different outfits before the clock even approached the eight o'clock hour; four from the former life and two from the new one. She finally landed on a combination of the two. Symbolic, she hoped.

She slipped on a pale pink long-sleeved tee shirt underneath the cute cotton tank dress she'd bought on the way to Izzy's barbecue. The hem of the dress landed a few inches above the knee, and she grabbed the beaded shade of the floor lamp, flicked on the switch and tilted it so she could double-check to make sure she hadn't missed anything on the three rounds of leg-shaving in the shower. She stood in front of the full-length mirror to determine whether she looked more appropriate for Sunday morning services than for, say, a lakeside picnic. Shannon slipped her feet into navy blue platform sandals.

Just after she'd added a couple of bangle bracelets, and a pair of rhinestone stud earrings and the thin silver thumb ring that had caught her eye while checking out at the boutique, the front bell rang to announce Daniel's arrival. Rodney greeted him with a peal of loud and intense barks.

Her stomach tumbled into somersaults as she made her way to answer the door, and she wondered if seeing Daniel had inspired the nervous reaction or if the idea of going to church was the culprit. It felt to her a little like visiting an estranged relative, wondering all the while how they might react. Would there be tension between them? Or was she the prodigal daughter returning home?

She pushed the dog aside with her foot and tugged the door open.

"Wow, look at you," he exclaimed, and she grinned triumphantly.

"This is okay for church? Not too casual?"

"It's perfect."

"Just one second," and she headed for the back door, slapping her leg as she went. "Come on, Rodney. You're out back for a couple of hours."

The dog sauntered along behind her and lumbered straight through the door when she slid it open.

"Okay! I'm ready," she announced, and her heart jumped as Daniel placed his hand on the small of her back and guided her through the front door.

17

"**Good to see** you again. We met at Barton Springs. I'm Daniel's friend, Josiah Rush."

"Yes, I remember you, Josiah. How are you?" Shannon asked the man who towered over her.

"Well, thanks. How'd you like the service?"

The three of them strolled down the winding sidewalk toward the parking lot. At five-foot-seven, Shannon didn't normally think of herself as short, but she felt a little like a miniature between Josiah and Daniel, both of whom probably exceeded the six-foot mark.

She smiled and stared at the sidewalk ahead of them as she answered him. "I liked the pastor's message about new beginnings. It was very timely for me."

Josiah grinned and slapped his thigh with his large hand. "I guess it was. So what do you two have planned now? Interested in grabbing some lunch?"

"Sorry, bud, we can't," Daniel replied. "Shannon has a meal with her aunts on Sunday afternoons, and I was just lucky enough to horn in on it."

"Would you like to join us?" she asked him. "It's just Daniel and me and my three elderly aunts. Not very exciting, I'm afraid."

"But the chow will be good," Daniel chimed in.

"I really appreciate that, but I have to be at the hospital by four today. I'm covering for Victoria," he explained to Daniel. "Her daughter's birthday."

"Your good deed for the year?" he teased.

"Yeah, I like to do something nice every now and then, just to throw people off the scent."

"Another time then," she interjected.

"Thanks. I'd like that."

Once they said their goodbyes, Daniel opened the door for Shannon and she slid into the passenger seat. She watched him jog around the front of the SUV and wave to a family gathering at a sedan across from them. He seemed well-known and liked here. Had Edmund become so casual and entrenched in life at United Point of Grace Church too? Had he gotten to know Josiah Rush, or the family in the black sedan? Obviously, he'd gotten to know Emily Dawson and her family and helped them in a truly remarkable way. Maybe he went out to lunch with select groups sometimes, or had been invited to supper now and again by churchgoers who felt sorry for the young groom whose bride lingered in a coma year after year.

Now it was her turn to blossom in an unexpected new environment—but she wasn't alone. She waited for the pang of guilt to come, but she realized she didn't feel it. This was her life now, and she was moving forward. She only hoped that Edmund had been able to do the same in some way. From what the church people had been telling her, it sounded like he had.

"Do you need anything from the store before I get you back to start your cooking?" Daniel asked as he snapped the seat belt into place.

"Nope. I have everything I need. I've got the turkey roasting . . ."

"And it's not even Thanksgiving."

"I figure I missed enough of them. I may as well make up for it. Do you like turkey? I guess I should have asked you."

"I certainly do."

"I found a recipe for dressing that kind of appealed to me," she explained as he drove out of the lot and onto the main road. "I put it together last night, and all I have to do is bake it today. It has a cornbread base, which Aunt Mary is going to love because she has a weakness for all things cornbread. And it has all sorts of fresh things in it, like onions and celery, raisins and walnuts, even some cranberries and orange juice."

"Orange juice," he repeated.

"Don't question my OJ, Dr. Petros," she warned him with a scowl. "You didn't think you would like risotto with lemon slices in it either, did you?"

"You knew?"

"Mmm. Something about that hint of horror in your eyes when you saw it helped me figure it out. I'm a crime-solver that way."

"A crime against lemons? Really?"

"Well," she said with a chuckle, "it would have been a crime not to taste it and see how delicious it is, right?"

"Worth a sentence of ten-to-twenty years at the very least."

Shannon giggled and leaned her head against the window. What was it about Daniel Petros that made her feel as if they'd known one another their whole lives? Not like with Edmund. He'd been the electrical outlet she plugged into, and their combined current coursed through her. With Daniel, beyond the foundational flames of attraction, something else slow-burned. With Daniel, it was easier. Comfortable. He gave her the odd yet relaxing feeling of . . . home.

I did not just think that!

● — ● — ●

Just a couple of hours later, the reason she felt like she'd known Daniel for a very long time was unexpectedly revealed after the whole group of them sat down to enjoy a well-trimmed turkey dinner.

"Okay," Daniel admitted, and he raised his right hand in a solemn vow. "I repent of ever doubting your orange juice stuffing."

"I warned you," she said, shaking her head at him. "It's pretty good, right?"

"It's heavenly," Mary sang. "Just heavenly."

Shannon surveyed the table and smiled. Candied sweet potatoes, steamed string beans, cucumber and tomato salad, and fresh strawberries and a pumpkin spice cake for dessert: a delectable combination of Thanksgiving fare and seasonal fruits and veggies. Aunt Lonna had brought along her buttermilk biscuits, and Lora made sweet apple butter to accompany them. Just one whiff of that warm butter, and Shannon had been transported back to a happy holiday table surrounded by her parents, aunts, and grandmother.

"You sure can cook, Missy," Lonna told her between bites, and she smacked her lips. "That nap you took really did transform you, didn't it?"

"I guess it did, Aunt Lonna."

"Any more sweet tea?" Lora asked.

"Let me get it," Daniel said, and he hopped up from his chair.

Lonna leaned toward Shannon and whispered, "He's a honey-pie, isn't he?"

Shannon giggled. "Maybe I can fix you two up on a date."

"Someone at this table should make the most of him anyway," her aunt cracked. Raising her voice, she asked, "Daniel, what's your last name again? Petros? That's Greek, isn't it?"

"Yes, ma'am," he said, giving them all refills from the glass pitcher. "Short for Petropoulos."

"Petro-poul-os," Mary repeated.

"Pop shortened it when I was a kid."

"I never knew that was your given name, dearie. There used to be a Petropoulos family that lived in my neighborhood."

Daniel sat down again and nodded. "Yep. That was us. We were a few streets over from where you are now."

"Daniel, you lived near Aunt Mary?" Shannon inquired.

"For a couple of years. I told you that. Remember, in the garden? I said my mom had a vegetable garden at our house too, and that it wasn't far from where we were standing."

"Did we go to school together, too?" she asked.

"I doubt it. My family was Greek Orthodox back then. While we lived on Beaumont Street, I went to Holy Trinity."

"Oh."

"Your father was Constantine, and your mother Irini?" Mary inquired.

"Indeed!" he exclaimed. "You knew them?"

"Of course. We all did."

"I didn't," Shannon said.

"Shannie. You did. In fact—wait a minute!—I think you and Daniel may have played together. Yes, you must have! There was a Petropoulos boy in that secret club you children formed. Was that you, Daniel?"

"Daniel?" she repeated. "No, we never . . ." Sudden realization dawned, and it made a distant crackling sound as it emerged over the horizon of her brain. "*Danny Petropoulos*? That was you?"

He chuckled. "Still is. But I didn't remember you being in our club?"

"The Adventurers. Yeah," she muttered. "You were *one of us*?"

"I think you and Daniel were actually married," Mary told her, "right there in the woods behind my house." She narrowed her eyes playfully at the memory. "Yes, and you tore my best lace tablecloth when you wore it as a veil."

Daniel turned toward Shannon, a sort of panicky confusion burning in his brown eyes.

"*You're* Danny Petropoulos?" she asked him.

"You're—my . . . *bride*?"

"Well, technically, I think it was the Professor and Mary Ann that got married, but we were pretending to be them." Shannon chuckled.

"Wait! I remember Gilligan. Yeah, he—or she?—performed the ceremony for us, didn't she?" Daniel suddenly recalled. "Who was that kid again? I can't remember her name. That girl with the braces who looked like a boy and insisted on being Gilligan."

201

"You're right! She lived next door to my best friend Caitlyn. Debbie something."

"Right." He leaned back against the chair and heaved a deep, thoughtful breath. "Oh, man. I remember playing in those woods with a whole group of kids. Sometimes we were the Swiss Family Robinson, and sometimes we were lost on *Gilligan's Island*. Donny Labecki was Thurston Howell III."

"Donny Labecki!" she exclaimed. "What ever happened to him?"

"His family moved to Minnesota."

"That's right. Funny, I can remember that summer like it was yesterday. . . ."

● ⸺ ● ⸺ ●

The sudden flash of Shannon playing the part of Mary Ann from *Gilligan's Island* still stung in Daniel's eyes. Wearing knee-length blue jean cutoffs, pigtails with bright red bows and a checkered blouse tied at the waist, she'd placed a remnant from a lace tablecloth over her head like a veil for their fake wedding in the woods. And when Gilligan/Debbie pronounced them husband and wife, he'd lifted that veil and . . .

Good grief. He'd kissed Shannon as they were pronounced Professor and wife. His family had moved across town a few weeks later. Shaking his head swiftly, Daniel exclaimed, "Shannon. That was *you?*"

Rodney stood close at Daniel's feet as he poured coffee for everyone while Shannon cut and served the pumpkin cake. They'd only lived on Beaumont Street for two years, but they'd been happy ones where he recalled having a lot of school and neighborhood friends. How bizarre that Shannon Malone—now Ridgeway—had been one of them.

"I just can't get over the fact that we knew each other all those years ago," Shannon said once they'd all convened at the table again.

"And that we played together," he added. "I have really fond

202

memories of the adventures we had in those woods." He glanced at Mary who grinned at him like a cat with a secret. "Donny and I would fight with wooden swords made out of fallen branches, and we'd tie ropes to the trees and swing along like clumsy Tarzans." A memory suddenly occurred to him. "Shannon, were you the girl who loved to play Robinson Crusoe?"

She guffawed at the memory. "Yes! That was me! Daniel, how strange. . ."

Daniel turned toward Shannon, and the two of them just stared at one another wordlessly. But the silence was just as noisy as any roar Daniel had ever heard.

Aunt Lonna elbowed her sister and they shared a smile.

● — ● — ●

"You came to the hospital on your night off just to tell me about your dinner with Shannon and her family?" Josiah recapped once they'd settled at a cafeteria table.

"Well, come on. Were you listening? It's not about the turkey, bro."

"She made turkey? Like Thanksgiving?"

"Yeah. But how weird is it that we played together when we were kids?" Daniel exclaimed.

"That's weird, all right. Dressing, too?"

"Yeah. It had orange juice in it, but it was better than it sounds."

"Sounds pretty good."

"Back on the track, freight train."

"Sorry. Yeah. Weird."

"And the thing is, I can almost remember her now. She was younger than me, played Mary Ann to my Professor."

Josiah chortled. "You're joking."

"No. And we even had this pretend wedding—"

"I don't think the Professor ever married Mary Ann."

"—and afterward . . . I kissed her."

Josiah grinned and raised his hand into the air, awaiting a

high-five. Daniel just glared at him until he dropped his hand and shrugged.

"How was it?" he finally asked.

"She was like . . . *eight*!" Daniel exclaimed.

"Still."

"You're a hopeless case. I don't know why I came over here."

"So I could tell you my news."

"You have news?"

Josiah fidgeted with his plate and glanced away before answering. "You know Emily Dawson?"

"From church?"

"Yeah. When you bailed on me for lunch, I met up with her in the parking lot and we got to talking . . ."

"Oh, no." Daniel recalled a couple of casual conversations with Emily over the years. In particular, he remembered that Edmund had met her at Draper and brought her and her family to United Point of Grace.

"Anyway, we decided to go grab some lunch together . . ."

"Oh, come on, Josiah," he said, leaning forward seriously. "She's a sweet kid."

"She is. I know. She's very sweet."

"Don't do your Josiah thing on her. She goes to our church, man."

"My Josiah thing!" He laughed. "What's that supposed to mean?"

Regret tinged the echo of his words, and Daniel smiled. "I'm just saying . . . you've dated just about every nurse in this place."

"So? I'm single. They're single. I'm not doing anything wrong, Daniel."

A spark in his friend's eyes told him he may have gone too far, miscalculated the depth of Josiah's feelings. "Sorry, man."

"Look, I'd love to have my future all figured out the way you do."

"Wha—"

"But I'm not mooning over some girl I kissed when we were in grade school."

"Come on, now."

"The thing is," he said with a somber tone in his voice that Daniel had never heard before, "I'm just looking for it like everyone else. And I felt a little something between me and Emily at lunch today. So I asked her to go out with me Friday, and she agreed."

Daniel flopped back in his chair and grinned. "Where're you taking her?"

"Jazz night at La Zona Rosa."

"Nice."

"You and Shannon want to come? We'll make it a foursome."

"Ooh, jazz night with Shannon? I think it's a little soon for that."

"Yeah," Josiah said, nodding his head slowly. "I can see that. It's been—what?—twenty-five years since you kissed her the first time? You give new meaning to *taking your time*, bro."

● — ● — ●

With a fire roaring in the pit and a fat, happy dog curled around her feet, Shannon sat on the patio reading *Robinson Crusoe* on her tablet. The egg timer on the sofa next to her ticked down the seconds until she would remove the strawberry cupcakes from the oven, and the silver stars twinkling through the slats of the pergola seemed to keep time with it. A bright crescent moon floated there like a swing in the sky.

She hadn't heard from Daniel in days, and she'd begun to really feel his absence. Since the revelation about their past on Sunday afternoon, memories had been flickering often. Maybe that was why she'd felt such a connection to him since waking up in his care. Or maybe it was just attraction. Maybe both.

Shannon stared at her phone where it sat idly on the table in front of her. She'd resisted the urge to call . . . text . . . Skype . . .

She leaned back and groaned. Maybe Daniel was right to stay away.

Still.

With a sigh, she leaned forward and grabbed the phone and laid it to rest in the palm of her hand. After several minutes of pensive consideration, she typed in a text.

The mere mention of kissing sent u running, huh? Thinking that might sound too strong, she added a smiley face.

She waited. The egg timer let out a shrill *ding* next to her, and she jumped.

She waited. Twenty seconds. Thirty.

"Fine," she said, tossing her feet to the ground and leaving Rodney sleepy-eyed and confused at the other end of the patio sofa. A few more seconds, and she got up and stomped into the house to remove the cupcakes from the oven, muttering as she went. "You want to disappear as soon as you feel a little uncomfortable, fine. You just do that, Daniel. I don't care. It's not like I didn't live most of my life without you just fine. And I'm still getting over Edmund. What was I thinking? I certainly don't need—"

When she heard the tone of an arriving text, she dropped the muffin tins to the stovetop, threw off the quilted oven mitt, and raced back out to the patio.

Sorry. Just busy. How r u?

"Busy. The universal excuse of a man in hiding."

Strawberry cupcakes cooling. Want some?

Nothing.

Trapped under something heavy?

Still nothing. She gave up.

I know. You're busy. Catch you later.

She put the phone down and jumped when it buzzed again.

Be there in 30.

She grunted. "What, years?"

● — ● — ●

Daniel had heard Shannon was in the building just that afternoon for her physical therapy session with Carrie, and he'd avoided leaving his office at all until he finally left for the day. He'd driven as far as the entrance to Briarcliff on his way home too, but he'd thought better of it and made a U-turn beyond the stone arch. Torn between his enthusiasm about the news he had for Shannon and his concern about the growing feelings between them, he'd chosen to simply avoid her until he decided which won out.

Come on. Meeting when we're kids? A pretend wedding? Cut to a couple of decades later and she lands in my care at Draper? With a husband who becomes my friend and suggests that we might end up together?

He'd never been much of a conspiracy theorist, but it felt like a colossal setup. Before, he had just felt concern over her vulnerability, wanting to go slowly for her sake. Now he wanted to slam on the brakes for his own sake; for his own sanity.

"Come *on*," he exclaimed aloud as he turned into Shannon's driveway and parked. He closed his eyes and tilted his head upward. "What's going on here, Lord?"

When Rodney barked out the announcement that he'd arrived, his eyes jolted open and he reluctantly climbed from behind the wheel.

Just the sight of Shannon standing there in the doorway grinning at him made his pulse quicken—and made him want to turn around and get back into the Lexus and drive away. Away from those beautiful red curls dancing on the evening breeze, and away from that little button nose smeared with pink icing—or maybe it was strawberry batter.

Why does she have to be so adorable?

And with that very thought, Shannon's lovely beaming face seemed to drop, and she scowled at him.

"You look like you're marching to meet the death squad, Daniel."

He didn't even know how to respond, so he didn't.

"How are you?" he asked as she closed the door behind him.

"Peachy." As she marched away from him, she added, "You?"

He followed her into the kitchen, reaching the island just as she filled two mugs with steaming black coffee.

"Have a cupcake," she said in monotone, and she grabbed one of the coffees, plucked an iced cupcake from the platter on the counter and set it into a napkin, and then stalked away.

When he caught up to her on the patio, she'd already settled into one of the chairs. Rodney groaned as Daniel exited the house, and he somehow got to his paws and growled.

"It's okay, Rodney. Sit."

The dog made no move to obey. Instead, he stood his ground in protecting Shannon from the intruder. Daniel stepped over the basset hound, sat down on the cushioned sofa, and crossed his legs. The pink icing had bits of fresh strawberries in it, and he recognized it as the imperfection on Shannon's otherwise perfect complexion.

"You have icing on your face," he said, and he took a huge bite of the cupcake while she rubbed one cheek and then the other. "The side of your nose," he added, tapping his own.

She grazed her nose with a napkin. "Is it off?"

He nodded. "Yeah. These are great, Shannon."

"Thank you." Her voice had a grudge in it.

"I have—"

"Look. Do we need to talk about our marriage, Professor?"

"—some news."

"Do you want a divorce? What news?"

"Did I tell you I'd been named to the governing board at Draper?" He knew he hadn't.

"No," she said, brightening slightly. "That's wonderful, Daniel. Congratulations."

"My first board meeting was today."

"Oh." She looked confused at the course of the conversation, but tried to just go with it. "How did it go?"

"Really well, I think. I mean, I'm still wondering what I'm do-ing there."

"Don't be silly," she said, and Daniel had the feeling that she couldn't quite decide between congratulating him and willing a large wart to pop up on his face. "You're a wonderful addition, I'm sure."

"Well, among other things, I learned that one topic of con-versation for the past year has been that there's nowhere on-site for the families to have a meal. Some of them are sitting there for days on end, keeping a patient company, and all they have are the vending machines. They have to leave the facility to get something solid to eat."

"I don't think I knew that," she said. "Or even thought about it. Poor Edmund."

"We've been negotiating with a few vendors, trying to provide something better. But as the building stands now, we just don't have the room for a cafeteria."

She stuffed the last of her cupcake into her mouth and grinned at him. Through a full mouth, she said, "*Theesh* are good, huh?"

"Very. So I pitched them the idea of someone with a mobile trailer," he said, and Shannon perked up. "They could pull it right into the courtyard where the stone benches and tables are. Instead of vending machine food, people—and Draper staff—can get a hot, healthy meal."

"Ooh!" she exclaimed. "I could do that!"

Daniel chuckled. "Well, that was my thinking."

"Really?"

"I told them about you this afternoon, and they're looking for a proposal from you."

She shot to her feet, hopping from one to the other. "Okay. I can, uh, put together a proposal." She hesitated. "Right?"

"Sure. Draper won't charge you anything to be there as long as you're consistent about showing up on agreed-upon days and hours and obtain your own licensing and the like. You can charge whatever you want but—"

"Daniel, is this really happening?" Her enthusiasm cast sparks bigger than those from the fire pit.

"Well, it hasn't happened yet. There is one other provider we've approached for a proposal. But I was thinking about what you said, about wanting to do something bigger, serving a greater purpose. Anyway, I thought maybe you could include so many free meals per week for needy families in your proposal. I think that would do it for the board—not to mention the fact that you're a former patient. And we have some families of patients at Draper that can hardly afford the gasoline to drive out and see them every day or so, sometimes for months or years on end."

Shannon went suddenly silent and folded down into the chair again without making a sound. She just stared straight ahead, her eyes wide and round, her ruby lips barely closed. After a couple of minutes of that, Daniel shifted.

"So? What are you thinking?" he prodded.

Shannon looked at him for a long, crackling moment before she shot to her feet again. This time, she walked straight toward him with her hand outstretched. When he took it, she tugged him up to his feet and Daniel stood in front of her, curious.

"Don't freak out," she whispered. Then she folded her arms around his shoulders and pulled him into an embrace. "Thank you."

The prince stood in front of her, his sword drawn
and his shield raised, protecting her from the approaching enemy.
"Stay behind me!" he declared. "I've sworn to do battle for you."

"But Prince," she whispered into his ear from behind,
"While I certainly appreciate your valiant bravery on my behalf,
perhaps I should raise my own sword
so that I might do battle at your side?"

The prince frowned,
charging forward as the enemy approached.
"How will I know you're safe," he bellowed over his shoulder,
"if I don't protect you myself?"

18

Shannon's eyes burned even more when she closed them. She'd been staring at that computer screen for hours upon hours, debating a truck versus a trailer . . . pricing licensing, fuel, cooking supplies . . . putting together menu possibilities . . . researching health department restrictions. She'd awoken with her brain bulging with questions that morning, and she'd grabbed a cup of coffee and rushed to her laptop before she'd even dressed for the day. With the recollection of how bad the coffee at Draper had been, she started out by looking into commercial coffee and cappuccino makers.

By noon, her stomach reminded her that she hadn't eaten, and she stopped for a quick shower before pulling a container of turkey leftovers from the refrigerator and heating it up in the microwave. She twisted her wet hair into a nest and ate lunch over a phone conversation with Izzy about the opportunity Daniel had relayed to her.

"I'm thinking—since I'll be mobile and all—I could do even more. Maybe park at homeless shelters on weekday mornings and serve free breakfasts before driving over to Draper."

"You'll want to hire someone to help you so you're not shouldering all of this on your own."

"You could do it with me."

"I have a job. Oh! But we should do a press release," Izzy suggested, "so we can let people in Austin know about it. Maybe it will bring in some donations. You know, you need to consider talking to an attorney about this. What if you started a nonprofit?"

And that's the way their conversation went for the next hour or more as Shannon scribbled notes, typed into search engines, bookmarked pages and emailed links to Izzy for a second look, all while rubbing her very tired eyes.

"Check you out with all the technology!" Izzy cried as she opened the third or fourth email from Shannon. "It's like you never left us."

Shannon hesitated a moment. "Hey, Iz?"

"Yeah."

"Can I tell you something?"

"Yeah."

"I kind of . . . I'm having thoughts about Daniel."

Izzy's delighted gasp sounded in her ear. "You *are*?"

"Really a lot. I mean, am I a horrible person?"

"Of course not. This is progress. I mean, you need to move on, right? Maybe this is a good thing."

"I nearly kissed him."

"What?!"

Shannon chuckled. "Well, I already have, if you count when I was nine."

"What!"

"Tell me when you're finished reading the email. I have a story for you."

"I'll read it later. Tell me."

"Well. Once upon a time, on *Gilligan's Island*, a certain professor and a girl named Mary Ann—"

"Shannon. Tell me the real story."

"Patience, grasshopper. All will be revealed."

"In this millennium?"

●—●—●

"Aunt Mary? Are you up there?"

Mary had called Shannon to ask for her help in moving her spindle out of the attic, and Shannon had hurried over to talk her out of it. The thing was an antique, retired to its attic home where it belonged.

She climbed the ladder stairs to the attic and spotted her aunt's puffy ankles and rubber-soled Mary Janes before she surfaced.

"Aunt Mary?"

Her aunt looked up at her and smiled, but Shannon sensed something amiss.

"Are you all right?"

She nodded strangely. "Yes, dearie. I just got cracked on the noggin and I'm gathering my senses."

Shannon noticed the large overturned spindle blocking her aunt from getting up from the chest on which she sat. A carton that had been on the shelf overhead now lay sprawled at their feet, its contents—a dozen or more leather-bound books—spilled out on the floor beside it.

"Let me see," Shannon said. The chest groaned under the weight of both women when she sat down beside her aunt. "Does it hurt?"

"Not too much. Look what I found up here, Shannie."

Mary picked up a small padded envelope with SHANNON'S THINGS printed across the front in slanted black letters.

"What is this?" she asked as her aunt handed it to her.

"The stretchy bracelet you were wearing when you had your diving accident," she said. "And your wedding ring."

Shannon's heart raced as she slipped open the flap and poured the contents out into the palm of her hand. She'd forgotten all about that bracelet, made for her by one of her third grade Sunday school students out of a stretch of elastic and some shiny blue beads. She grinned as she slid her hand through it and examined her wrist.

"None the worse for wear," her aunt commented.

Shannon opened her palm and gazed at the rose gold band, simple and plain except for the subtle vine carved across the top. She'd nearly forgotten this ring and all that it had meant to her; such a diminutive symbol of so much more than just a marriage.

"Ohhh," her aunt whimpered, and she leaned toward Shannon. "What is it?"

"Just feeling a little strange."

Shannon tried slipping the ring onto its rightful home, but it slid right off again. Instead, she pushed it down her larger index finger before raking through her aunt's gray hair to feel for a lump or an abrasion.

When her fingers returned with blood on them, Shannon's heart sank.

"I don't want you climbing down the ladder," she said, pulling her phone from the zippered pocket of her jacket. "I'm calling an ambulance."

"No," her aunt protested, but not vehemently enough to deter Shannon from dialing 911.

In less than fifteen minutes, the EMTs had assisted Mary down the ladder and into a waiting ambulance. Shannon followed behind them in her car. In no time at all, they both sat inside a curtained cubicle awaiting a doctor's attention.

"I'm Dr. Rush," the handsome doctor said as he entered. He looked at them more closely. "Shannon?"

She blinked several times before realization dawned. "Josiah. How are you?"

"I'm good," he said, "but more importantly, how are you? This must be one of your aunts?"

"Aunt Mary. She was working in the attic and a box of books fell from an overhead shelf," she told him, nerves jumping around inside her stomach like grasshoppers. "Her head is bleeding."

Josiah pointed a penlight at Mary's eyes. "Follow my finger without turning your head, okay, Miss Mary?"

"Do I know you?" she asked as she did what she'd been told.

"Sort of," he said. "I'm a buddy of Dr. Petros."

"Oh, Daniel. We do love Daniel."

"I'll tell you what. After I stitch you up, I'll call and let him know you're here. He performed a very long surgery this morning. You'll be a breath of fresh air."

A few stitches and a CAT scan later, Shannon paced inside the curtained cubicle while a nurse tended to the scrape Josiah had noticed on the back of Mary's hand. She said a quick, silent prayer of thanks while the after-care instructions were delivered, and she smiled somewhat vacantly when the nurse told them they were free to go, her thoughts trained on how much more of a tragedy it might have been to awaken after ten years to find her sweet aunt gone as well. Shannon couldn't even imagine what she'd do without her. "Ready to go, Aunt Mary?"

"What about Daniel?"

"We'll see him later. Let's get you home for some rest. The nurse is going to help you into a wheelchair and bring you out front while I go and pull the car up to the door. All right?"

"All right," she replied.

Once they reached Mary's house, Shannon helped her aunt inside to her very floral bedroom.

"You sit down on the bed and slip off your shoes," she told her. Her aunt didn't argue or mention some important task that required her immediate attention, so Shannon felt like a victor. "Once you're settled, I'll make you a cup of something warm and you can snuggle up in here for a nap, Aunt Mary."

"Okay. But you'll sit with me for a while, won't you?"

"Of course."

With Mary nestled underneath the blanket and leaning back on a mountain range of ruffly floral pillows, Shannon rested her back against the headboard beside her and stroked the woman's bandaged hand.

"It's a shame we didn't get to see Daniel while we were there," Mary remarked.

"I saw him last night."

"Did you?"

Shannon softened her voice. "Yes, he came to see me with some lovely news."

"Oh?"

She glanced over at her aunt to see that she'd closed her eyes.

"I may be allowed to cook some meals for the families of some of the patients at the Draper facility. It's too early to know the details yet because I'm still working them out, but I'm putting together a proposal for them and, if they like it, I'll start a whole new endeavor."

Her aunt moaned softly. "New endeavors are good."

"Well, they can be. I'm a little nervous about it, actually."

"Are you?"

"Edmund never really wanted me to work. He wanted me to leave my job after the honeymoon so that I could devote all of my time to starting a family. We were going to think about it for a few months after the wedding. I guess I never really got the feeling that he understood my desire to have something of my own, apart from everything we might have together. But at the time, I was okay with that. You know—just happy to be with him. All of a sudden, I'm thinking about striking out on my own in this completely new thing. I don't know if the cooking thing is just some momentary miracle that will go away as quickly as it came, or if I'll even be any good at running something all on my own. But I feel like I need to try, you know?"

"Mmm." It had emerged as more of a soft rumble than an actual reply.

Mary had drifted off, of course, but Shannon hardly noticed. She twisted the hem of her blouse around two fingers as she continued. "I'm starting to have all sorts of feelings like these, feelings I don't know what to do with, really. I mean, I'm having these strange yearnings about my future. Stirring, from somewhere deep inside of me, like something . . . God-like, if that makes any sense. Daniel has prayed with me a couple of times. Did I tell you that? And whatever these stirrings are, I really feel like Daniel is a big part of it. I mean, aside from the obvious attraction—now there's another thing I feel sort of guilty about but also not guilty about—but aside from that, I sometimes think about him and feel like he's supposed to be way up there—" She waved her hand at the inexplicable future far in front of her. "Yet here he is, right here." She tapped the bed beside her. "And just when I feel like I want to run ahead as fast as I can to catch up to him, I look up and there he is already. Right by my side. It's disconcerting, you know, Aunt Mary?"

Her aunt's breathing had grown rhythmic and deep, and Shannon snickered and kissed her on the forehead.

● — ● — ●

"Thanks for seeing me, Dr. Benedict."

Daniel sat down in the plush, overstuffed wingback chair across from the psychiatrist as she adjusted her thick black glasses.

"I'm happy to," she replied. "My secretary said you wanted to discuss a personal matter. Are you interested in scheduling therapy sessions with me, Dr. Petros?"

He shifted in the chair and set his hands to rest on the padded arms. "No. That's not it, exactly."

"Is this about Shannon Ridgeway?"

He'd never noticed before how her eyes bulged behind those glasses of hers.

"It is," he admitted.

"Of course you know I can't discuss—"

"No, no," he stopped her. "I'm not asking for anything like that."

She crossed one leg over the other and waited for him to expound.

"The thing is, Shannon and I have been seeing a good bit of each other since she was released from my care."

He glanced up at her and spotted no emotion or reaction whatsoever. He'd almost expected her chastisement, but it didn't come.

"I'm concerned about her," he explained. "She's had an awful lot to deal with, waking up to the loss of her husband and trying to navigate back into some semblance of a life. It's really quite impressive how well she's done . . . from the outside, at least. But I'm not entirely certain she's as ready to move on as she thinks she is."

"What makes you say that?"

Such a therapist thing to say. Next thing, you'll be asking me how I feeeel about it.

"She's exhibited some . . . romantic tendencies toward me."

"Are these tendencies mutual?"

"Ha!" It just popped out of him. Nodding, Daniel grinned. "Definitely. And I'm not convinced that she's ready for that, with me or anyone else. What I was hoping to get from you, Doctor, is some sort of recommendation about how to proceed. Or whether to proceed at all." When she remained thoughtfully silent, Daniel sighed. "I'm not asking for you to breach confidentiality. I'm just trying to look out for Shannon's best interests."

"I'll tell you this," she began at last. "Shannon is conflicted about the relationship she had with Edmund. There is a good bit of guilt involved with dealing with his death, and my professional opinion is that, until she comes to terms with that and has worked it through for herself, a new relationship is ill-advised."

Daniel's stomach dropped, and he felt the thud all the way to his soul. Hadn't that been exactly what he feared she would say?

"I'm not saying that a relationship between the two of you should never be pursued, Daniel. I'm only suggesting that you give it some time before you attempt to move forward beyond your friendship. The world is spinning fast for Shannon right now, and I think it's all she can do to get her bearings on her own. Adding another person into that mix could be . . ."

He lifted his hand and nodded. "Yeah. I get it. Thank you. That's what I needed to know. The truth is I've been approached about another three-month stint with Medical Mercy, and I wondered if a little distance between the two of us might be good for Shannon. Maybe help her to put her life into perspective."

"I couldn't really say how she might respond to news like that. But if you'd like me to be involved when you discuss it with her, I can certainly make myself available."

● — ● — ●

The pretty young woman behind the reception desk looked up at Shannon as she entered and smiled, bearing slightly crooked teeth. She tucked her straight brown hair behind her ear and grimaced as the phone rang.

Holding up her index finger toward Shannon, she answered, "Law offices of Rivera and Knutson. How may I help you?"

She pointed at the blue leather sofa, and Shannon went over to it and sat down.

"Yes, you're due in court tomorrow at eleven," she told the caller. "Mr. Knutson will meet you there thirty minutes beforehand to go over what you can expect."

As she waited, Shannon mindlessly paged through a magazine.

"I'm sorry to keep you waiting. Are you Shannon Ridgeway?"

She stood up and approached the desk. "Yes. That's me. I have a nine-thirty appointment with Beverly Rivera."

"Right. You can have a seat, and she should be right with you."

Shannon returned to the leather couch and sat down again. No sooner had she done so than a smiling Hispanic woman with pretty brown hair and wearing a navy blue skirt and jacket opened the large wooden door behind the receptionist.

"Shannon?"

"Yes," she said, popping to her feet again.

"Come on into my office."

She followed the woman down a short hall and past a makeshift eat-in kitchen until they reached a bright, open office at the back of the suite.

"First, let me say what a pleasure it is to finally meet you," Beverly stated. "Have a seat and let's chat."

Shannon sat down on the narrow, uncomfortable chair. "Daniel tells me I have many things to thank you for, Ms. Rivera."

"Beverly, please. I was happy to do it. I met your husband toward the end of his life, and he asked me to advise Daniel until you were able to take care of things on your own."

"Well," she said with a grin, "as you can see, I'm back among the living and ready to do that. The first thing I'd like to discuss is my sister-in-law, Millicent, and whether she actually has any claims on the inheritance left to me by my late husband."

"She does have the right to fight it," Beverly said, and a flock of butterflies flapped their wings inside Shannon's stomach. "Whether she can actually win . . . I don't think so."

"Really?" she said with a sigh. "That's a relief."

"I'm going to do everything I can to defuse the situation, Mrs. Ridgeway."

"Shannon, please." She smiled at the woman.

"Shannon. In fact, I have a meeting scheduled with her representation this afternoon to discuss it further. They do seem very intent on making as many waves for you as humanly possible. Do you have any idea why, exactly? I mean, with you just coming out of a ten-year coma, it seems a little unjustified."

"I wish I could offer you some sort of explanation, Beverly. She wasn't keen on me when Edmund was alive. Now I think she just sees me as the person who drained the family bank account for my medical care."

"Have you had any contact with her?" she asked, and Shannon nodded.

"She came and asked me for some family heirlooms. Jewelry. Once I found it, Daniel went with me and I delivered it to her home."

"Oh," she said with a slight wince. "I wish you would have spoken to me first. I might have liked to have held on to those pieces for leverage."

"Well, they really did belong to her now that Edmund is gone. They were pieces that had been in the Ridgeway family for generations."

"I see, I see," she said, nodding. "But let's not hand over anything else without talking to me, Shannon."

"Okay." Shannon swallowed around the lump that rose in her throat. "Am I in any jeopardy of actually losing the house Edmund and I purchased before the accident?"

"I don't think so. She does have her sights on it, but I can't see that happening."

"Also, I'm considering starting a small business of my own," Shannon told her. "I'm hoping to cover the start-up with funds Edmund set up for me. Do you see any problem with that?"

"Not at this time," she replied. "But it's not out of the realm of possibility that she'll try to freeze those accounts until a final decision has been handed down in court."

"Based on what?" Shannon exclaimed.

"Based on the fact that those monies were derived from Ridgeway family money, and you were only an official part of that family for such a short time. A couple of weeks until your accident?"

"Six days," she muttered in defeat.

"In the eyes of the law, however, you and Edmund were married for eight years before his death. I can't see any judge overlooking that, but why don't you hold off on any further plans until after my meeting today. I'll give you a call in the morning so we can discuss it further."

"Beverly—should I be worried?"

"No," she stated confidently. "But I'm a lawyer. Caution is part of my makeup."

Shannon sighed.

"We're just sweeping up the floor here. Let me do the worrying. You just try to enjoy your second chance at life."

"Funny thing about second chances," she said, taking a stab at a smile. "They're sometimes not all they're cracked up to be."

Her meeting with Beverly Rivera had been enough to suck the sunlight straight out of her day. But Shannon had yet another disappointment waiting for her at home. Having changed clothes and taken Rodney outside for a walk, she came face to face with a furious young boy.

"Hey! That's Freckles!" the boy shouted at her from across the street on the other side of the block. "You stole Freckles!"

Rodney wagged his tail so hard it looked like he might fall over to one side and then the other as the boy approached. Shannon didn't feel quite so enthusiastic about him.

"That's my grandpa's dog, lady. What are you doing with my grandpa's dog?"

"Oh, he is?" she replied. "He wandered into my backyard, and I posted a notice on the community Facebook page, but I haven't heard from anyone about him."

"You never heard of puttin' up signs, lady?" the boy exclaimed, and his abundant orange hair flopped as he yanked the leash right out of her hand. "My gramps ain't got the Internet."

"Well, hang on a minute," she cried, but the boy just kept right on walking. And Rodney-turned-Freckles didn't seem to mind following him either. "Wait!"

"I'm takin' my grandpa's dog home, lady. And you ain't stoppin' me."

Shannon just stood there on the sidewalk, the leash-burn on her hand scalding hot, and her grief-laden disappointment nearly at the boiling point as well. He wasn't exactly a dog worth crying over or anything, Shannon knew that. But it didn't stop the tears from flowing just the same. She sniffled and sobbed all the way back home.

● — ● — ●

As he drove around the curve and prepared to make the turn to Shannon's, Daniel spotted her as she ambled up the driveway, hunched over and red-faced, crying. She started as he stopped the car, hastily wiping away tears as she waited for him to join her in the driveway. He suddenly felt as if he'd taken a swift punch to the gut.

"Shannon?" he yelped as he flew from the car. "Are you *cry-ing*?" She backed away slightly as he hurried toward her, wiping the tears from her face with the back of her hand. "What is it? Is Mary all right?"

"Oh," she said, sniffling, "yeah, she's fine."

"Josiah said you two were in the ER yesterday, and—well, I rushed over—and now you're crying. What is it?"

"It's Rodney."

He looked around the yard and cringed, myriad scenarios flashing through his thoughts. "Where is he?"

"He went—" She couldn't seem to keep the emotion at bay. Putting her hands up to her eyes, she broke into fresh tears. Daniel couldn't take it anymore. He took her into his arms and stroked her hair soothingly. "It's okay. Tell me what happened."

"This little kid took him away from me, right on the street," she sobbed into his shoulder.

"What do you mean? What kid?"

"He said Rodney belongs to his grandpa, and he took him. Look," she said, showing him the crimson burn on the palm of her hand. "He pulled the leash right out of my hand! The little brat just took him."

"Oh, no." With his arm around her shoulder, he led her toward the front door. "I'm so sorry."

"And he's not even Rodney either," she whimpered. "He's . . . he's . . . *FRECK-LES!*" she said, hiccupping.

"Fred what?"

"Not Fred. *Freckles.* They called that poor dog Freckles. Isn't that some sort of animal cruelty or something?"

"No more than naming him after Rodney Dangerfield, I don't think."

Once inside, she couldn't appear to make it any farther than the living room. She just collapsed over the sofa and let the tears flow.

"You really liked him, huh?" Daniel commented, just standing there in the middle of the room like a stone statue dropped out of nowhere. "Maybe you should get a dog of your own."

"I don't want another dog," she cried. "I want Rodney. I know how stupid it sounds, so don't mock me over it, Daniel."

He lifted both hands in surrender and shook his head. "I wasn't—"

"I know he was ugly and he smelled, even a little bit after I had him groomed, but—I can't help it. I want Rodney."

Daniel made no move to comfort her, or even to sit down. When she looked up at him a few minutes later, he just stood there staring at her with a stupid face filled with . . . what? Pity, he guessed. And he didn't know what else.

"I'm just so tired of losing things," she muttered, and Daniel inched toward her and sat down on the edge of the coffee table in front of her and took her hand.

"Losing things?"

"Ten years of my life, for one. And then Edmund. Now Millicent wants to take my house . . . and Aunt Mary took a hit on the head and scared me half to death. I didn't know if I was going to lose her too."

"But you said she's doing fine."

"Yeah. She's okay. And I met with Beverly Rivera today. She thinks Millicent might try to freeze my bank accounts so I won't be able to start something new. And now Rodney. Why do I have to keep losing things, Daniel? When am I going to feel like I'm making some progress? Like there's a life ahead for me without people and things and situations being snatched away every time I turn around?"

Daniel didn't have any answers for her, but one thing he knew for sure: this was the wrong time to talk to her about leaving the country for three months.

"What?" she exclaimed, and he darted his attention back to her. "What's that on your face?" she asked accusingly.

He raised his hand instinctively, wiping away whatever remnant of lunch might be left on his cheek.

"No, there's nothing on your face." With a sigh, she sank back into the sofa cushion. "I meant, what haven't you told me? They don't want me at Draper after all?"

"No, no," he reassured her. "I told you, they're waiting for your proposal."

The way she looked at him, with her narrowed green eyes shimmering that way, Daniel couldn't tell whether she might be ready to start crying again or if she was a heartbeat away from throttling him.

"Go ahead, Daniel. Out with it."

Man, she's good.

"I can see there's something on your mind. Don't leave me in suspense. Just spit it out."

He sat down beside her on the sofa. With his hands folded in front of him, he tried to gather the right words.

"I'm concerned that whatever this is—this thing happening between you and me—it might be too much, too soon for you."

She looked up at him vacantly, her eyes wide and her lips slightly parted, and for a moment he swam around in the notion that she didn't have one clue what he meant.

"I mean . . . You've felt it too, right?" he asked, and he wanted to kick himself for it.

She swallowed a little cough. "Yes. Of course."

"Oh. Good. Then you can understand—"

"And I don't get to decide what's too much for me?"

"Shannon, I just think you have past issues to work through before you safely dive into the future too quickly."

She widened her eyes.

"Is that what you are, Daniel? My future?"

"I don't know," he admitted. "I care for you, Shannon. Deeply." He hesitated. Did he dare tell her how deeply?

"But?"

He swallowed the lump in his throat, willing the right words to surface.

Help me here, Lord. Please.

Nothing.

He took a deep breath.

"The only hospital in Pibor Town in South Sudan has been destroyed. There are thousands in Sudan's Jonglei state without medical care, and I've been asked to give ninety days to one of the Medical Mercy teams . . ." Not sure what to say next, he let his words trail off.

"Oh. So . . . you're going then?"

"I still have to work out the details with the hospital, but yes. I'm going."

The house fell so silent that Daniel thought he could hear the traffic all the way out on the main road. Suddenly, Shannon stood up and walked halfway across the room before she stopped in her tracks. When she finally turned around toward him, one lone tear cascaded down her already tear-stained cheek.

"Shannon . . ."

"If you're going because you want to help those people, Daniel, I think that's pretty remarkable, actually. But if you're going as an excuse to run away from me, there's really no need. I think I can manage to stay away from you, if that's what you want."

"Shannon. Come back here. Sit down and let's talk about this."

"I really can't, Daniel. Sitting so close to you, I might not be able to control myself. I—I'm afraid I'll just lean over and—and—it's better that you go now. Really. You're just too much temptation for one vulnerable woman to stand."

And with that, she calmly walked out of the living room, down the hall, and into her bedroom. The door closed softly behind her, and the gentle click of the lock echoed against the silence.

Daniel was left all alone on the living room sofa.

"Thanks loads, Lord," he muttered.

19

"**I was thinking** this morning about how you loved purple when you were a little girl."

"Did I?" Shannon asked her aunt. "I don't remember that."

"Oh, you certainly did. Everything had to be purple. Your bedroom walls had to be purple, and your bedspread and the curtains. You said it was a royal color, and every princess should be surrounded in purple. You told Auntie Lonna that all you wanted for your birthday was a purple tiara like the one you'd seen someone wearing at the fair. She searched high and low for a purple tiara that year. I think it was your sixth birthday. Or fifth?"

Shannon paused, trying to remember . . . but . . . Nothing. Instead, she leaned over the pot simmering on the stovetop and dipped a wooden spoon into the brew. She blew on it first before taking a taste, and disappointment curled her nose into an upward wrinkle.

"What am I missing, Aunt Mary? I followed your recipe to the letter. Why doesn't it taste like yours?"

Mary looked up at her from the dining room table where she'd been embroidering for an hour or more.

"Oh, dearie, I don't really follow the recipe that closely any more, I suppose. I toss in a dash of this and a pinch of that."

"Great," she said on a chuckle.

"I'm sure it's perfectly lovely."

"I think I'll let it simmer for another hour or so. Then we can have some with a baguette for lunch."

"A baguette?"

"I couldn't sleep last night, so I made some French bread . . . And some vegetable lasagna. Oh, and a pot of turkey chili. Anyway, I brought a loaf of the bread with me, and I'll warm it up to have with our lunch."

"That sounds very nice, Shannie. That was a lot of cooking when you should be sleeping."

"Yeah. I've had a lot on my mind."

"This new business of yours has you very excited, doesn't it?"

"Yes," she admitted. "The last couple of weeks have been crazy, but it's all starting to come together. The board at Draper has approved my proposal, and the attorney's taken care of the paperwork, so I'm ready to go ahead with my plans. Oh, and I can pick up my tricked-out food truck next week. I've got my menu plan, and I've found a wonderful wholesale produce company that's going to let me order every other day and they'll deliver it right to me. I'm going over to Izzy's again later so she can help me plan out a press release and such."

"Does she know about that?"

"Izzy's in public relations. I think she's the perfect person to help me."

"Well, isn't that nice?"

Shannon stirred the pot one more time before replacing the lid. She turned down the heat as she told her aunt, "I'm going up to the attic to get those recipe cards I saw up there a while back. Grandma Malone had one for breakfast cupcakes. Do you remember those? The omelets in a cupcake tin? Anyway, I saw the recipe on a card, and I really want to try it out."

"Oh, dearie, it's such a mess up there. I've never cleaned up the books that fell and conked me on the head."

"I can do that while I'm up there then."

"Be careful, Shannie. It can be dangerous in the attic."

She giggled as she shuffled toward the stairs. "Apparently. Don't get into any trouble down here while I'm gone."

"I'll give it my best effort."

At the top of the stairs, Shannon tugged down the ladder to the attic and climbed it to see the books and cardboard carton still sprawled across the floor. The antique spinning wheel—the culprit that had started it all—looked innocent and casual angled into the corner as if nothing had ever happened.

She stepped over the books and sat down on the Malone family hope chest. Clutching the colorful vintage hat box with the blue velvet cord, she poked through the photos and index cards tossed inside. She found the one she wanted in just a few seconds.

BREAKFAST CUPCAKES.

A wave of sweet memories of cold winter mornings washed over her as she reviewed the baking instructions. Small cheese and egg omelets baked into muffin tins, served warm with blueberry compote and tender, flaky biscuits.

"Who wants hot chocolate?" Her grandmother's gravelly voice came back to her out of her past.

She ran a finger over the shaky writing on the card. "Nutritious breakfast on-the-go," she read out loud. Her grandmother had scribbled the words at the bottom of the recipe. And on the back, suggestions for possible variations.

"Stick to just three added ingredients per cupcake," she'd written. "Sausage, mushroom, and onion. Ham, feta, and spinach. All veg—onion, tomato, and bell pepper."

Shannon tucked the card into her pocket with a sigh and dragged the cardboard box on the floor toward her. She gathered an armful of the books that had spilled from inside it and sat down to review the titles as she packed them away again. There was *Jane Eyre, The Adventures of Tom Sawyer, Anne of Green Gables, Little Women, Pride and Prejudice.*

It suddenly occurred to Shannon that this one particular box of books didn't belong to her aunt at all; these books had been hers. They were books that her mom had passed on to her, books they'd shared together. These were the books that had ignited something inside Shannon; something that had never left her. But there were still a few corners of her mind where coma-webs still lingered, and she looked down at the books in her arms and realized that all she had left of them were vague impressions. Emotions. Distant fires clouded with distracting smoke.

When she picked up the copy of *Emma* by Jane Austen, this one was different. The smoke cleared in front of this one, and Shannon grasped the recollection of the plot, the humor, the love she'd had for the main character. She opened the book and thumbed through the pages, inhaling the underlying mustiness, the top notes of grassy paper and tangy printing ink. In this new age of Kindles and tablets where one could carry around hundreds of books that weighed no more than a few compact ounces, nothing could ever replace the fragrant reminder of adventures long past.

As she stacked them, one after the other, into the thick cardboard box that had housed them for she-didn't-know-how-many years, she strained her memory trying to remember when—and more importantly, *why*—she'd given them up to a sealed box instead of an open bookshelf. Determined to lug the box of books home with her, she picked up the others from the floor.

When only two odd-shaped bundles remained, Shannon retrieved them and sat down on the chest again. One of them, the package of colorful books tied together with a faded blue ribbon, lifted both sides of her mouth in an unbidden grin at the mere sight of it.

"Dr. Seuss," she said on a sigh.

They were all there; her whole collection.

Cat in the Hat. One Fish Two Fish Red Fish Blue Fish. And the one that made her heart sing, even all these years later: *Green Eggs and Ham*.

"I do not like them, Sam I am. I do not like green eggs and ham."

The words had popped out of her memory and flown across her lips, and Shannon sat there in the afterglow feeling a little stunned. Were there any more bizarre little flashes she hadn't even known were hovering, waiting to jump out of her?

"I would not like them in a house, I would not like them with a mouse," she blurted, and then she cracked with laughter. "I can quote Dr. Seuss, but I can't remember that purple was my favorite color."

She set the Seuss books into the box with loving care before picking up the second packaged bundle from the floor. As realization dawned, Shannon gasped and her hand flew to her heart before she sank into a deep and cleansing sigh.

"My fairy tales."

The collection of her favorites—bought for her by her father on her fifth birthday. She untied the bow and loosened the long piece of twine holding them all together in one tidy little package. The cardboard books with fragile white pages came in a variety of sizes, and she flipped through them, examining the covers with fresh eyes.

The Princess and the Pea. Snow White and the Seven Dwarfs. Cinderella. The Ugly Duckling. Thumbelina. And yes, *Sleeping Beauty.*

She opened the book and flipped to the last page, just to make sure the snoozing princess actually had a happy ending. Spotting the magic words, *happily ever after*, she sighed. "Well, that's a relief, at least."

She stacked the books again and tied the twine around the bundle once more, this time with *Sleeping Beauty* on the top. As she set the final bundle into the cardboard box and folded over the flaps, Shannon's thoughts wandered toward Daniel and lingered there. She hadn't heard much out of him since that day she'd left him in the living room, holding nothing but the news of his abandonment plans while she walked away. A few text messages, an email congratulating her on the board's acceptance of her proposal, but no phone calls or visits or late-night Skype chats.

During her physical therapy session, Carrie had mentioned a going-away cake the staff planned to give him sometime before he left for Africa. Or Zimbabwe. Or wherever it was he was going. She couldn't remember. But she knew she wouldn't be attending any such cakefest, that week or any other. Especially when he'd grown so distant after the declaration of his plans to sever their ties.

For my own good, she thought bitterly. *Coward.*

The notion of Daniel flying to the other side of the world induced a mist of tears that stung her eyes. She'd come to depend upon Daniel so much since awaking from her coma; not the kind of dependence that stemmed from desperation or incapacitation. Shannon was getting stronger all the time. She didn't *need* Daniel Petros.

But she sure did miss him.

Before she even knew it, she'd placed the box of books on top of the chest and slipped past it to the floor . . . and to her knees. With her face planted in her hands, and her hands resting on the rug, the dam broke and she let the tears loose . . . and allowed the prayers in her heart to find their voice.

"Lord, help me," she softly cried. "Don't let me put my eyes on Daniel—or anyone else—as my salvation in this new world. Let me keep my eyes on you. Help me to wipe away the frost on the windows of my mind and fully remember what we had before, you and I. If Daniel is supposed to go away, then send your angels with him to keep him safe. But whether he goes or doesn't go, I need you. I can't do all of this without you . . ."

"Shannie? Are you all right up there, dearie?"

Her aunt's voice cut through her spirit and Shannon sat upright. "Yes. I'll be right down."

Once the thump of Mary's footsteps indicated that she'd retreated down the hall, Shannon covered her face again and clamped shut her eyes.

"I used to know you so well," she prayed in a whisper. "I depended on you for everything. I think Edmund thought I was a little crazy that way, but I didn't care. You were my everything." She opened her eyes and dried her tears with her sleeve. "I want that again. I want *you* again. I need you, God."

Izzy and Shannon saddled up to the counter between Izzy's kitchen and dining room, their two tall barstools moved close together to allow them to share a glimpse of the very large screen on Izzy's laptop.

"Did Carrie say where he's headed?" Izzy asked, her fingers frozen in a holding pattern over the keyboard. "Or did Daniel tell you?"

"I think so," she said. "Honestly, I don't think I even heard everything he said. One minute, I was just whining to him about everything I've lost, and the next minute he was telling me I'm losing him too."

"Temporarily. And this doesn't seem like it's such a terrible thing for you, honey. It'll give you a chance to sort things out without him."

"That's why I'm here," Shannon said with a smile. "I'm hoping you can help me focus on regaining my life, or even creating a whole new one so I won't have time to miss him any more than I already have."

"That's the spirit."

Izzy continued tapping out the rest of the press release she'd agreed to write for Shannon's new endeavor. At the final key stroke, she swiveled her chair and started talking a-mile-a-minute.

"So we've got two shelters onboard, and all you have to do is call them once you're all set up so you can work out a schedule with them. Do you have your schedule with Draper?"

"Yes. I'll be in their courtyard from noon until six on weekdays."

"Then let's tentatively plan for you to serve breakfast to Shelter #1 on Monday and Wednesday, and to Shelter #2 on Tuesday and Thursday. How does that sound?"

Shannon nodded. "Okay. Good."

"You should probably suggest a timeline of eight o'clock until ten. You don't want to be there too long, and that will give you a couple of hours for clean-up and lunch prep."

"Listen to you," Shannon teased her. "You've got the whole food truck lingo down."

"Honey, I've been eating and breathing this for two straight weeks," Izzy replied with a chuckle. "Now let's talk PR."

"You mean the press release?"

"That, yes. But I've also got you set up for a few interviews—"

"Interviews?" Shannon's heart started pounding double-time.

"Just a few of them. A local radio spot, and some face time with a couple of food bloggers out there with some interest in what you're doing."

"Do I have to travel to do that? When will I have the time with all of the—"

"You'll do them via phone and Skype, honey. And we'll get them out of the way before you even launch your endeavor." Izzy touched her arm and gazed seriously into her eyes. "This is what I do, Shannon. You don't have a thing to worry about, okay?"

Shannon inhaled sharply and nodded. "Okay."

"Now let's go over the release and make sure we've covered all the points. If we can generate a buzz and get some local sponsorship for the breakfast program—"

"Oh! About that," she cut in. "Remember how you said we should give the program a catchy name?"

Izzy nodded. "What are you thinking?"

"How about *Urban Manna*?"

She tried it on for size. "Urban Manna. Urban Manna . . ." A smile rose over the horizon of her face. "I like it. Let me just revise this a little . . ." Her fingers flew over the keyboard as she made changes to the press release, muttering as she did. "Dine-1-1, offering meals to . . . adding a non-profit breakfast program for needy Austin residents . . . Urban Manna will bring much-needed relief to . . ."

Izzy interrupted herself, ripped a page from the notepad next to her computer, and handed it to Shannon. "Here's the names and contact info for the two shelters. Why don't you call them and arrange the schedule we discussed."

Before Shannon could even reply, Izzy had released the torn page into her hand and returned her laser focus to the press release on the screen. She read—or muttered—it back to herself, and Shannon only caught bits and pieces of it as she retrieved her cell.

" . . . homeless and battered women shelters . . . hot meals . . . giving back to the facility that provided care . . . languished in a ten-year coma . . ."

Oh dear, Shannon thought as she took her phone into the next room. *Nobody spins a story like Izzy. She's a born publicist.*

She plopped into a chair and stretched her aching legs. The strain reminded her to make time for a PT appointment with Carrie. Mobility sat up there at the top of her list of priorities these days. She couldn't accomplish everything she had planned if her broken-down body gave out on her. Calling to mind some of the strengthening stretches Carrie had taught her, she carefully lifted her leg and flexed the muscle as she dialed the first number on the list Izzy had given her.

"Yes!" she exclaimed as the party answered from the other end of the line. "Marlene Vaughn? This is Shannon Ridgeway from Dine-1-1 . . ."

Shannon Ridgeway from Dine-1-1.

It gave her a little rush to say it out loud.

"I believe you've been in contact with my PR representative, Izzy Rojas?"

237

20

Shannon's stomach rumbled, and she tried to silence it by pressing both hands against her abdomen. She'd accomplished nearly everything on the list Izzy had emailed to her.

A phone call with Rachel Maxwell, a food blogger with over twenty thousand followers on Twitter, a platform Shannon had yet to decipher. *Check!* A quick five-minute radio spot with a local Austin talk jock. *Check!* Skype chat with Dale Madden from Texas Pipeline, a blog about the variety of ways small business owners reached out to fellow Texans in need. *Check!* Three more quick phone calls with smaller bloggers that Izzy had chosen from a Twitter search based on content and the demographic of their followers. *Check! Check! And check!*

And all from the comfort of her patio.

Just one more interview remained. As the otherworldly tone sounded on her laptop to announce the incoming Skype call, Shannon imagined foraging for sustenance and tried to picture the contents of her refrigerator to formulate a plan for lunch.

"Shannon?" A pretty young woman with wire-framed glasses and long brown hair appeared on the screen. "Can you see me?"

"Yes," she replied. "Can you see me?"

She nodded. "It's a strange way to meet someone, isn't it?"

Shannon chuckled. "It is. But it's good to meet you, Janice."

"Oh. No, it's Janese. Like *ja-NEES.*"

"That's pretty. Hey, are your glasses pink, Janese?"

The woman cast a sort of shy glance into the camera. "Yeah."

"Like your blog," Shannon observed. She'd checked out the

Loving Life in Pink blog just that morning. "So what's the connection to pink?"

"I don't know, really. In fact, when I was in high school I was sort of anti-pink. But for some reason, it just grew on me. And now it's my signature."

"I apparently went through the same thing with purple," she confessed. "I can't remember it, but that's what my aunt tells me. Anyway . . ." She shook her head hoping the webs might clear. "Janese, I love the look of your blog. It seems like you cover a little of everything, from your favorite books to cooking and baking to cleaning tips and crafting. I like the idea of the diversity of your readers. I'm sure that's why Izzy chose you to help us spread the word about what we're doing here in Austin."

"Thanks," Janese replied. "Izzy and I discussed spotlighting your plans so that it might spark other people to give back the way you plan to do. So how about we start with the details of your accident. In a coma *for ten years?*"

Shannon laughed out loud.

"And you're able to laugh about it," she commented. "I'm not sure I'd ever be able to make sense of something like that, much less laugh about it."

Over the next forty-five minutes or so, Shannon really enjoyed her conversation with Janese Lopez. Their chat wove a tapestry— beyond the basics of her accident and coma . . . to Dine-1-1 and the bizarre attraction to cooking that had birthed it . . . past the breakfast program for two local shelters—and they progressed in a back-and-forth pattern that felt more like two friends catching up than an interview with a blogger from North Dakota!

Shannon recounted her time with Edmund in Fiji before the accident, and she learned about Janese's seven-year marriage to Keenan after they met in college through a mutual friend; unlike Shannon and Edmund, Janese and Keenan had enjoyed a long courtship of a couple of years before they finally sealed the deal. Just as their chat drifted from their shared infatuation with a "ruggedly handsome" and lovable television writer named *Castle*—her newfound and present-day equivalent to her beloved Rob Petrie— Shannon asked, "Have I distracted you too much, Janese? Have you gotten everything you hoped out of our interview?"

"And more," the charming young woman assured her. "I'm particularly impacted by your URBAN MANNA food program. Do you have a logo or anything for that?"

"We have a preliminary one. I'll have Izzy email it to you with everything else once it's finalized."

"I was thinking maybe you could send me a couple of your favorite recipes. Something unique that will be on your menu."

"I know just the thing," she replied. "It's my grandmother's recipe really. But it's nutritious and fun, and I'd like to incorporate it into the meals I take to the shelters. She called it a breakfast cupcake, but it's really a sort of omelet baked into a muffin tin."

"That sounds great. Thank you so much for taking the time to talk with me, Shannon. And uh . . ." She gave a one-syllable giggle as she added, "Welcome back to the world."

"Thank you. Happy to be back."

Janese Lopez had been a pleasant note on which to conclude the half-day interview junket. Shannon closed the laptop and, just as she allowed her thoughts to swerve back to her quest for lunch, a rustle in the foliage on the other side of the gate drew her attention. She leaned forward and took a closer look, and she jolted when one large eye peered back at her from beneath a flowering bush with low-hanging leaves that looked like cabbage.

"Rodney?"

And with that, her wandering dog buddy shook his head so hard that he slapped himself in the face with one long velvet ear and he emerged from the garden.

"Rodney Dangerfield, is that you?" she cried as she hopped to her feet and slapped both thighs excitedly. "Come over here this minute."

Rodney scampered across the pavers toward her and thumped

into her leg, wagging his tail with happy exuberance.

Shannon leaned down with the intention of scooping him up into her arms and sitting with him on the couch for a bit. Instead, she groaned at the effort.

"Whoa!" she exclaimed. "You are short, but you're certainly compact!"

So instead of picking him up, Shannon dropped to the ground and sat next to him while Rodney applied layers and layers of sloppy, dog-spit kisses to her face and throat.

"You missed me too?" she sang. Sidetracked by his terrible breath, she shook her head and coughed. "Anyway, it just hasn't been the same without you. So much has happened."

In that moment when she realized how ridiculous it might have seemed to anyone looking on—that she had greeted a dopey dog with all of the enthusiasm of finding a long-lost family member—Shannon also thought about the old man a couple streets over, probably grieving the loss of his dog. Again.

"I'll get you back to him," she told Rodney as she lifted his ear into the palm of her hand and nuzzled it. "Just not right now. It's been so lonely around here without you."

After a few more minutes of getting reacquainted, Shannon's stomach rumbled again, and Rodney cocked his head and glared at it as if he might have to fight something off.

"Let's get some lunch first," Shannon suggested. "What do you say?"

●　—　●　—　●

"Let's everyone start with the stick in your left hand," Josiah instructed them, and the boys followed his instruction as Daniel laid out the last of the small red cones on the field. "This is a zig-zag exercise where we'll go forward, slow down, shuffle our feet, and split. Got that? Watch me and Daniel. Forward, slow, shuffle, and split."

"Hey, Daniel," the kid called out as he whipped his trained

hair to the side. "Where'd you get those moves? New Kids on the Block?"

"Hardee-har-har," he returned. "Laugh it up until someone comes at you and you can't maneuver out of their way, pretty boy."

Josiah shot him a grin before turning serious on the players. "Big words, Brandon. If you don't want to take this seriously, buddy, you can sit this one out."

"Nah. I got it. Forward, slow, shuffle, split."

"All right then. Let's give that a try."

The teens lined up and faced Daniel and Josiah.

"Get your sticks to your hips, and get your shoulders into the turn. Like this."

Over the next hour, they drilled the boys on roll dodges, stick handling, and combination moves. When Josiah finally called the end of practice and told everyone to grab a drink and a snack, Daniel twisted open a bottle of water and plunked down on the nearest bench. He hated to admit how tired he felt from just an hour on the field with Josiah's group of teens. It had been the first physical exercise he'd gotten in at least two weeks.

It was also the first thing that had distracted his thoughts away from Shannon.

"I want you all to practice the moves we taught you this week, you got me? And Trevor, you need to focus on keeping your feet choppy."

"Sure, coach."

"Right, Doc."

"Got it."

When they dispersed to stow the equipment, Josiah dropped to the bench beside Daniel. "So you shove off soon, huh?"

"Yep. Sure do."

"You planning to see Shannon before you go?"

"I'll call her."

"Not stop by?" Josiah pressed. "Don't you think you should stop by?"

Daniel didn't betray any hint of how many times he'd driven over that way with the thought of a casual visit. "Nah. I don't want to stir it all up again, man. She's had time to come to terms with it, and Izzy says—"

"You talked to her friend?"

"Well, yeah. I just wanted to check in and see how she's doing. Izzy says she's positive and focused and looking toward the future. She's been helping Shannon set up her new business, and . . . she doesn't need me tripping into the picture and making a mess of things again, just when she's started to feel clear."

"Yeah. Wouldn't want that."

Daniel glared at Josiah, weighing his meaning.

"Emily and I are going to dinner and listen to some music down on Sixth Street tonight. Why don't you go home, catch a shower and change, and join us."

Daniel shook his head and slapped Josiah's shoulder. "Nah. Thanks, but I have some things to get ready for the trip."

"Daniel—"

"Have a good time, buddy," he interrupted and stood up. "Give my best to Emily. I'm glad you two are doing so well."

"Thanks, man. She's something special."

"I'll see you at the hospital in the morning."

Daniel debated all the way home whether to swing back in the other direction and stop by to see Shannon, but his own words echoed back at him and kept him from doing so. He'd been meaning to check on her aunt, however, and it would hardly be out of his way at all to do it right then. He probably should have showered and changed first, but something just compelled him to follow the lead of his inclination, and he headed south toward his old stomping grounds and Mary's house.

He could have easily mistaken his relief for disappointment when he pulled down her street and didn't spot Shannon's BMW parked out front. Somehow, those two emotions felt the same these days.

"Daniel!" Mary cried when she opened the door and saw him standing there on her front porch. "What are you doing here? Shannon's not here, dearie."

"I came to see you," he told her with a smile. "And you're looking pretty great."

"Fit as a fiddle," she said. "Come in and let's have some iced tea."

He followed her inside and insisted she sit down and let him serve her, but Mary popped to her feet several times inside of a minute.

"I'll just get some sugar in case it's not sweet enough for you."

"Oh, you know, Shannie brought over the most lovely cookies. Let's have some, shall we?"

Once they had settled in the dining room, Mary reached across the corner of the table and squeezed his hand. "How nice to see you, dearie. How are you doing? Shannie tells me you're headed off on quite an adventure. Tell me about it."

"First, you tell me about you. How's that bump on your head? Have you had any residual problems?"

"I'm right as rain, sweet boy. Shannon's taken very good care of me."

"How is Shannon?" he asked, and it felt as if the entire world had gone silent, just those three words singing from a nearby hilltop. "I mean, how's her new business venture coming along?"

Mary took a long draw from her glass of tea before she answered him. "You don't really want to talk about her business, do you, Daniel? What you really want to know is whether you made the right decision in stepping back and letting our butterfly take flight all by herself. Isn't that right?"

Daniel tried to swallow, but his tight throat wouldn't cooperate. It didn't matter anyway with his mouth lined in sandpaper the way it was.

"How is she?" he rattled out.

Mary stroked his hand. "She's just dandy, dearie. But she misses you. We all do."

"I haven't gone anywhere."

"No. You're just right across town," she said, nodding. "Just on the other side of the big wall between you two."

Before he could respond, the front door creaked open and a familiar, sweet voice rang out. "Aunt Mary?"

She must have seen his car out front, but she came in anyway. Daniel wondered if she expected a confrontation or a reunion.

"Hello, Daniel," she said, tucking a wavy strand of copper hair behind her ear, revealing her Audrey Hepburnesque neck.

Was it his imagination, or had the cavernous two weeks since he'd seen her actually transformed her into this beautiful creature before him? *Shut up and get a grip. She's the same girl.*

"How are you?" she asked when he sat there like a bump on a rotting log.

"Good," he finally said, his voice coming out as a croak. He pressed his hands on the edge of the table and pushed up to his feet. "What about you?"

"Right as rain," she said, and he grinned.

"That's just what your aunt said. 'Right as rain.'"

Willing himself not to fumble it, he gave her a quick, awkward hug. "Good to see you."

"What are you doing here?" she asked, pulling away from him and heading to the kitchen to grab a glass from the cabinet. "Come to say goodbye to Aunt Mary?"

"Daniel came to check after me," Mary told her as she filled the glass with tea.

"I guess you're leaving any time now, right?"

"Yes. Very soon."

Shannon stood casually behind Mary's chair, staring down into her glass. "Well, be careful over there," she finally said. "Where is it again?"

"South Sudan. Pibor Town."

246

She replied with a simple nod before asking, "Aunt Mary, do you need anything? Are you set for your supper?"

"No need to hover, Shannie. You heard Daniel. I'm right as rain."

Shannon lifted her eyes, their green light casting a sudden spotlight over Daniel that left him feeling strange, fighting against the curious and bitter urge to apologize to her.

Sorry for having your best interests at the heart of things . . . So sorry that you're beginning to find out how strong and equipped you are . . . Oh, and really sorry that I've—

"Well, I'll leave you two to have your visit then."

His heart rate kicked it up a notch when she turned to go.

"Can I walk you out?"

"No need. Safe travels, Daniel."

When the front door clicked shut behind her, Daniel still stood there like a dope. As he turned and glanced at Mary, her face contorted and she rolled her entire arm toward the door.

"Do you need a bee to sting you in the behind, boy? Go on. Go after her."

The princess groaned softly and wiped her brow
with the sleeve of her dress.
"That should do it," she declared. "What next?"

The prince peered up at her from the ground.
He'd never met anyone like her.
"We'll want to ride back to the castle," he suggested,
"to see how they're faring."

She mounted her white steed,
grasping the reins with both hands.
"Well, come on then," she called to him over her shoulder.
"Are you going to sit there all day?"

No indeed. He'd surely never
met a princess like this one before.

21

As she turned the key in the ignition, Shannon noticed Daniel racing across the lawn toward her. She thought about pretending not to notice and just pulling out of the driveway, but curiosity got the better of her and she rolled down the window and watched him rush to the car.

"Shannon. Don't leave things like this."

Seriously?

"What *things*, Daniel?"

She wanted to hear him say it right out loud. When she folded her arm over the window ledge and leaned into it, Daniel covered her wrist with his hand.

"I'm sorry if I hurt you."

"So why did you?" she asked sincerely. "Here's how I see it: a couple of close moments between us and you're suddenly fleeing to another country. Please tell me there's more to it than that. And if there is, explain it to me, will you please? Did I need a breath mint? Because that's easily solved without leaving the country over it."

Daniel sighed and looked off into the distance for about two hundred years while Shannon waited for him to speak. She used the time to mold her expression into a mixture of disinterest and curiosity.

"I had a conversation with Dr. Benedict," he said.

"You spoke to my *therapist*? Can you do that?" she asked. "I thought our sessions were private."

"They are!" he exclaimed. "I just wanted to know how she

thought you were processing everything. I mean, Shannon, you've been through more than the average—"

"You talked to my therapist about me."

He tightened his grip on her wrist and leaned forward, parking his face about twelve inches from hers. She turned away from the closeness. "We were moving into something, Shannon. I had to know if you were ready for it yet."

"Moving into something." She hadn't meant to repeat it aloud, but the words just sort of floated out. "Can you define that for me, Daniel?"

He let out a rumbly sigh and backed up slightly. When he lifted his hand from hers, she quickly snatched his wrist and shook it.

"So what did Dr. Benedict tell you? That I'm too feeble and ill-equipped for a relationship with you, or with anyone? So—what? You dropped the coma girl and ran?"

"It's more complicated than that," he insisted. "I just want you to have the time and space you need."

"For what?" She wanted to tell him that she'd never felt *less crowded* than when she was with him; that he was the only man on earth who ever made her feel . . .

She resisted.

"To get over losing Edmund," he snapped. "To adjust to losing ten years of your life. To get your feet on the ground before you—"

"Let me tell you something, Daniel. Edmund was my first love. Losing him was terrible. But he's gone, and I can't bring him back. And I don't even know if . . ."

She choked back her own words. Was she really going to say she didn't know if she'd bring him back even if she could? Just the thought of saying such a thing burned her vocal cords. And it wasn't true anyway. Of course she would will him back to life if she could!

It's just that—

"I'm not the same person now that I was ten years ago," she said instead, and her throat felt raspy and sore. "I was barely in my twenties when I married Edmund. Are you the same person you were in your twenties?"

"Of course not."

"Well, me neither. Apparently, I continued changing while I slept because I woke up a whole different person. And you know what, Daniel? I feel pretty good about her. I kind of like her! The truth is . . . I don't know if Edmund would have liked this woman very much, but I was kind of thinking you did."

"I do."

"Then why aren't you sharing all of this with me?" she asked him. "I would have thought you'd be interested in what's going on, maybe want to cheer me on a little bit."

"You have no idea how much I'm doing that."

She let out one bitter laugh. "Well, I hope you cheer loudly from the other side of the world then, Daniel. It's going to be a little hard to hear you from here."

And with that, she rolled up her window and drove away.

● — ● — ●

She'd seen enough *Don't text and drive* ads to know better than to pull out her cell phone on the drive home, but Shannon did it anyway. At least she'd waited until she stopped at a light, she rationalized as she dialed her aunt's number.

"Aunt Mary, it's me."

"Did you forget something?"

"Just to tell you that I love you. And I'm sorry if Daniel and I made you feel at all uncomfortable."

"Not at all, dearie. Were you uncomfortable?"

"A little." If she wanted to describe the awful ache in her stomach as merely "uncomfortable."

"Oh, Aunt Mary. Do you have any suggestions for me?" she asked somberly.

"I suggest The Beach Boys."

Shannon blurted out a laugh. "Seriously?"

"'Barbara Ann' works wonders for me," she said and she began to sing.

"I'm going to listen to it on my computer the minute I get home," she said, chuckling. Her mood had lifted a bit just hearing her elderly aunt sing the first few silly lyrics.

"You know what else might work, Shannie?"

The mischief in her aunt's voice signaled a warning for Shannon. Heading off the inevitable reference to resolving things with Daniel, she said quickly, "Enjoy your evening, Aunt Mary."

She couldn't help herself from humming "Barbara Ann" for the rest of the drive, but she stopped abruptly when she turned into Briarcliff and headed for her own street. A shock of bright orange hair caught her attention, and Shannon steered over to the curb and rolled down the window.

"Hey!" she called, but the boy didn't glance in her direction. "Kid! Hello."

He moved toward the car, still keeping a safe distance as he leaned down and looked at her. "You stoled my grandpa's dog again, didn't you, lady?"

"No, I did not. And I didn't steal him the first time. If you would help your grandpa keep him in the yard, he wouldn't come looking for my house."

"Hey, Grandpa!" the boy hollered. "This is the lady who stoled Freckles."

Freckles. The disagreeable moniker just didn't fit her Rodney.

An elderly man with a thick head of wavy silver hair leaned on a broom and angled down to glare at her. When he made a move toward the car, Shannon climbed out to stand and greet him.

"My name is Shannon Ridgeway," she said as he reached her. "I live two streets over."

"Dog escaped again," he declared. "Dumb dog."

She grinned. "He's at my house, probably asleep on the patio furniture. I just wanted you to know he's safe, and I'll bring him over to you in about an hour if that's all right."

"You don't gotta."

She lifted one eyebrow into an arch. "Pardon?"

"Grandpa, Freckles is your dog," his grandson objected.

"Here," the old man said, pushing the broom toward him. "Go on, git. Driveway won't clean itself."

Once the boy had retreated, the man shook his head and chuckled. "Never liked that dog. More trouble'n he's worth. Smells like my first wife."

Shannon giggled, trying not to imagine the woman who smelled like Rodney.

"You sent him back smellin' like a flower though."

"Oh. Well. I just had him groomed."

"Musta run him pretty good too. Looked like he took off a pound or two."

"The pet store suggested weight management kibbles. I can bring you the rest of the bag. I still have it."

"You don't want him neither?"

"No, that's not it. I rather like him, but . . ."

"Keep him then, would ya?"

Shannon's heart soared slightly. "Really?"

"Never been a dog person," the old man declared. "Got three cats. They don't like the dumb dog much neither."

Shannon instinctively reached forward and took the man's hand between both of hers and began shaking it. "Yes. If you don't mind, I'd love to keep him. I really would. You see, I was in a coma and my husband died . . ." A snowball, rolling down a mountain; she just couldn't stop. " . . . and I've had to adjust to a whole new world on my own, and Rodney . . . that's what I call him because he looks a little like Rodney Dangerfield, don't you think so?...he was pretty good company for me. To be honest, when he went back to you, I kind of missed him."

"Never thought of it, but I guess he does look like Dangerfield. Acts like it too. Dumb dog thinks he *gets no respect*."

Shannon cackled. "That's funny! That's what Rodney Danger-field used to say."

The old man looked at her strangely.

"Anyway. Thank you so much. If you're sure."

"I'm sure."

"I'll take really good care of him, I promise."

"Yeah. You do that."

He turned away and plodded back to the driveway where his young grandson had just finished the sweeping.

Shannon rounded the car and, just before sliding back behind the wheel, she waved her arm. "Thank you!" The man didn't even glance back in her direction. She closed her eyes and said it again, this time to God. "Thank you so much."

The oddity of the thought didn't escape her as it formed in her head, but . . . she could hardly wait to get home and tell Rodney. "Finally," she said, sending the word upward in a prayer. "Something I've lost is returned to me. Keep that up, will you, please?"

As she pulled into the garage, Shannon's phone rang. She answered it and depressed the button to close the overhead door.

"Shannon?"

She didn't recognize the voice. "Yes?"

"Shannon, this is Emily Dawson. We met at the baptismal out in Barton Springs. Do you remember?"

"Umm . . ."

"I told you about meeting Edmund, and how he'd helped me and my family?"

"Oh! Of course, Emily. I'm sorry. What can I do for you?"

"Josiah is here, and he was just telling me about your new business venture. First of all, I just wanted to say what a wonderful thing you're doing. I don't know what's more needed; providing meals for Draper families, or the breakfast program you're starting. It's just amazing, Shannon."

"Thank you." She tried to think of something else to add, but nothing came to her.

"I was wondering—hoping, really—that maybe you need someone to help you."

"Well, I have been thinking about that. I just haven't had time to act on it."

"Daniel gave Josiah your number, and he suggested maybe I give you a call. I have a lot of cooking and serving experience. I've been waiting tables since I was sixteen, and I've been a sous chef at The Bristol Inn for the last two years."

"I don't know what a sous chef is paid these days, Emily, but I'm just starting out and—" Rodney's high-pitched howl from the other side of the door sliced her thought right in two.

"Are you all right?" Emily asked her.

"Yes," she said with a chuckle. "That's my dog."

I have a dog!

"He sounds very unhappy."

"It's hard to tell with him," she joked. "Can you email me a resume with three references, Emily?"

"Yes!" she exclaimed. "Thank you. What's the address?"

Rodney wailed throughout the last few minutes of their conversation, and Shannon disconnected just before she opened the door. The dog tossed himself at her leg in a happy display.

"Wait until you hear this, *Freckles*!" she teased. "Hey! How did you get into the house? I left you out on the patio."

His wide, bloodshot eyes betrayed nothing beyond subdued excitement to see her. The glass slider, standing open no more than six inches, told the rest of the story anyway.

I'm going to have to start locking that door.

"You figured out how to push the door open?" she asked him, and Rodney plopped his behind down and sat there staring at her. "Well, that just means you're hiding genius tendencies, doesn't it? Either that, or my suspicion that you can walk through doors and closed gates is correct. Is that your secret doggie super-power?"

He followed her to the table, thumping down to his wide behind again once she settled into the chair and opened her laptop.

Two minutes later, The Beach Boys serenaded her, and Shannon bounced into the kitchen—thankfully, with her legs cooperating!—and she yanked open the refrigerator door as she sang along.

"Bah-bah-bah bah-bahber Ann . . ."

● — ● — ●

Shannon drummed her fingers on the arm of the leather chair for several minutes before she finally recognized the rhythm she'd been tapping out, and she sang along in her head.

"Barbara Ann" sure had a catchy tune to it. She wished she could find the button in her brain to turn it off after more than twenty-four hours of it dancing around up there.

"Sorry to keep you waiting, Shannon. How are you today?"

She gazed at Dr. Benedict as she descended into the hard leather chair behind her desk.

"I'm actually pretty great," she replied.

"My secretary said you asked for an immediate appointment. Is there something particular that you'd like to discuss?"

"Yes. Daniel told me that the two of you had a conversation about me."

The doctor shifted in her chair. "Only to the extent that he wanted to know how you're navigating through the adjustment process."

"And did you tell him I might not be ready for a close relationship?"

"I may have indicated my concern about it, yes."

Shannon inhaled sharply and let it out slowly, controlling her breathing before she replied. "I appreciate your concern. But I don't feel like it was your place to make a judgment like that, or specifically to express it to a third party."

"Shannon—"

"My feelings for Daniel are admittedly confusing," she interrupted. "But I'm navigating alien territory here. Does that make sense?"

"Certainly."

Over the next fifty minutes, Shannon filled the time with wonderings about the future, insecurity, and questions about her new venture. She talked about her inability to connect the dots between her newlywed status with Edmund and the monstrous task of moving forward without him. She did almost all the talking, in fact, and she felt comfortable with the way Dr. Benedict heard her. She realized she could trust her.

Afterward, she wondered as she stepped onto the elevator whether the surge coursing through her consisted of anxiety or adrenaline. She pressed the button for the lobby and decided it might have been a little mixture of both.

Before reaching her destination, the elevator car stopped at the third floor. To Shannon's surprise, Josiah Rush stepped onboard. Dressed in well-worn jeans and a long, somewhat oversized gray Henley, he tapped the lobby button several times.

"Josiah?"

He glanced over at her and pulled an expression of complete bewilderment. "Shannon? He called you?"

"Pardon?"

"Daniel. Did he call you?"

"N-no. Today? No. Why? Is everything all right?"

"He had an accident, and I brought him into the ER. I'm headed back down there now."

Her pulse accelerated at an alarming rate, and her heart began to beat out thudding sounds deep inside her ears. "An *accident*? What kind of accident? Is he okay?"

"It looked pretty bad initially, but—"

When the elevator doors slid open, Shannon took off at a full run, leaving Josiah behind her. By the time she reached the emergency room check-in, every horrible outcome had splayed across her mind like a Technicolor disaster movie. With the fleeting thought of a broken arm or leg, she nearly catapulted across the desk at the poor girl seated there.

"Daniel Petros," she shouted. "Where is he?"

When the intake nurse didn't answer quickly enough, Shannon groaned and darted around the desk, through the ER doors.

"You can't go back there unless—"

"I got this, Donna," Josiah stated from behind her. "Shannon! Shannon, wait!"

But she couldn't wait. She had to see for herself. Pulling back curtains and peering into cubicles as she went, she plowed through the emergency room with all the determination of a mother bear in search of her cub. She thought she heard someone mention applying a cast to someone's broken leg, and it drove her anxiety up several notches.

"Over here," Josiah said, and she raced into the direction of his outstretched arm.

Had they already managed to get a cast on his leg? Would there be surgery involved? He wouldn't be able to walk around at first, even with crutches, depending on the extent of his injuries . . .

"Shannon?" Daniel peered up at her through one swollen, disfigured eye. "Is that you? What are you doing here?"

"You didn't break your leg?"

"My leg? No. What made you think—"

"I ran into her in the elevator," Josiah explained as he stepped up behind her.

"And you told her I broke my leg?"

"She didn't give me time to tell her anything at all. She concocted the leg scenario all on her own. I just said you were hurt out on the lacrosse field."

"Lacrosse?" she exclaimed. "I thought . . ." Embarrassment doused her with a large barrel of ice, and she cringed. "I don't know what I thought. What happened, exactly?"

"Look at you," he teased, but when his smile lifted enough to push on the upper side of his face, he groaned and winced, and that silly grin of his evaporated in no time at all.

"Look at you," she retorted. Mounds of swollen flesh around

the outside of his eye looked discolored and painful, and one of them resembled a chunk of raw meat that had been treated with clear ointment. She turned around and glared at Josiah. "What happened to him?"

"He was clocked in the eye with a lacrosse stick."

She wheeled around to face Daniel again and placed her hands on her hips.

"What did the doctor say? You look awful."

"Yeah, that's pretty much what she said. She said I look awful."

"She also told him it's a good thing he's not as pretty as *me* or it might really make a difference," Josiah chimed in. "As it is, no one will really notice another layer of hideous on *his* mug."

"Are you through?" Shannon asked.

The two of them exchanged glances before they burst out laughing.

"I suppose you can take him home?" she asked Josiah. "Make sure he's got what he needs?"

Josiah looked to Daniel, and Shannon caught Daniel shaking his head wildly out of the corner of her eye.

"Well, if you're available to give him a ride, I'd really appreciate it because—"

"I saw that," she stated. "You shook your head to get him to say he can't take you. Well, guess what. I have to go, and you're stuck with him. You two deserve each other."

Their laughter echoed down the hall after her as she stalked away. She heard that laughter for hours afterward, and she was safely home with Rodney on the patio by the time she finally relaxed and found the perspective to join in.

22

"**So you've got** everything you need, right?"

"Except for sight out of *both eyes*, you mean?" Daniel quipped. "Yeah, I think I'm all set."

Josiah headed for the front door, and then he stopped in his tracks. "While you were waiting on your walking papers at the hospital, I got a call from Emily. She's having breakfast with Shannon tomorrow."

"Job interview?"

"Yeah."

"I'm glad they connected. Give her my best. I think the two of them might work well together."

Josiah nodded. "You know who else works well together, Daniel?"

He glared at his friend for a long minute before nodding toward the door. "Go ahead and take off. I'm good."

"Just one thing?"

Daniel groaned. "What."

"I should have said this to you when you told me about your initial walk-off with Shannon, but . . . I don't know. For whatever reason, I didn't."

"Spill it."

"I know you said your main concern was her not being ready for something new so soon after everything, right?"

"Yeah."

"Well, I know you might *think* that's why." He paused for a moment before sighing. "But I think there's also the issue of the dead husband."

"Edmund."

"Right. Edmund. And I don't mean her issue with him. I mean yours."

"What issue do I have with Edmund, Dr. Freud?"

"You always said, once he was terminal, you thought he was grooming you to be the next guy in line for the throne."

The conversation started to feel a little like a stiff collar around his neck. Too much starch. "What's your point?"

"I think you're intimidated about living up to it, that's all. You see them as this great romantic tragedy, and I think that's a bit much for you after all this time on your own."

He nodded in the hope of moving the conversation along. "Finished?"

Josiah opened the front door. "I'm just a text away."

The minute he left, Daniel pushed up from the sofa and shed his clothes as he lumbered down the hall, through his bedroom, and into the bathroom. The shower had been calling his name since before that kid had sucker-shot him with his lacrosse stick. When he caught a glimpse of himself in the mirror on the path to the shower, Daniel backtracked and leaned across the sink to get a closer look. A couple of stitches, a black eye, and wedges of swollen flesh that looked a bit like kneaded bread dough streaked with red color. No wonder the look of him had scared Shannon half to death.

Once under the hot water, he found himself chuckling over the way she'd raced into that exam cubicle expecting to find him laid up with a broken leg; or something worse. His pulse raced just thinking about it. He'd begun to wonder if she'd have cared if a meteor flew out of the sky and reduced him to ashes. But of course she would have, even though she wouldn't have dared to show it.

After toweling off, he threw on a cotton tee shirt and the ever-faithful pair of navy sweats. He grabbed his phone and located his tablet before heading into the living room to sack out on the couch and watch some television. Nothing much looked good on network TV, so he mindlessly flicked through the upper cable channels until he landed on one of the classic movie networks.

Breakfast at Tiffany's.

He'd watched that movie only a few short months back while a silent redhead occupied the hospital bed a few feet away. It was a rather silly movie really, and he recalled wondering why he'd spent his dinner break watching it with a comatose patient. He wondered again now why he kept it on.

He picked up his tablet to consider some reading, but he noticed an interrupted game of Words with Friends that he'd started with Shannon. He studied the board for a minute before playing *exudes* off her *ponds* for forty points. Just as he decided to start a game against a random opponent, the familiar airy pops of another move drew his attention back to their game. She'd played *max*, but before he had a chance to consider his counter, the chat box ignited.

Skype?

He grinned—and then winced—as he typed in his reply. *Sure.*

Daniel quickly initiated a video chat, and Shannon appeared on his screen in under two minutes.

"Wow," she said, shaking her head. "You're really not easy to look at, Daniel."

"Yeah, I get that a lot."

"How are you doing? Does it hurt?"

"Compared to what?"

"Aah," she sympathized. "Do you need anything?"

"Nah. I'm good. Dr. Rush has me all squared away."

She hesitated for a moment before arching one eyebrow and grinning. "Well, you're grounded from playing lacrosse, young man. If you can't keep out of the way of the puck, you're not allowed to play anymore."

"Yes, ma'am. Except a puck is used in hockey. Not lacrosse."

"Oh. Well, you get my meaning."

"Yeah. I'm grounded." He casually ran his thumb along the

outline of her face on the screen, admiring the wayward spiral curl that molded along the top of her right shoulder. "So I didn't get to ask you. What were you doing at the hospital today?"

"Firing my therapist," she replied.

"You're joking."

"Only partly. I went there to give her a piece of my mind for discussing me with you. She had no right to do that."

He fell back into the cushions with a groan. "You don't think you need someone to talk to, Shannon?"

"Well, you'll be happy to know I changed my mind and we actually had a pretty good session."

After a brief silence, Shannon clicked her tongue and sighed. "So how long before you leave?"

"Couple of days."

"Sudan, huh?"

"Yep."

"They have wild African dogs there, you know."

"Is that so?"

"And giant forest hogs. And lions. You could easily be eaten by a lion."

"I'm fairly sure that's not going to happen. Have you been googling again?"

"Yes. Is it dangerous?"

"You mean Africa, right?"

"Yes."

"Well, it can be. But in this world, not many places are guaranteed safe, not even America."

"You're comparing the United States to the Sudan."

"I just mean there's a need there," he explained. "And I can help."

"So I was thinking about this today and I wondered . . . What does a neurologist do in the Sudan? I mean, it seems like you'd need imaging equipment and the like to do the job that you do."

"I'm also a medical doctor, Shannon," he said with a laugh, and his hand jerked toward his eye in the same instant.

"Oooh, it hurts?"

"Only when I laugh."

"Well, stop laughing then."

"My second time out with Medical Mercy, I worked with a civilian nurse who also served as a translator," he explained. "Since there were no MRI machines or X-ray capabilities, we sometimes had to rely on guerilla warfare."

"A tin can and a string?"

"Good old medical bag."

"Really? So if they can't move their neck, you take their temperature? A bold move, Doctor."

Daniel lifted only one side of his mouth in a fractured smile. "Flashlight, stethoscope, reflex hammer. You'd be surprised what you can learn with just those few things."

"I guess you rely a lot on your experience and intuition."

"They're in the process of rebuilding the hospital there, and they'll continue that work while we're there assessing injuries and treating malaria—"

"Malaria!" she exclaimed. "Daniel. Have you had your shots?"

"They're kind of sticklers about that, yes."

"Malaria."

"And we'll train some of the medical personnel that will staff the hospital when it's finished."

"Malaria," she breathed, her beautiful face corrugated with worry. "I know we're sort of—I mean, we were never—although . . . Anyway, will you email me every now and then to let me know you're all right?"

"I won't know what the connection challenges will be until we arrive."

"Oh."

"Are you worried about me, Ms. Ridgeway?"

"A little. But don't let it go to your head. I'm nice like that."

Daniel heard a strange sort of yowl. "What in the world was that?" he asked.

"Oh. Rodney. He's sacked out at my feet and I'm keeping him awake with all this yacking."

"Rodney?"

"Oh, yeah. Turns out the old guy didn't want him back. Freckles is all mine!"

The laughter that blasted out of him sent waves of pain shooting through his entire face.

"Ooooh, sorry," she said, cringing.

"You're not going to call him Freckles now, are you?" he asked.

"Only when I'm mad at him. He's Rodney Dangerfield Ridgeway. I think it suits him."

Daniel shook his head and tried to avoid smiling. "Were you even alive when Rodney Dangerfield was popular?"

"Yeah, sort of."

"But then *The Dick Van Dyke Show* was on in the sixties, and you somehow manage to know every show backward and forward. I think you were just born too late, Shannon."

"You're questioning God's wisdom now?" she teased. "So unlike you. Get some rest, One-Eyed Jack. And . . . will you call me before you leave?"

He nodded. "I will."

"Thank you." She tilted her head slightly, and her sweet, timid smile shot through him like an arrow. "Goodnight, Daniel."

"Goodnight, Shannon. *Goodnight, Freckles.*"

As he disconnected, her throaty laughter sent a shockwave of electricity straight through him. Leaving her for three months might be even more of a challenge than he'd anticipated.

● ─ ● ─ ●

"So it's the basics of any omelet," Shannon explained as she and Emily stood side by side at the kitchen counter. "But you have to keep the added ingredients down to a maximum of three or else they'll get weighted down and fall apart. You want them to keep their shape after you remove them from the muffin tin."

"That makes sense."

"So I thought I'd let you choose the additions from those set out on the counter. Then take a little flag toothpick," she said, displaying one of them and twirling it between two fingers, "and put a little sticky dot on the flag for each ingredient you use. So for veggies only, it's a green dot. If it has meat in it, use a red one. If it has both, use both dots. Make sense?"

"Absolutely."

Shannon returned to the dining room table and sat down in front of her laptop to review Emily's resume displayed on the screen.

"You used to work at Francine's down by the park," she observed. "Edmund and I used to go there all the time."

"Yeah," she said over the sound of the chopping. "It was my first kitchen job. I was so sad when they sold the place."

"They sold it? Who's there now?"

"I don't know. They tore it down and rebuilt something there. I think it's a BabiesRUs."

"Well, that's just sad."

Emily chuckled, and Shannon looked up from the computer screen and watched her. She used to wonder what it would be like to go through life with a perfect body, shampoo commercial hair, and big blue eyes instead of thick red hair, pasty skin, and freckles.

"So Josiah told me about Daniel's accident," Emily said. "I'm so sorry."

Apparently, there were a few things Josiah hadn't told her, like that little factoid about how she and Daniel had pretty much gone their separate ways.

"I guess you're going to miss him when he leaves on his medical mission, huh?"

Shannon inhaled a sharp, bracing breath. "I have a lot going on here to keep me focused."

"Still, I'd be beside myself with worry every minute Josiah was gone if he went somewhere dangerous like that, and we haven't even been dating that long."

It took a second for Shannon to determine that the patter in her ears came from her accelerating heartbeat.

"Are you trying to scare me?" she asked Emily with a broad smile.

"Sorry." A moment later, she lifted the muffin pan to show the finished product to Shannon. "Put them in the oven?"

"Yes, it's already preheated. You can set the timer for twenty minutes, and we can grab some coffee and chat out on the patio."

"I don't drink coffee," she said, "but I'd be happy to get you some."

"How do you feel about dogs?"

"I love dogs. Barney and I made friends while you were busy in the kitchen."

Shannon chuckled. "Rodney."

"Oh, right. I'm sorry. I'm terrible with names."

"He's named after Rodney Dangerfield," she tested. "Do you know who he was?"

"Sure! He's that comedian who got no respect, right?"

"Yes."

"Your dog does kind of look a little like him, doesn't he?"

Shannon's heart sang. "Thank you. Yes, he does."

Twenty minutes later, after an amiable conversation where Emily's demeanor sold Shannon on the idea of making her a job offer, the breakfast she insisted on finishing off while Shannon enjoyed her coffee pushed her right over the edge.

"I hope you don't mind . . . I saw the pink grapefruit in the refrigerator," Emily said as they sat down to a breakfast table that looked like a photograph in a foodie magazine. "This is one of my favorites that we serve at The Bristol. Chilled grapefruit sections topped with just a drizzle of honey. Normally I'd add a few blackberries when they're in season."

The more she talked, the higher the corners of Shannon's mouth arched upward.

"I gave you two of the little omelets," she continued. "One with Swiss cheese, spinach, and mushrooms. And the other has turkey sausage crumbles, diced red onion, and cheddar."

"Perfect," Shannon commented. At first bite, she repeated the sentiment more enthusiastically. "Emily, it's perfect."

Her blue eyes glistened as her beaming smile seemed to take over her entire pretty face.

"I'm so glad."

"Let's talk the specifics of the job, shall we?"

Two hours later, Emily had agreed to give two weeks' notice to her employer, they'd ironed out the schedule, and Emily asked if she could tag along when Shannon picked up the food truck she'd purchased. A match made in heaven . . . she hoped.

"Emily, you're sure you want to leave a prestigious position like sous chef at The Bristol?" she asked her at the door.

"I really love cooking," the young woman told her sweetly. "But I have a six-year-old, and the job just isn't a good fit for me now that she's in school. I've known that for a while, but when Josiah told me about what you're doing, about the breakfast program and the service to the people at Draper, I just knew I wanted to be involved."

Shannon smiled and took Emily's hand. Shaking it, she warned, "We could very well crash and burn, you know."

"Maybe. But you have a real entrepreneurial spirit, Shannon. I share that, and I'm so honored to be part of what you're doing. I just feel like God's hand is on this whole thing, don't you?"

Shannon had to admit that she did. And she treasured the return of that feeling after so long.

She stood in the doorway and watched after Emily as she climbed into her car. The moment she pulled out of the drive, a different car pulled into the place Emily's green Toyota had occupied. Shannon stood there waiting to see what the young man in the brown sedan had on his mind.

"Shannon Ridgeway?" he asked as he made his way up the sidewalk.

"Yes."

With a smile and a nod, he placed a thick envelope into her hand. "You've been served."

"What?"

"Have a nice day."

●　—　●　—　●

"Thank you, Beverly. I'll see you tomorrow morning then."

Shannon disconnected the call and tossed her phone to the cushion next to her. After taking a moment to lean back and stare at the gloomy sky beyond the pergola overhead, she unfolded the paperwork in her hand and scanned it for the hundredth time since the cute young guy in the brown car had handed them to her.

"You've been served."

The words scorched her ears with the same effusive and brash fervor as the legalese that burned her eyes as she read through the papers yet again.

Rodney sat down very close to her foot and nuzzled her leg. When she glanced at him, she noticed a certain alarm in his eyes as he lifted his double chin and glared at the fast-moving gray clouds blocking the midday sun.

"Looks like rain, huh, boy?" She scratched his velvet ear with two fingers and patted him on the head. Her phone rang at the same moment that the first droplets of rain plunked down over them.

She grabbed the court papers and her phone and slapped her thigh as she hurried toward the house. "Come on, Rodney. In the house."

He obediently followed her, and she closed the sliding door behind them.

"Hello?"

"Shannon? It's Daniel. You sound out of breath. Is this a bad time?"

"The baddest," she replied, and then thought better of it. "Sorry. I was just racing against the rain to get into the house with these ridiculous court papers just delivered to me."

"Court papers? What kind of court papers?"

"It seems Millicent has been polishing her broomstick again."

"Oh no. What's she after this time?"

"My wedding ring, for one thing."

"Your . . . Your what?"

Shannon dropped to the dining room chair and stared at her closed laptop. "Edmund gave me this ridiculously expensive diamond when we got engaged. It was too big to even wear on a regular basis. It kept catching on everything, and I felt like it tilted me to the left side all the time."

Daniel chuckled, and his laughter came through the phone like a comforting embrace.

"So I asked him to choose a really simple wedding band, something I could wear all the time . . . and he did the most amazing thing. It was so unlike him, actually. He said if he was going to give me something small and unremarkable, he wanted it to carry some weight of a different kind." She paused to wipe away the tear that ambled down her cheek. "He had his mother's original wedding band restored and sized for me."

"And Millicent wants it back."

"Yes." The stream of tears flowed freely now, and Shannon propped her elbow on the table and leaned into her hand. "I can't do it, Daniel. I won't give it up. His mother left it to him when she died. It was Edmund's to give, and he gave it to me."

"I'm so sorry, Shannon."

"There are other things listed, like Edmund's mahogany desk and his clothes. I don't even know where his clothes *are*."

"In boxes on the shelves in the garage."

"That's what those are?"

"I didn't know where else to put them, and I didn't know if you'd want to get rid of them."

"Thank you, Daniel."

"What's she want with his clothes?" he asked her. "She doesn't look like the Armani suit kind of guy."

"Why does Millicent want anything she wants!" she exclaimed, and she jumped up from the chair and began pacing in front of the glass door. "Frankly, I don't even care. She can have it all. But she's not taking my wedding ring. It's all I . . ."

Shannon allowed her words to trail off. It wasn't all she had left of Edmund. She knew that. But it symbolized something so much greater than all of the money or the heirlooms or the useless items on the long legal list. That ring symbolized a confirmation for Shannon. A validation that she'd desperately needed at the most crucial time in her life.

When Edmund had put that ring on her finger, he'd proven to her for the first time in quite a while that he'd really *heard her*. He heard what she had to say about wanting something simple—even though there wasn't a simple gene in the man's body—and he'd delivered in a mind-blowing, sentimental, more-than-she-could-have-imagined way. That simple, thin, engraved band had been the answer to a month of prayers for a sign that marrying Edmund was the right thing to do. Shannon refused to give it up now.

"Is there anything I can do?" Daniel asked, interrupting her thoughts.

"I don't think so," she admitted. Standing at the slider, she watched the thunderous torrent of rain pour down on the patio beyond the door. "I'm sorry. Did you tell me why you called?"

His silence spoke volumes, and her heart dropped slightly.

"Oh. You're leaving."

"You asked me to call and say goodbye. I'm out on the first plane in the morning."

Something inside Shannon wrenched, and she backed up to the nearest chair and folded into it. "You'll be careful, won't you?"

"Of course."

"And email if you can?"

"If I can."

There were those tears again. Shannon thought how tired she'd grown of tears, when suddenly Millicent materialized in her mind again in an evil cloud of smoke.

"Shannon?" he said, as if he'd heard her mental change of gears.

"I'm fine," she said, not wanting to burden him with her decision on the brink of his departure. "I just have something to do." But he must have sensed her determination and realized she was hiding something significant.

"You're not going over to see her, are you?" And when she didn't answer: "Shannon, tell me you're not going over there. Aside from the fact that it's a colossally bad idea, there's a severe thunderstorm warning in effect."

She wasn't worried. In fact, she felt completely calm about her decision. "I need to confront that evil woman and tell her what she can do with her lawyers and demands."

"Shannon, calm down. Why don't you put in a call to Beverly."

"I am calm, actually. And I've already spoken to Beverly. I've got an appointment with her in the morning."

"Then just hold off doing anything rash, and talk to her tomorrow."

"Not about this, Daniel," she stated. "This is between me and Millicent, and I'm going to—"

"Shannon."

"Listen, you have a wonderful trip," she said, cutting him off. "Save a lot of Sudanese lives. Build a hospital and take care of yourself. And come back safely, please. Avoid the lions, okay?"

"Shannon, I just don't think—"

"I know you don't, but you're going to have to let it go. Take care, Daniel."

Fifteen minutes later, Shannon left Rodney cowering in his new blue dog bed in the corner of the bedroom and headed for Lake Austin. About a mile down Lamar, it suddenly struck her quite odd that the normally busy road hosted so little traffic for the middle of a weekday. She guessed the terrible weather had a lot to do with it. She flicked the windshield wipers to their fastest speed, and she still had to work hard to see the road ahead of her as the swirling greenish-black sky whipped the falling rain into wind that pelted and rocked her car with its force.

Perhaps getting out on the road hadn't been the best idea she'd ever had, Shannon mused, and she sent a quick prayer into the churning sky that God's protection might trump her questionable timing.

Her ringing phone, muted through the pocket of her bag, drew her eyes in a quick dart to the floor of the passenger seat where the strewn court papers ruched over the bulge of burgundy leather.

"Sorry," she said aloud, returning her laser focus to the road ahead. "Nobody home."

Something enormous flew across the road in front of her at an oblique angle, and Shannon pressed down the brake until it—an aluminum trash can, as it turned out—crashed against a slanted street sign and rolled back into the street. Convulsing wind howled and screamed at her from outside the rattling windows, solid sheets of sideways rain let up only in swift increments, and the usual under-thirty drive out to the Ridgeway estate took almost twice as long. When she finally pulled into the circular drive, Shannon felt exhausted.

She pulled the key out of the ignition and tucked it into her pocket, making the choice to leave her bag behind in the dry, safe haven of the car. She flipped up the hood of her shiny red rain jacket and tucked her long hair into it, tugging on the toggled string to tighten it around her face. She thought about waiting for the rain to let up but realized it had hardly done so at all since she left her house, and she took a deep breath, yanked open the door and raced up to the front door. She rang the bell and turned into the jamb to shelter her face from the driving rain. The moment the door opened, she angled upward and looked into the face of Reginald's son.

"Miss Shannon," he exclaimed, opening it wider to let her inside. "What are you doing out in this storm?"

"I need to see Millicent," she told him, wishing she'd thought to ask his name the last time she'd paid this house a visit. "Is she here?"

"What on earth do you want, Shannon?"

"Question answered," she muttered to the man who wore his father's familiar features as she loosened the hood and flipped it back. "I need to speak with you."

"You may speak with me through my attorney," she said, and she turned and clicked away on short, thin heels.

Not to be deterred, Shannon followed her into the great room flanked by massive floor-to-ceiling columns and a wall of glass windows that framed the frenzied storm just beyond them.

"You shouldn't stand so close to the window when the weather looks like this," Shannon remarked, but Millicent didn't cast her even the most furtive glance.

"What do you want?"

"I came to tell you . . . that I miss him, too."

Millicent turned slowly around, her cat eyes narrowed and burning with almost-frightening flames.

"I beg your pardon."

"I know he was your brother, and you had a complicated relationship. I never really understood it, in fact, but I can tell you this . . . that he loved you very much. And I think everything you're doing to me is a strange, distorted way of saying that you miss him. Well, I miss him, too."

It wasn't what she'd meant to say, not what she'd practiced in her head all the way out there, but it's what came out just the same.

"You probably think I married him for money or something," she continued, and Millicent sniffed as she turned away. "But I didn't. I married Edmund because, despite all of our differences—of which there were many, I can assure you—I loved him."

She hesitated for a moment as she gathered the words to follow.

"I know your mother's wedding ring symbolizes something for you, and I understand why you might want it returned. But the thing is . . ." A clutch of raw emotion clawed its way over her, and a mist of tears rose in her eyes that she willed into submission. "That ring represents something for me, too. I'm not going to tell you what, or explain why, but in many ways it's the most important thing that Edmund ever did for me, giving me that ring." She swallowed around the lump in her throat and inhaled sharply before adding, "I'm not giving it up."

Millicent continued to face the window, but the way her entire frame straightened, her reaction translated without words.

"You can have the clothes and the desk and anything else you want of the material items. But you can't have the provisions he made for me before he died, because he did that so I could have a shot at making a life again while I tried to figure out how to live without him. And you and I both know you don't need the money anyway, don't we? You're just determined to be hateful. But over and above anything else you might want to argue over in the courts, you can't have my wedding ring, Millicent. I'm not giving it up, no matter what you do."

She turned around toward Shannon, not a trace of reaction showing on her harsh face as she asked, "And if you remarry one day?"

"Especially not then," she said with resolve. "That ring symbolizes something you'll probably never understand. Something I'll take with me into whatever relationships, ventures, travels, or frightening realities I face for the rest of my life. It's a tiny gold life preserver for me in a way, and I just can't—I won't let it go."

The front bell rang at just that moment, but before Shannon could even process it, a detonation of thunder roared in her ears like an approaching freight train.

She gasped, clapping her hands over her ears and looking wildly out the window.

Suddenly everything happened at once. Like a classic disaster movie—but without the benefit of slow-motion movement—a cacophony of noise, wind, screams, and weather converged, and Shannon watched in horror as a large tree with thick, dark branches crashed through the window, its foliage absorbing Millicent in one hungry bite, and she disappeared from view with a disturbing shriek.

"Millicent!" Shannon cried. Without a moment's thought, she dove straight into the tree that now occupied two-thirds of the living room. Shards of broken glass and severed branches sliced at her arms and face as she worked her way through the wreckage like a human machete, calling out, "Millicent! Can you hear me? Millicent?"

She spotted an arm clothed in torn fabric. As it reached out to her, Shannon struggled to free her former sister-in-law. She lifted a section of tree with a guttural groan, and Millicent looked up at her from beneath it, a spatter of blood staining her cheek.

"Help me!" she cried out.

"Hang on. I'm going to try and work this limb free . . ."

The wood punctured her hands as she tugged and tugged. When it slipped away and Millicent screamed, Shannon went back at it again, yanking and pulling with all her might.

"I don't know if I can do this on my own," Shannon yelled above the roar of the storm that had invaded the house.

"Vincent!" Millicent called. "Vincent, help us!"

Reginald's middle-aged son called back to them. "It's wedged in from this side!"

As he continued to communicate with them from behind the mass of leaves and branches, a strong hand grasped Shannon's upper arm and yanked her back. She spun around and found herself face to face with Daniel and his horrible, mangled eye.

"Daniel?!"

"Get out of there. Let me try from this angle."

As if in a daze, Shannon trudged backward out of the foliage as he supported both of her arms. When she finally emerged, she stood back watching as Daniel and Vincent worked together to inch a section of the tree away from Millicent. Beyond them, the whirling storm raged on and the darkened sky glared down at the whole scene from behind a thick cloak of dark rain.

Now that she'd stepped back, Shannon had the chance to take in what was happening outside. The scene had changed to one of drama, with the sky a snarl of storm clouds and wind-whipped debris. She gasped as a large outdoor lounge chair tumbled across the landscape like a cotton ball caught up on a cross-breeze.

"I can't get it," Daniel shouted. "Millicent, can you move in either direction?"

"Only back," she returned, "but there's a very sharp section of broken window behind me."

Shannon surveyed the scene in front of her and spotted an opening off to Daniel's right.

"Hang on!" she exclaimed as she rushed into the break.

She pulled back on one of the thinner branches with all her might, and she watched as Millicent saw her chance, thrusting herself through the opening Shannon had created. They both had to crawl on their hands and knees to clear the debris, and Daniel stood there waiting for them. He lifted Shannon into his arms and carried her to safety before returning and doing the same for Millicent.

"Are you hurt?" he asked her as he carried her out. "Is anything broken?"

"I don't think so," Millicent called back over the roar.

"Vincent?" Daniel called.

"I'm okay," the butler called out from where he stood.

Millicent looked up at Shannon from the floor where Daniel had placed her before he hurried to the other side of the tree to check on Vincent. Standing over her, she saw something there that she'd never even imagined lingered within Edmund's horror of a sister. *Gratitude?* Could it be?

Shannon considered her next move thoughtfully. With a smile, she extended her hand. "Do you need help? Can you stand?"

Millicent's eyes blazed suddenly with sheer terror, and she only had time to scream her name. "*Shannon!*"

23

Daniel's heartbeat defined an all-new meaning for the concept of racing when Millicent screeched out Shannon's name. By the time he and Vincent had climbed free, they found Shannon sprawled on the floor a good five feet back from where he'd left her, motionless, her face bleeding and Millicent kneeling at her side.

"What happened?" he demanded as he joined her.

The woman gave her head a frantic shake as she pointed at an enormous framed painting lying broken and crumpled on the floor against the front door.

"It hit her?" he asked, and she managed a spastic little nod.

"Okay, move aside." When she didn't budge, he repeated his demand. "Millicent! Move aside."

Vincent grabbed her arm and helped her up. She limped away with him as Daniel examined the gash on Shannon's head. He pulled his phone from the pocket of his jacket and tossed it to Vincent. "Call 911. We need an ambulance."

As the man complied, Daniel leaned in close to Shannon's face. *Still breathing. Thank you, Lord.*

He peeled her blood-soaked hair away from her face and stroked it into place so that he could get a closer look. With his thumb, he lifted her eyelids one at a time and examined her pupils.

Only slightly constricted. That's good.

Daniel took her hand between both of his and shook it gently.

"The ambulance is on its way," Vincent told him. "The woman said the tornado touched down in three spots over here."

"Shannon?" Daniel said, praying for a response. "Shannon, can you hear me? Open your eyes."

Vincent and Millicent stood behind him, looking at her over his shoulder.

"She risked her life to save me," Millicent said, and Daniel noticed the tinge of disbelief in her voice.

"Shannon?" he repeated.

The sirens in the distance brought him a certain degree of relief, and he turned back and asked Vincent to go and flag them down. Just as he returned his focus to Shannon, her eyes gave an odd little flutter, and they drifted open.

"Thank God," he said with a smile. "Shannon, can you see me?"

She didn't reply, but after a moment her lips quivered and broke into a wide smile.

"Hi," he cooed. "You had us all pretty scared, young lady."

Shannon looked over his shoulder and grimaced when her eyes landed on Millicent looking down at her.

"What happened?" she finally whispered.

"Tornado," Daniel answered, smiling with relief. "I told you the weather was bad."

"Am I alive?"

"Yes," he answered with a chuckle.

"Are you going to kiss me?"

When he lifted one eyebrow in surprise, the pain of it caused him to wince. As soon as he recovered, he asked, "Do you *want* me to kiss you?"

"That's how it goes when the prince wakes Sleeping Beauty, silly. I swear, sometimes it's like you don't know anything at all."

Daniel leaned down and pecked her lips, but Shannon lifted her arms and slid them around his neck, drawing him into a deeper kiss. When they parted, she grinned at him.

"And they all . . . lived *happily ever after*," she said with a happy laugh.

"Promise?"

She nodded. "I think it's my turn."

"You know what?" At the sound of Millicent's voice, sounding completely unlike the Millicent they had known, Daniel glanced over his shoulder at her. "It certainly is," she said.

"Millicent smiled," Shannon observed, and he nodded. "You should do that more often," she told her directly. "It looks good on you."

And with that, Daniel realized nothing could have astonished him more as The Evil Queen burst into a laughing fit of tears.

Now I've seen everything, he thought.

"Okay. Now I've seen everything," Shannon muttered, and he laughed right out loud. "Daniel? You know how there are giant hogs and stuff in Sudan?"

"Yes."

"Don't go there, okay?"

Daniel sighed and cradled her in his arms. "You know I have to now."

"Yes, okay. You gave them your word," she sputtered. "But . . . anyway . . . don't go." When he didn't reply, she piped up, "I'll go with you then."

"No, you won't. You have things to do. Besides, there are lions in Sudan."

"Oh. That's right. Yeah, I've had enough adventure I think. I'll just stay here."

He kissed her again as he held back a laugh. When they parted, Vincent had opened the door to the drenched EMTs.

"Promise me you won't get eaten by a giant hog or something," she said to him as they lifted her to a gurney.

"I promise."

"And don't drink the water unless it's bottled. It's very bad there, you know."

"So I've heard."

"And come back in one piece, Daniel . . . because if you let a

283

lion tear you to shreds and I lose you too, I'm going to be so mad at you."

"I know. I'll come back in ninety days, right as rain."

As the EMT raised the gurney and they prepared to roll her out the front door, Shannon looked up at him and smiled. "Don't say rain."

He wanted to laugh, but the overwhelming relief pushed it out of him in a sort of cackle.

"In fact, let's not refer to water of any kind," she called back to him. "So are you coming, or what?"

"I'm right behind you."

"She's quite the little fairy tale heroine, isn't she?" one of the EMTs remarked as they prepared to transfer the gurney to the ambulance.

"You have no idea," he replied.

Once upon a time, a writer was given a set of
extraordinary blessings named Rachelle and Marian,
and a team of kind, loyal elves called Launchies.
The support of these women drove her forward
and helped her become the best writer she could be.
And because of them, the writer grew stronger
and far more grateful than she'd ever been before.
And because of them, the writer continued to write
and learned to live Happily Ever After.

Special thanks to
Deb and Michele
at River North.

IMPACTING LIVES THROUGH THE POWER OF STORY

Thank you! We are honored that you took the time out of your busy schedule to read this book. If you enjoyed what you read, would you consider sharing the message with others?

- Write a review online at amazon.com, bn.com, goodreads.com, cbd.com.

- Recommend this book to friends in your book club, workplace, church, school, classes or small group.

- Go to facebook.com/RiverNorthFiction, "like" the page and post a comment as to what you enjoyed the most.

- Mention this book in a Facebook post, Twitter update, Pinterest pin or a blog post.

- Pick up a copy for someone you know who would be encouraged by this message.

- Subscribe to our newsletter for information on upcoming titles, inside information on discounts and promotions, and learn more about your favorite authors at RiverNorthFiction.com.

Shriek with laughter—and embarrassment—as your
new best friend, Julianne, goes on
a collision course with God's impeccable plan!

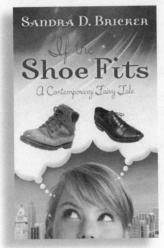

ISBN-13: 978-0-8024-0628-6

Another contemporary fairy tale by Sandra D. Bricker . . . Julianne used to
believe in fairy tales, but she's never come any closer to finding the perfect
man than tripping over her childhood best friend, Will. And now she and
Will are attorneys, joined up in private practice.

On her way to court one day, Julianne runs right smack dab into Prince
Charming: The Prince's toolbox has fallen off the back of his truck, and
one work boot along with it. What better way for God to grab her attention than to show her a glass slipper . . . errrr, work boot?

Julianne is on a collision course with God's perfect plan for her life—if
only she could open her eyes and see it before it's too late. After all, who
finds their Prince Charming on a 10-speed bicycle on the other side of the
cul-de-sac? Well, Julianne does. Only she doesn't have a clue.

Also available as an ebook

midday connection

Discover a safe place to authentically process life's journey on **Midday Connection**, hosted by Anita Lustrea and Melinda Schmidt. This live radio program is designed to encourage women with a focus on growing the whole person: body, mind, and soul. You'll grow toward spiritual freedom and personal transformation as you learn who God is and who He created us to be.

www.middayconnection.org